DOMESTIC MALICE

I was taken aback by how disheveled she was. When we'd met other times, she'd always appeared to be meticulous in her dress and personal appearance, her brunette hair shining and nicely cut, her makeup judiciously applied. But that wasn't the woman who sat before me on this night. Whatever makeup she'd applied had been watered down by sweat and tears. Her eyes were bloodshot, her mascara smeared. Her hair hung in lank strands. Her red blouse was wrinkled and she wore flip-flops, an odd choice for such a chilly night. She looked as though she'd dressed hastily, in whatever was close at hand. There was no question why she was there.

Domestic Malice

A *Murder, She Wrote* Mystery

A NOVEL BY

JESSICA FLETCHER & DONALD BAIN

Based on the Universal television series created by
Peter S. Fischer, Richard Levinson & William Link

AN OBSIDIAN MYSTERY

OBSIDIAN
Published by the Penguin Group
Penguin Group (USA), 375 Hudson Street,
New York, New York 10014, USA

USA | Canada | UK | Ireland | Australia | New Zealand | India | South Africa | China

Penguin Books Ltd., Registered Offices: 80 Strand, London WC2R 0RL, England
For more information about the Penguin Group visit penguin.com.

Published by Obsidian, an imprint of New American Library, a division of
Penguin Group (USA). Previously published in an Obsidian hardcover edition.

First Obsidian Mass Market Printing, September 2013
10 9 8 7 6 5 4 3 2 1

ISBN 978-0-451-41481-6

Printed in the United States of America
10 9 8 7 6 5 4 3 2 1

For Maria Morey,
for her selfless dedication to helping people
who have suffered at the hands of those they loved or trusted.
Her assistance with this book was invaluable.

ACKNOWLEDGMENTS

It has been our good fortune not to have had firsthand knowledge of domestic abuse, so we relied on input from experts who help those who've gone through that experience. Our thanks to Patricia A. Zachman, executive director; Alex Lopes Massa, director, Facilities and In-Kind Donation Program; and the entire staff of the Women's Center of Greater Danbury, who make the world a safer place for men, women, and children.

Thanks also to Lisa Marchese, assistant attorney general, state of Maine, for giving so generously of her time in explaining how abuse cases are handled in her state and what constitutes self-defense.

We hope that we have portrayed what we learned accurately. Any errors are ours alone.

Part One

Chapter One

I don't know how much longer I can stand it—try so hard to make him happy, meals he likes, house spic-and-span, good mother to our children—nothing I do seems to please him.

Shouldn't have confided in my mother. She never liked him from the day we started dating—when I announced we were getting married she went into a depression—lasted for months, maybe she's still depressed—wants me to take the kids and leave him, but I can't do that. Where would we go? How would we live? He wanted me to stay at home and be a full-time mom to the kids, and I've done that. How can I make a living after being a stay-at-home mom so many years—no training, no job experience—we'd have no money—can't even type anymore. I wanted to work but it made him mad when I said that—always mad—acts like he hates me sometimes—names, the nasty curses and names—not true that names don't hurt. Always threatening to hit me. Sometimes he does—he has no right to hit me. I have to stay in the house till the bruises fade. I'm so ashamed, don't

*want someone I know to see—even hide them from the kids.
—MW in Maine*

*MW in Maine—You sound at wit's end. Don't try to be
a hero (or heroine). Don't think it's better for the kids to stay
married to this guy. Get out while the getting is good. Take
it from me. I know. My sister was murdered by her live-in
boyfriend after an argument. I never knew what was going
on. She never said a word. Please, please escape before something terrible happens to you. Take the kids and start a new
life where you don't have to be abused. —Janet*

"The only thing that this so-called women's shelter
does is to foster disharmony in otherwise harmonious
households here in Cabot Cove. For the Cabot Cove
town government to be providing financial support to
it is a travesty, a prime example of the misuse of taxpayer funds."

The speaker was Richard Mauser, owner of a
metal-fabricating factory in an industrial park along-
side the Cabot Cove River, and an elected member of
the town council. Mauser, age sixty, was a bombastic
naysayer whose fiery speeches during council meetings were often the butt of jokes for those in attendance, but this didn't deter him from offering his
opinion on anything and everything. He was a large
man with a shock of copper-colored hair fringed with
gray, and whose suits—he always wore a suit and tie
to meetings—tended to be a size too small for his
bulky frame. His white dress shirts pressed into the
folds of his neck, and his face reddened whenever he
took the floor and railed against whatever was being
considered, shouting down those who disagreed with

his positions and disparaging anyone who dared challenge him.

This night was no different.

I'd had a previous engagement and hadn't planned on attending the meeting, but when I heard that renewing funding for the women's shelter would be on the agenda, I canceled my plans. Now I sat in the front row along with Edwina Wilkerson, a former social worker at the hospital and a friend of many years, who'd spearheaded the establishment of the shelter two years earlier. Edwina was one of those women who seemed to be in perpetual motion, and her wiry frame attested to her active life. She was coiled like a snake as Mauser spoke; I was ready to grab her should she leap up and attack the man.

"We've been sold a bill of goods," Mauser shouted, "told by the usual do-gooders in town that we even *need* a shelter for"—he paused and smirked—"for the fair sex. Well, let me tell you the facts. Let me differentiate between reality and fancy. The only thing the women's shelter accomplishes is to give women an excuse for leaving their hardworking husbands and adding to the divorce statistics. You want to talk about family values? I'll tell you about family values, and this shelter isn't it. Now, frankly, I don't give a damn whether these do-gooders want to run a shelter and pay for it out of their own pockets or collect donations from anyone they can hoodwink, but Cabot Cove has no business allocating funds to help sustain this travesty of morality." He glared at our mayor, Jim Shevlin, who sat with a small smile on his lips. Jim had had to put up with Mauser's mad rants for the years that he'd been mayor, and I admired him for his calm patience.

Mauser ran out of steam and sat heavily in his chair.

"That man is a heart attack waiting to happen," Dr. Seth Hazlitt, who sat on the other side of me, muttered.

"The man is despicable" was Edwina's whispered editorial comment in my ear.

"We've heard from Mr. Mauser," Mayor Shevlin said. "Let's open the discussion and hear other viewpoints."

Edwina quickly got to her feet. "First of all," she said, "I deeply resent the way Dick Mauser has characterized me and others associated with the shelter as do-gooders who are out to hoodwink donors. The fact is that the shelter provides a much-needed haven for women and their children who have been subjected to domestic abuse. Whatever funds the town contributes to the shelter each year help save lives, something that can't be said for Mr. Mauser's plant, which pollutes our river and *threatens* lives."

Mauser stood and shook a finger at Edwina as he boomed, "I won't allow this meeting to turn into a forum for the dissemination of lies and character slurs."

"Sit down, Dick," Mayor Shevlin said. "You've had your say. Now it's Ms. Wilkerson's turn to have hers. Ms. Wilkerson, please confine your comments to the subject at hand."

Edwina gave an impassioned defense of the shelter and the need for it. When she was finished, the mayor asked whether anyone else wished to address the subject. I was about to stand, but Seth Hazlitt was on his feet and facing the forty or so people who'd attended the hearing. The room was silent as one of our town's leading citizens took the floor.

"First of all," he said, "I've been one of those people

who, some say, have been 'hoodwinked' into donating money to the shelter—and I've done so with pride, and intend to donate more. Now, I know where people who oppose the shelter are coming from. There are folks, and well-meanin' ones I might add, who view having a women's shelter as sayin' something negative about the town they've grown up in. But let's face the facts. Cabot Cove is no longer a sleepy little town bypassed by the problems larger cities have. Sure, we're still blessed compared to lots of other places. Our problems are relatively minimal. But that doesn't mean we can sweep 'em under the rug. And unfortunately domestic abuse is one of these problems. I'm not sayin' it's an epidemic, but it exists, and anyone who denies it has blinders on. Mayor Shevlin and the council are doin' the right thing by supporting the shelter despite Mr. Mauser's protests."

There was a smattering of applause as Seth sat. I patted his arm. Although doctor-patient confidentiality prohibited Seth from naming names, he had confided in me that a few of his patients were women who'd been abused, and said that he'd even treated a man whose wife had the habit of striking out at him physically, causing bruises as well as humiliation. Seth said the man was grappling with intense shame at having been hit by a woman, even though he hadn't provoked her attacks, nor had he responded in kind.

The mayor called for a vote on whether to provide funding for the shelter for the upcoming year. The measure passed with Richard Mauser the lone "nay" on the council. He grabbed the briefcase that sat next to him and stormed from the room, muttering under his breath.

"That man!" Edwina exclaimed.

"Just your typical, run-of-the-mill blowhard" was Seth's evaluation. "Coffee, anyone?"

The three of us went to Mara's, on the dock, where Edwina and I asked for decaf lattes, a new offering by the town's favorite eating establishment. Seth specified a cup of regular coffee—"I never did understand this latte business," he said—and added a slice of lemon meringue pie to his order.

"Well," I said to Edwina, raising my cup to her, "we have something to celebrate: another year of funding for the shelter."

"No thanks to our favorite council member," she said.

"Forget him," said Seth. "Likes to hear himself talk."

"He's so self-righteous."

"The pie is delicious," Seth said. "Anyone like a taste?"

We declined.

I deliberately shifted the topic of conversation from the shelter to less contentious subjects, and Edwina calmed down. As we stepped out into the cold, humid, March night air, she thanked Seth and me for our support. "I'll see you tomorrow night?" she asked me.

"I'll be there," I said. As a member of the shelter's board, I'd volunteered to be on hand one evening a week in case anyone walked in seeking services.

Later that night, as the final scenes of the original black-and-white version of *Brief Encounter*—the Technicolor remake for television starring Sophia Loren and Richard Burton was, in my humble opinion, dreadful— faded out and THE END came up on the screen, I reflected on the events of that evening and my involvement in them.

The Cabot Cove women's shelter had been founded two years earlier. While Edwina was the public face of the committee formed to establish the refuge for abused women, it had been Seth Hazlitt's brainchild. The genesis of the idea had surfaced at a dinner party at my house attended by Seth; Edwina; our sheriff, Mort Metzger; his wife, Maureen; and a few other friends. Seth had cited statistics he'd recently read—twenty-five million American women are the victims of domestic violence each year, resulting in more than two thousand homicides. Mort reminded us of a murder that had taken place only one year earlier in the next town down the coast: A drunken husband had killed his wife in the midst of a violent argument.

"I heard that their cops knew something was going on," Mort said.

"Well, couldn't they do anything?" his wife asked.

"They answered a couple of calls, but the wife, she always refused to press charges. Their hands were tied."

"How awful," Maureen said.

"The point is," said Seth, "Cabot Cove isn't immune to domestic violence. Seems to me that it might be time for setting up a place here where women can come if they need to escape trouble at home."

"Unfortunately, I know someone who would benefit from such a place," Edwina said. "Her husband treats her like chattel. He's always putting her down in front of others, and I'm certain that he's hurt her more than once when she stood up for herself. I won't mention any names, but some of you certainly know her. Of course, she's too proud or ashamed or scared to allow the truth to come out, stays at home so her friends won't see the marks he left on her."

The topic had been bounced around for another hour, until it was time for my guests to leave. As Edwina was on her way out, she'd turned to me and asked, "Would you be interested in joining a committee I'm going to form to get us a women's shelter right here in Cabot Cove?"

"Count me in," I'd said.

And so I became part of Edwina's tenacious drive to raise private funding and to persuade the town council to back the plan financially. She was successful. The Cabot Cove women's shelter became reality. Edwina immersed herself in domestic violence counseling courses, and an anonymous donor put up enough money to purchase a small house in an area zoned for commercial use—even I didn't know where it was. The location was kept secret, or as secret as possible, to avoid having an irate husband arrive on its doorstep in search of a wife who'd run from his abuse. I did know that three women and their children were currently residing there until they could move on to something more permanent. Two were from Cabot Cove, but the third had come from a village down the coast, having been reluctant to involve her friends in her troubles, and fearing that her husband would be able to track her down too easily if she remained in her hometown. An office was leased in town as the public face of the shelter, where women could drop in for an initial consultation, solace, and advice. The office was staffed by a cadre of volunteers, yours truly included. Private donations coupled with a yearly sum from the town's operating budget kept things afloat, along with funds allocated by the state legislature, a federal stipend dispensed under the Congressional Victims of Crime Act, and, later, increased funding when the federal Violence Against Women Act was passed in Congress.

Cabot Cove was late in joining the statewide network of shelter programs for those who are abused, primarily because people were hesitant to acknowledge that such things existed in our tranquil small town. But Maine had recognized it as a serious problem as far back as 1973, and the movement to address domestic violence really picked up momentum in 2000 when then-governor Angus King declared violence against women and children "Maine's Public Enemy Number One" in his State of the State Address. He dramatized his remarks by pointing to seats in the hall that had deliberately been left empty to represent those who'd been killed by domestic abusers.

I turned off the TV and climbed into bed. A feeling of well-being swept over me. As I often do, I thought about how fortunate I was to live in a place like Cabot Cove and to have so many wonderful friends. The town's strong sense of community has always been alive and well, and the establishment of the shelter is but one example of that spirit of reaching out to the less fortunate and more vulnerable.

My final thought as I closed my eyes and allowed sleep to wash over me was that life was good in Cabot Cove. I had no reason to think otherwise.

Chapter Two

Hate hunting but glad when he goes away for a weekend with his buddies—wish he would go away forever—leave me alone—leave the kids alone—what did they ever do to make him so mad? He wasn't like this when we met—nice and gentle—except for the hunting—killing defenseless animals—makes my skin crawl—no pets for us—he never let us have pets—maybe just as well—he wouldn't be kind to them. —MW in Maine

Hey, MW in Maine—Sounds like you're in a bad situation. I know what you're going through. Been there, done that. Janet is right. Get out!!! It'll only get worse. They always do. Get out now. Your kids are suffering, too. Wish I could help but I'm on the other side of the country. —JS in Oregon

I spent part of the next afternoon catching up on correspondence and other paperwork before whipping up a simple dinner for myself. Although I'd worked behind the scenes to raise funds for its establishment, it was my first evening to volunteer at the women's shelter's downtown office, and I considered riding my bike into town. But the sky was threatening (March is one of those months in Maine when you can never accurately predict what the weather will be day to day), which ruled out using my trusty two-wheeled transportation. I called a taxi (*One of these days I really should learn to drive*, I thought) and arrived composed and dry. Edwina was already there reading the newspaper.

"Feels good in here," I said, referring to the warm air that was oozing from the ceiling vents. "What's new in the paper? I never got a chance to read it this morning."

"Evelyn was kind to Mauser. All she wrote was that he voted against funding for the shelter, not a word about his rant."

"Just as well," I said. "Do you know his wife?"

"Met her once or twice. You never see her in town. A real homebody. Seemed nice enough, kind of shy, quiet."

"I wonder if she ever gets a word in at home," I said.

Edwina laughed. "Can you imagine being married to a bully like that?"

"Not a pleasant contemplation," I said. "I've never met her. Is she his first wife?"

"I'm sure she is. She's about his age, give or take a few years. Not a young 'trophy' wife, if that's what you're wondering."

I settled into a small club chair and reviewed some of the training material I'd been given. "Think anyone will walk in tonight?" I asked.

"You never know. Some nights it's quiet and sometimes two calls come in just as someone walks in the door. Remember, if someone phones in looking for support, use language that's full of empathy and reassurance, but nothing judgmental, no questions asking why she did or didn't do something."

"Because 'she's doing what she needs to do to survive,'" I said, quoting from the sheet in my hand. "I was just rereading those instructions."

"Exactly! By the way, Jessica, one of the women is moving out of the shelter tomorrow. We've found a new home for her and her teenage son. We're delivering furniture to their new place tomorrow afternoon."

Aside from cash donations, the shelter was the repository of contributions of clothing and furniture, baby items, food, and other necessities for those who didn't want to return home to an abusive environment. But it was only temporary quarters. Edwina and others working at the shelter helped them find and move to alternate lodgings.

"That's great," I said. "Anything more they need?"

"I'll know once they're moved in. I'm so excited for her. It'll be a new life for her and her son, safe from battering, new credit card, new untraceable cell phone, new PO box address, like the witness protection program."

"I suppose it is," I said. "Hopefully she'll pick up the pieces and build on her new life."

Edwina had brought with her homemade cookies that she put on a paper plate. We made cups of tea on a one-burner hot plate and nibbled on the sweets while filing a week's worth of forms and correspondence. I was on my knees putting papers in a low file drawer when the doorbell sounded. We both looked up. "I'll get it," Edwina said, and went to the door. She returned seconds later with a woman I almost didn't recognize. Myriam Wolcott was a friend of my neighbor Tina Treyz. We'd met at several of the bake sales Tina often organizes to benefit her favorite charities. I stood, schooled my expression so it wouldn't reflect my shock at her altered appearance, and extended my hand. "Hi, Myriam," I said. "Jessica Fletcher."

She took my hand but did it in a way that mirrored the fright in her moist eyes, tentative, as though touching me would injure her. "Jessica?" she said in a voice that was at once surprised and unhappy.

"Hi, Myriam," said Edwina.

"I—I think I shouldn't have come here," Myriam said, glancing in the direction of the door.

"But now that you're here, you might as well have a cookie, and tea or coffee," I said.

Edwina quickly pulled a chair from the corner and invited Myriam to sit. She looked as though deciding whether to stay represented a monumentally important decision. I smiled encouragingly. She sat.

I understood her unease. She'd undoubtedly expected to see only Edwina, whose work at the shelter was well-known around town and who could be counted on to keep confidential whatever nasty secrets Myriam brought with her. Could she count on me? I tried to put her mind at ease by saying, "I'm a volunteer here, Myriam, and I'm obligated to keep whatever transpires private. I promise you. But if you're uncomfortable with me being here, I'll leave, of course."

"No, that's okay."

"You're sure it's all right for Jessica to stay, Myriam?" Edwina asked. "It's your choice."

"She can stay. I just wasn't expecting her, that's all."

"We have tea and coffee. What would you like?" I asked, busying myself with the refreshments.

"Ah, neither," she replied. "No, I guess coffee would be nice." She looked down at her lap and smoothed her skirt.

Edwina and I glanced at each other. There was no mistaking the angry red-and-purple bruise beneath Myriam's left eye. I was taken aback at how disheveled she was. When we'd met other times, she'd always appeared to be meticulous in her dress and personal appearance, her brunette hair shining and nicely cut, makeup judiciously applied. But that wasn't the woman who sat before me this night. Whatever makeup she'd applied had been watered down by sweat and tears. Her eyes were bloodshot, her mascara smeared. Her hair hung in lank strands. Her red blouse was wrinkled, and she wore flip-flops, an odd choice for such a chilly night. She looked as though she'd dressed hastily in whatever was close at hand. There was no question why she was there. It wasn't a social call, and she didn't want to volunteer at the shelter. Myriam Wolcott had come because she'd been assaulted.

Before Edwina or I could initiate further conversation, Myriam doubled over, her head in her hands, and wept. I wanted to put my arms around her to comfort her, but I didn't know whether she was injured or bruised. Edwina had instructed that it was best not to hug the shelter's clients unless they initiated it. Instead, I sat in a chair close to Myriam's and said in a soft voice, "It's okay. You're safe here."

When she'd managed to stem the tears, Myriam looked up at us and said, "I'm so ashamed. I never should have come here. I didn't think I'd know anyone and—"

"As Jessica said, anything that happens here is strictly confidential," Edwina assured her. She laughed to lighten the atmosphere. "We're like those ads for Las Vegas. Whatever happens in this room *stays* in this room. Water's ready for coffee. Have a cookie."

Nothing was said as Myriam took a small bite and sipped her drink. Edwina broke the silence by saying, "It's very brave of you to be here, Myriam. It took a lot of courage. What made you decide to come tonight?"

Myriam drew a breath, winced, and touched her abdomen.

"Did someone hit you there, too?" Edwina asked gently.

She nodded.

"Do you need medical attention? If you'd like me to accompany you to the emergency room, I will do that."

Myriam looked up sharply. "No! No hospital. I don't need a doctor."

"All right," Edwina said soothingly, "no doctors. You know, you've taken an important step to protect yourself and your children just by coming here."

I remained silent, allowing Edwina to set the pace. She'd received extensive psychological training in how to handle battered and abused women. I'd attended several training sessions with her but was well aware of my limited knowledge. I knew my role was to be an attentive listener and to observe Myriam's demeanor and body language.

Edwina got right to the point. "Who hit you, Myriam?" she asked.

"I—Josh."

"Your husband?"

She mouthed a silent "Yes."

"He hit you in the face and in the stomach?"

She nodded. "And over here." She indicated her shoulder, then brushed away the tears that had started again.

"Has he ever done that before?"

The question caused Myriam to screw up her face as though a new, more intense pain had emerged. Judging from her reaction, Edwina and I knew what the answer was, but we waited to hear it from her.

She swallowed hard and nodded again.

"Many times?" I asked.

Myriam blotted her tears with the napkin, shrugged one shoulder, and winced.

"What provoked him to hit you tonight?" Edwina asked.

She blew her nose with a tissue. "He was angry about something. He always seems angry lately. He'd stopped after work at a bar and had a few drinks with some friends. I'd had dinner ready on time and the kids were hungry, and . . ." She shook her head. "Does it really matter? He was late and I said something. Maybe I shouldn't have."

"I don't know what you said," Edwina said, "but whatever it was didn't give him the right to lay a hand on you in anger. No husband ever has the right to hit his wife."

There was a lull that I filled by asking, "What about the children? Did they see him hit you?"

She drew in a deep breath before answering, "Yes, they did. My daughter, Ruth—she's twelve—she became hysterical, screamed that she hated him, and ran up to her room. She's always been her daddy's little girl. I don't want her to hate him."

"It's not unusual for a child to love a parent, yet hate what he does. You have a son, too, if I remember correctly," Edwina said.

"Mark. He's sixteen. He left and went to his friend Paul's house. I called the Hanleys and confirmed that he was there. They're a nice family. He arrived just in time for dinner." She managed a smile. "Mark has a good appetite. He eats us out of house and home. You'd never know it, he's so small for his age." Her smile turned to laughter. "I sometimes wonder where he came from. Everyone in my family is tall, and Josh is over six feet."

"Where's Ruth now?" Edwina asked.

"She's at a friend's house, too. I dropped her off before coming here. I didn't know what to do, where to go. I didn't want to come here, but it seemed the only place that I . . ."

"That you could feel safe and secure," Edwina filled in.

"Yes."

"That's what it's meant to be."

She visibly relaxed.

Edwina drew her out, asking about her life, and Myriam responded enthusiastically. She talked about their home, her garden that she took pride in, how well her children were doing in school, and how she'd been working on a sewing project to enter in the blueberry quilt contest. Edwina gently tried on a few occasions to get her back on the topic of having been assaulted by her husband, but Myriam resisted revisiting it. She looked at a clock on the wall. "I'd better be getting home," she said, standing and smoothing her skirt. "I can't thank you enough," she said.

"Before you leave, Myriam, I should ask you a few more questions," Edwina said. "Are there weapons in the house?"

"Yes. Josh is a hunter. I hate hunting, but it's his hobby. He has a gun collection that's kept locked up in a cabinet." Her brow furrowed. "Only . . ."

"Only what?" I asked.

"Oh, it's nothing, really. Josh has a couple of hand-guns that he keeps in the cabinet, too, but he's been leaving one of them in different rooms lately."

"A loaded handgun?" Edwina asked, her voice mir-roring her concern.

"No, of course not, never with the children around," was Myriam's response. She quickly added, "And he has permits. Josh is law-abiding."

Edwina and I avoided looking at each other. There was no need to verbalize what we were thinking. He was "law-abiding" except when it came to assaulting his wife.

"Has he ever used a gun to threaten you?" I asked.

Myriam shook her head vehemently, but I wasn't certain I believed her.

"Is Josh a heavy drinker?" Edwina asked. "Does he use drugs?"

"Well, he has a couple of drinks before dinner, and sometimes before going to bed." Her posture said that she was now anxious to leave, to get away from the questions. She edged toward the door.

Edwina looked at Myriam with her head cocked. "Do you feel it's safe enough to go home now?" she asked. "We can provide a haven for you and your children. He won't know where you are, and you'd be safe from any further abuse."

Myriam forced a small laugh. "Oh, I'm sure Josh has gotten over whatever he was angry about and everything will be fine. She managed a wide smile. "He's always so sorry after something like this, like a little boy who got caught doing something naughty."

Edwina nodded slowly, but I knew what she was thinking, that she'd heard this too many times from too many women. "Even so, you may want to have a safety plan in place."

Myriam swallowed audibly. "What's that?"

"Keep a small bag stashed away with a night's clothing for you and the children, and some cash or a credit card, just in your name. Set up a code word with the children, in case of an emergency, in case you need to leave quietly and quickly."

A small moan escaped Myriam's lips.

"And please keep in mind," Edwina continued, "if ever you decide you want to move out permanently, your new address can be kept private by law, and the state has a victims' compensation program, so some of your expenses could be covered. And we're here to help you in whatever way we can."

Myriam shook her head. "I don't think it will have to come to that. I love my husband and he loves me. He's just going through a difficult time, and sometimes he . . . he . . . Well, he's just going through a hard time right now."

"This is not about him," Edwina said urgently. "It's about you and the kids. We have programs to help them, too."

"Please don't tell anyone that I've been here. I'd be so embarrassed," Myriam said.

"You don't have to worry about that," Edwina said. "There's always someone at this number if you need us." She pressed a piece of paper into Myriam's hand.

"Do you feel well enough to drive?" I asked as we walked her to the door.

"I'm fine," Myriam said. "I'm sorry to rush out, but I have to pick up Ruth. Mark can walk home. It isn't far. Thanks again."

We watched her get into her car. She started it, waved at us, and pulled from the curb.

"She'll be back," Edwina said.

Chapter Three

He says I spend too much on groceries—I don't!—I try to scrimp and save, always using coupons and looking for sales—I hate him—forgive me—it's not right to hate anyone—but could kill him sometimes—no, don't mean that—I just feel trapped, nowhere to go. The kids—he's their father—doesn't hit them, not yet anyway—but they're scared of him, I can tell. They hate it when he yells—always cruel to me. Should talk to someone—not mother. Don't really want anyone to know—have to keep things together for the kids. —MW in Maine

Hello, MW—My family used to vacation in Maine when I was a kid. What part of Maine are you from? I really ache for the spot you're in. Isn't there some sort of shelter or other agency you can turn to for help? We have a shelter in my town in Ohio. Please seek help, MW. It sounds like you're in a dangerous situation. —Jill in Ohio.

Back home, I reflected on the evening.

I'd met Myriam's husband, Josh Wolcott, on a number of occasions—brief encounters around town. I'd attended a few Little League baseball games at which Josh had coached his son's team when the boy was younger, and we'd run into each other in stores and at a few community events. But we did have one sustained conversation almost a year ago. It occurred at my house.

He had called out of the blue one morning. "Mrs. Fletcher?" he said. "This is Josh Wolcott. I wonder if you remember me."

"Yes, of course, Josh. How are you?"

"Couldn't be better, Mrs. Fletcher. May I call you Jessica?"

"Of course."

"Great. I don't know if you're aware that I'm a financial planner right here in Cabot Cove."

"Yes, I know that," I replied.

"Well, it seemed to me that I'd be remiss if I didn't make contact with you concerning your financial planning needs, and—"

"That's good of you, Josh, but I already have a financial planner."

"Do you mind if I ask who it is?"

"A firm in New York City."

"New York City," he repeated, enunciating each word as though to give them extra meaning. "You're comfortable having someone that far away handling your financial affairs?"

"Yes, I am. It's a very reputable firm. I've been with them a long time."

His silence had meaning. After the pause, he said, "I know you're busy writing your best-selling books, Jessica, but I really feel that I might have some sound ideas that would benefit you and your financial future. All I'm asking is that you give me a half hour of your time. I can meet with you whenever it's convenient."

"I appreciate the call, Josh, but I really have no intention of changing things where my finances are concerned."

"I understand," he said, "but I can't urge you enough to at least become aware of some outstanding investment opportunities that are newly available."

"I *am* busy, and—"

"You'd have nothing to lose by simply listening," he said. "Look, I'm going to be on your street tomorrow. One of your neighbors—I won't say who—has asked me to review his portfolio. I can ring your bell before I see him. Only take a little of your time. Just a half hour that could be *very* beneficial to you. No commitment on your part. Just let me tell you what I have to offer."

It was obvious that he was not to be put off, so I agreed to have him come to the house the following day at eleven. He arrived dressed nicely in a navy blue suit, white shirt, and red-and-blue tie, and he was carrying a briefcase. He declined my offer of something to eat or drink, sat at my dining room table, opened his briefcase, spread out an assortment of papers, and said, "You won't regret taking the time for me, Jessica."

"As you said, I have nothing to lose by listening, although I must tell you that I have no intention of changing financial advisers."

"I certainly understand your reluctance to change," he countered, "but sometimes we become complacent and avoid change because it seems complicated. That's not the case here. Your mortgage is paid off, I assume.

It would help me if I could see the investments your financial adviser has you invested in."

I shook my head. "I'd rather not do that," I said.

He shrugged. "That's your choice, of course. But I'm concerned that you've placed your trust in someone far away from here. There's a big advantage in having your adviser close by, available to you twenty-four/seven, a neighbor who shares your values. I certainly know how successful you've been as a writer—I've read some of your books and they're great."

"Thank you."

"And I'm sure you've been handsomely rewarded financially. But even if you don't have ready cash, we can arrange, say, a refinancing on this house, for instance, to give you money to invest. What's important is that the investments you make stay ahead of inflation and assure you a comfortable retirement when you've laid down your pen and decide to take it easy."

I felt myself becoming impatient but didn't want to be impolite. He was, after all, a member of the community with a family and someone about whom I'd never heard anything negative. But I was anxious to get back to the book I was writing. He saved me from having to cut the session short by saying, "I know that you don't have time to waste, Jessica, so I'll get right to the point." He leaned closer and his tone became conspiratorial. "I have some very credible sources of information within the financial community that I share only with special clients. These sources—and I'm talking about top people—enable me to buy stocks for my clients before they become available to the general investing public. I don't know what your investments currently earn—three, maybe four percent?—but the investments I'm able to put you into can earn as much as twenty, maybe even twenty-five percent. Think of that, Jessica. Instead of falling behind inflation, you can watch your hard-earned money grow into sizable figures, far more than what most people enjoy. *And*, as I've said, you're dealing with someone close to home, a neighbor and friend."

He sat back, a satisfied look on his handsome face, confident that he'd gotten across his point and had been persuasive. I don't know whether my expression and body language reflected what I was thinking, nor did I express it. What struck me was what my late husband, Frank, always said—that if something sounds too good to be true, it probably is.

"I can put you into some of these sterling investment opportunities, Jessica, but we'd have to move fast. They come along only so often, and—"

"I don't think so, Josh," I said. "It was nice of you to drop by, but as I told you, I'm very satisfied with my current financial adviser. I'm sure you're very good at what you do, but your services aren't for me."

He said that he understood, but his face testified to something different. He shuffled his papers back into his briefcase, stood, and thrust out his hand. I shook it.

"This may not be the right time for you," he said heartily, "but I'll check back in six months. I'll let you know how these opportunities have panned out. I think you'll be surprised how well they did and be sorry that you missed out on them. Thanks for your time, Jessica," he said.

"Please give my best to your family. I've watched your son play baseball. He's very good."

*   *   *

I was glad he was gone, although I was sorry about his obvious disappointment. He seemed like a nice enough young man who was only doing what he did for a living, trying to sell someone something. Nothing wrong with that. But aside from my not being interested in changing financial advisers, I was taken aback by his promise of inflated profits through some unnamed sources in the financial community. It made me uncomfortable. It smacked of a possible pyramid scheme, at least to this relatively inexperienced investor. I hoped that wasn't the case, for his sake and for anyone who might fall for such a pitch.

Chapter Four

Been crying all day—can't help it—have to stop—he hates it when I cry. I hear him in the driveway—hope his day at the office was okay—hope he isn't angry—got to get supper going—he gets mad when it's not ready on time. Thanks for listening, all of you—helps to vent with someone, whoever you are. —MW in Maine

MW in Maine—Listen to me. Your husband is dangerous. Kill him before he kills you! Make it look like an accident. He'll kill you if you don't. —Anonymous

I'd forgotten about my meeting with Josh Wolcott until Myriam's arrival at the shelter the previous night. I saw him around town, of course, and we'd had a few short but pleasant chats. Josh is a member of the Rotary and Lions Clubs and we exchanged pleasantries when I spoke at those civic association luncheons. He seemed to be popular with his colleagues and never brought up our conversation about my finances again; nor did I raise the subject.

But seeing Myriam's bruised face and hearing her story cast Josh Wolcott in an entirely different light. It's true that he had come off as a bit of a hustler that morning he paid me a visit, perhaps involved in shady financial schemes, but I was shocked to learn that he was a wife batterer. You just never know about people who can hide who they really are.

These thoughts occupied me as I cleaned out a utility closet, a project I'd been promising myself to get to. I'd started right after breakfast and was halfway finished when the phone rang. It was Evelyn Phillips, the publisher and editor of the *Cabot Cove Gazette*, and a friend.

"Hope I'm not taking you from something important," she said.

"If finding three different-sized mop heads is important, then you are."

"Huh?"

"Just kidding, Evelyn. I'm cleaning out a closet. Happy for the break. What's new in town?"

"Not a lot. The reason I'm calling is that Sheriff Metzger has sent me a press release. Seems that festivals and fairs around the state have seen an increase in pickpocketing incidents, and he's come up with a list of things we can do to keep our possessions safe when in a crowd."

"Good public service."

"That it is. I wanted to spice up the piece a little and wondered whether you've ever used a pickpocket as a character in any of your books. You know, add a little color to the article."

"I can't say that I have," I said. "My bad guys, or gals, are usually murderers."

"Just thought I'd ask. What did you think of the council meeting the other night?"

I smiled. I knew that Evelyn must have had another reason for calling. "I was happy that funding for the shelter passed," I said.

"And what did you think of Mr. Mauser?"

"Oh, he likes to let off steam and pontificate. Fortunately cooler heads prevail when it comes to voting."

She lowered her voice. "Keep a secret, Jess?"

I sighed. It looked like this was another day of secrets. "I'll do my best," I said.

"Edwina may not have had any proof behind her accusations at the town council meeting, but I hear that the federal government, the EPA, is getting ready to launch an investigation into Mauser's company and whether it's polluting the river, a follow-up to the state's investigation last year."

"If he's polluting the river, he should be investigated, but as I recall, the state decided that he wasn't, at least beyond acceptable EPA guidelines."

"Rumor has it that he bought off the state inspector."

"Rumors aren't fact, Evelyn, as you well know."

"Of course. I can't print it without a confirmation. Just thought you'd be interested."

"I am, and thanks for sharing it with me."

"Got to run," she said. "The library is exhibiting Richard Koser's photographs and there's a luncheon."

"Richard takes wonderful photos. I'll make a point of stopping by later in the week."

By the time I'd rearranged the closet and determined

which mop head actually fit the handle, on top of finishing other chores around the house, the day was gone. I met up with Seth for a quick bite before attending a meeting of the Cabot Cove River Preservation Commission, which I'd been invited to join. It was obvious from the opening minutes that I wasn't the only person in town sworn to secrecy by Evelyn Phillips about the possibility that the EPA might be poised to investigate Richard Mauser's factory and its alleged role in polluting the river. Everyone on the commission knew about it, and a spirited discussion ensued. It was eventually agreed that the commission should do nothing until the EPA formally announced its intention, at which time they would do what they could to support the investigation.

I sat on my glassed-in porch after returning home from the meeting, sipping a tall glass of lemonade, and finished reading a novel I'd started days ago. It occurred to me as I closed the cover and headed inside that it was possible to become so involved in a community's affairs that there was little room left for other things—like writing murder mystery novels—and that maybe it was time to start my next book. I'd been developing a plot for it, and its twists and turns kept me from falling asleep until long after I'd gotten into bed.

I would have slept a little longer the next morning were it not for the ringing phone. I glanced at my digital alarm clock: seven thirty. Who'd be calling at that hour?

I picked up the phone and heard Edwina Wilkerson say, "Jessica?"

"Hello, Edwina."

"I hope I didn't wake you."

"It's time that I was getting up anyway."

"I have terrible news."

I sat up straight and said, "What is it?"

"Josh Wolcott has been murdered!"

Chapter Five

It's me again. I was the one who suggested that you kill your husband before he kills you. Have you done it yet? Of course not. You don't even have the guts to leave him.
—*Anonymous*

There's nothing like being told that someone you know has been murdered to bring you fully awake and to get the blood flowing. Maybe "blood" is the wrong word to use. "Juices" would be more appropriate.

I sat on the edge of the bed. "How do you know?" I asked Edwina.

"My brother Alfred called me." Her brother, who lived outside of town, was a ham radio fanatic who spent time when he wasn't working tuned into police, fire, and aviation frequencies. "Alfred said that he heard a call go out to the police last night at about nine, nine thirty, for a possible gunshot victim at the Wolcott house. He stayed tuned and heard Sheriff Metzger call back to headquarters for the medical examiner and a crime scene unit to be dispatched. The sheriff said on his call that it *was* a homicide, and named Josh Wolcott."

"Do they have any suspects?"

"Not that I know of, but, Jessica, do you think that— I hate to even consider it—do you think that Myriam might have shot him?"

"Let's not jump to conclusions, Edwina."

She was not the only one to call about the shooting. By nine my phone was virtually jumping off its base. Every time I tried to squeeze in a shower, it rang, friends calling to ask whether I'd heard about Josh Wolcott. Each caller had information to impart, although it was obvious that just about everything they had to offer was based upon rumor and innuendo. They all wanted to know whether I had any information about the event, assuming, I suppose, that a writer of murder mysteries has some magical insight into real crime. I fended them off as politely as I could and finally grabbed a quick shower, dressed, and managed coffee and an English muffin before the next call.

It was Seth.

"Yes, I heard," I replied to his question. "Edwina called me earlier. Do you have any factual updates?"

"I notice you injected the word 'factual,' Jessica. I assume the rumor mill is running amok."

"That's putting it mildly."

"Well," Seth said, "I did have a brief conversation with Doc Foley." Dr. Rolland Foley was a physician in town who doubled as the medical examiner. Seth often filled in for him when he was away. "From what he says, Wolcott was gunned down in his driveway last night, single shot to the chest."

"What sort of weapon?" I asked.

"Not sure at this juncture, Jessica. I gather that the weapon wasn't found at the scene."

"The family must be devastated."

"Ayuh. Did you know the Wolcotts well?"

"No," I replied. I almost added that I'd been at the women's shelter two nights ago when Myriam Wolcott walked in, but held myself in check, certain it would constitute a breach of confidence, murder or no murder.

"I knew Mr. Wolcott," Seth said. "He wasn't a patient of mine, but he tried to get me to hire him as my financial adviser a coupla years ago."

"He did the same with me," I said. "He was nice enough, but I told him right away that I didn't intend to change advisers."

"Same here. I had a funny feeling about what he was trying to sell."

"You, too?"

"Ayuh. Whenever somebody tells me that he can triple my profits, it raises my wariness antenna."

"Frankly, Seth, I had the same reaction."

"I did a little checking after he left the house. He was a certified financial adviser, all right, but there have been a few complaints filed against him, claims that he misrepresented what he was offering."

"Sorry to hear that," I said, "but I suppose it doesn't make any difference now that he's gone."

"Unless somebody who filed a claim against him got sore enough to take drastic action."

I hadn't thought of that in the hubbub of that morning. Of the basic motives for murder, money ranks right up near the top along with jealousy, revenge, and envy, not to mention being a battered spouse.

Seth excused himself to answer another call but was back on the line quickly.

"Sorry, Jessica," he said. "One of those infernal telemarketers wanting to sell me some jo-jeezly thing I don't need or want. I told her that I was busy but that if she'd give me her home phone number, I'd call her this evening while she's eating dinner."

"What did she say?" I asked, laughing.

"She hung up."

"Good for you, Seth," I said. "I'll talk to you later."

I'd no sooner put the receiver down when I heard a plop at the front of the house. I opened the door and picked up that day's edition of the *Cabot Cove Gazette*. The bold banner headline screamed at me: "It Was Murder." I took the paper inside and laid it on my kitchen table. Evelyn Phillips must have been up all night putting together the story, although she shared the byline with James Teller, a young reporter whom she had hired fresh out of college with a journalism degree from the University of Southern Maine in Portland. I'd stopped by the office a few days after he'd started working there and Evelyn had introduced us. I was immediately taken with James's youthful exuberance and energy, which undoubtedly had been helpful in coming up with the story overnight.

According to their article, the 911 operator had received a call at 9:07 from the Wolcott residence. The caller was Myriam Wolcott. The conversation with the operator was replayed in the story:

"Nine-one-one."

"This is—oh my God—there's been a shooting," Myriam was reported to have said.

"A shooting. Where?"

"At my house. It's . . ."

"What's the address, ma'am?"

Myriam managed to get it out.

"Is the victim with you now?"

"Yes. No, he's in the driveway."

"Is he alive, ma'am?"

"No. I don't know. He's been shot."

"Do you know the victim?"

"Of course I do. It's my husband."

"Is the shooter still there? Are you in danger?"

"No, he's not here. I mean, I don't know who shot him. Please hurry. Send help. Please!"

"Can you see if he's still alive, ma'am, breathing? I'll notify the proper authorities. I'm sure they'll be there shortly."

According to the article, Sheriff Metzger was called at home and immediately met up with a deputy who'd responded to the 911 call. After surveying the crime scene, the sheriff called for backup, the medical examiner, and a crime scene team. Dr. Foley arrived fifteen minutes later and confirmed that the victim, Joshua Wolcott, was indeed dead.

Evelyn Phillips and her new hire, James Teller, had also gone to the scene and reported what they'd witnessed. Two patrol cars were parked at the foot of the driveway, their lights flashing. Evelyn and Teller were able to get close to the victim before another deputy arrived and helped establish an off-limits boundary using crime scene tape. Prior to being banished to the perimeter, the reporters were able to get off two snapshots in which the deceased was seen lying in a pool of his own blood next to his vehicle, his face covered with a cloth presumably placed there by the police. He was on his back; the driver's door of his gray SUV was open, leading the writers to speculate whether he was gunned down as he was about to get into the car.

Although neither Evelyn nor Teller was able to gain access to the house, an anonymous source—my guess would be one of the EMTs—said that the victim's wife, Myriam, and their two children, a teenage boy and a younger daughter, were huddled on a couch. Another couple was with them, later identified as Mrs. Wolcott's brother, Robert, and her sister-in-law, Stephanie, who lived sixty miles down the coast.

Attempts to question Sheriff Metzger were stone-walled. "I have nothing to say at this moment," the sheriff replied. "This is an ongoing investigation."

Evelyn and her new journalist had done a good job reporting the incident, considering its fast-breaking nature. Aided by the photos, I kept visualizing the grisly scene as I settled in my home office and checked e-mails that had come in overnight. I was in the midst of that task when the phone rang once again.

"Mrs. Fletcher. It's James Teller at the *Gazette*."

"Hello, James. I'm just reading your coverage of Josh Wolcott's murder. I must say that you and Evelyn did a thorough job."

"I spent most of last night at the scene of the crime and have been trying to dig up additional facts all day."

"Quite a baptism for you in your new position."

"You bet, Mrs. Fletcher. It's my first byline. I mean a real one. I had plenty on the school newspaper, but this is different."

I congratulated him.

"Ms. Phillips suggested that I call you."

"I'm afraid that I have nothing to offer, James. You know a lot more than I do. Everything that I do know comes from your article."

"But Ms. Phillips said that besides writing mysteries, you've also helped solve real murders."

"That's unfortunately true."

"Did you know Mr. Wolcott?"

"I'd met him a few times, but I wouldn't say that I knew him well."

"Ms. Phillips thought you might have a few insights or comments about the murder."

"Hold it right there," I said. "Writing about murder is one thing. The real thing is another. My only comment is that my heart and prayers go out to the Wolcott family."

"Oh, sure, no offense. It's just that we're working on a follow-up piece and are looking for some local color."

"Well, James, I appreciate the call, but I'm afraid you'll have to find your color elsewhere."

"Do you know *Mrs.* Wolcott?" he asked.

I hesitated before saying, "We've met. She's a lovely lady."

"She's being questioned as a suspect."

"Oh? I'm sorry to hear that."

"I have it from a good source."

"It's only natural that the police will want to hear from her."

"No, I mean she's a *suspect*."

While I admired his tenacity and youthful zeal for his job, I wasn't anxious to prolong the conversation. "I really must be going," I said.

"Okay, only I hope it's all right if I call you again, you know, as the case progresses."

"If you wish. Say hello to Evelyn for me."

Trying to put the murder out of my mind was like telling someone not to think of a green-and-white zebra. It stayed with me throughout the afternoon, helped along by more phone calls from friends. I spent time outdoors cleaning winter debris from my garden and doing other March chores. The light was fading when I came inside to answer yet another call. It was Edwina Wilkerson again.

"What a day," she said.

"A day we could all do without. Have you heard anything aside from what was in the paper today?"

"Yes, I have. I got up the nerve to call Myriam a half hour ago. She'd just gotten back from being questioned by the sheriff at police headquarters."

"How is she holding up?"

"As well as can be expected. Sheriff Metzger put her through quite a wringer, as she put it."

"Questioning her is routine," I offered. "After all, she was there at the time of the shooting. Did she say anything to indicate who might have killed him?"

"No. But she did tell me a little of what had happened. She and Josh had an argument that escalated into something more."

"Did he hit her again?" I asked.

"I believe so. Myriam says that it began to 'get out of hand,' which really upset their son, Mark. He walked out and went to a friend's house not far away. Myriam said that his friend's mother and father have become like a second family to Mark. He always went there when things heated up at home. Anyway, Mark left the house and the daughter, Ruth, fled upstairs to her room. Myriam says that her husband had been drinking before the argument and announced he was going out. She asked him where he was going, but he wouldn't tell her. She tried to stop him and he threw her down. He left the house to get in the car—this is what Myriam says—and after a while she heard a shot. She ran outside and found him lying there by the car, blood coming from his chest."

"What an awful thing to have to go through," I said. "The article in the paper says that Myriam's brother and his wife were there."

"That's true. She was in a panic and called them before dialing nine-one-one."

Before calling 911? Calling her brother first would certainly be viewed by some, especially anyone in law enforcement, as highly unusual and suspicious. Why hadn't she immediately sought medical help in the event her husband was still alive and might have survived with emergency care? But I wouldn't pass judgment on someone who'd just suffered such a shocking discovery. In her state of mind, it might have made all the sense in the world to reach out to a brother who lived relatively close by.

"Poor thing," Edwina said. "I just keep wondering if I should have been more forceful when she came to the office, insist that she leave the house and move to the shelter."

"Don't second-guess yourself," I said. "You couldn't have forecast and staved off this tragedy. Did she say how her children are doing?"

"She said that they've rallied around her. I hope she arranges for some sort of therapy for them. The impact of a tragedy like this can last a lifetime. Oh, Myriam's mother is on her way from Bangor to help with the kids. Myriam didn't sound too enthusiastic about it. Seems her mother was never a fan of Josh Wolcott."

"Be that as it may, it's good that Myriam will have some additional support. Thanks for the update, Edwina."

"I thought you'd want to know, considering we spent time with her the other night. And I wanted to talk to you because I'm not sure exactly what to do."

"What do you mean?"

"Well, the police ought to know that Myriam was a battered wife, that Josh hit her, don't you think? But I'm not sure it's ethical to tell them. I only know about it because she came to the shelter. But we promise confidentiality to all our clients. Do you think I should tell the police that Myriam had come to the shelter after Josh had hit her?"

"They may already know, but I'd ask Myriam how she feels about that," I replied. "I imagine it will come out anyway as the investigation proceeds, but ask her first."

I could almost hear her sigh over the phone. "Good advice," she said. "I didn't want to bring it up to the shelter board, but maybe after all this is over, we can straighten out what we do in cases like this. We're learning as we go. Thanks, Jessica."

I just had time to drop in at the library to see Richard Koser's photo exhibit before getting over to my local market. I had a grocery order I wanted to leave there for delivery the next day. Richard occasionally did work for the *Gazette*, but his loves in life were art photography, cooking, and of course his wife, Mary-Jane, not necessarily in that order.

Richard's photographs were mounted on foam board without frames and filled a whole wall in the front entrance of the library to the right of the checkout desk. His subjects varied from landscapes and architectural studies to candid scenes and portraits. I browsed pictures of places in Cabot Cove that were familiar to me, most of which were made all the more dramatic by being rendered in black and white, a few shots accented with color. Whether he still used film or used the computer to make his digital pictures mimic black-and-white film, the images were dark and mysterious.

"Nice, aren't they?" said a voice behind me.

"Wonderful," I replied, turning to see my friend Tobé Wilson. Tobé is married to Jack Wilson, Cabot Cove's most popular veterinarian, and works side by side with him at their animal hospital. Some years back, she'd made a name for herself and attracted quite a bit of attention by walking her pet pig, Kiwi, in town. Kiwi was now in hog heaven, having succumbed to old age, but people in Cabot Cove still remembered her fondly. Meanwhile, Tobé volunteered what spare time she had to civic activities. She was this year's chairwoman of the Blueberry Festival.

"Can I count on your being a judge in the blueberry pie contest this summer?" she asked.

"I will if you need me," I said. "I was debating whether or not to enter it myself."

"You can enter one of the other competitions," she said. "We're going to be inundated with blueberry pies, and I'm desperate for good judges. I've got Charlene Sassi, but everyone else I've asked turned me down."

"I'm sure Seth would help you out," I said.

"Already called him and he declined."

"He did?"

"He said he gained three pounds with last year's contest and still hasn't taken them off. He's not willing to add to the total."

"Well, that's prudent of him," I said. "He could stand to lose a pound or two."

"Or three. So are you in?"

"Tell you what," I said, not eager to add to my weight either. "If you can't find anyone else, I'll fill in, in a pinch. But I'd really rather not be a judge."

"Fair enough. I'll keep looking, but in the meantime, I'll send you the judging instructions. By the way, did you see Richard's picture of the river that runs behind Dick Mauser's plant?"

"No. Which one is it?" I asked, scanning the top row of photographs.

"This one down here," Tobé said, leading me to a photo of leaves floating on the water; the base of a brick building could be seen in the background. Richard had added color to the picture, tinting the rocks along the shore and several of the leaves spilling down the bank a bilious acid green.

"He's making a political statement, wouldn't you say?" I said to Tobé.

"No doubt about it, but it's hardly undeserved," she replied.

"Has anyone come up with any proof that Mauser's plant is polluting the river?"

"We should have it soon," Tobé said. "Jack says the team from the Environmental Protection Agency is expected to arrive any day."

"Is that official?" I asked.

"He heard it this afternoon from a councilwoman who brought in her corgi to be spayed."

"I wonder why the river preservation commission hasn't been informed," I said.

"You'll probably get the word in the morning," she replied. "Frankly, I hope they come up with a finding that really rakes Mauser over the coals, hits him with a hefty fine that torches his bottom line. And I'm not the only one to feel that way."

I was surprised to hear Tobé wishing a harsh result on anyone. Her kindness to four-legged creatures usually extended to the two-legged kind as well. Clearly, Mauser had alienated many in the community.

But later that night after I'd gotten home, changed for bed, and started reading my new Molly MacRae novel, *Lawn Order*, I was struck with how dramatically and swiftly events had occurred that would impact the town. Only a few days earlier, the most exciting news stories in Cabot Cove were plans for the upcoming annual lobster and blueberry festivals, high school sports, an occasional case of teenage vandalism, and other less-than-monumental happenings.

Now Josh Wolcott's murder, his history as a wife abuser should it ever come out, and a federal agency arriving to investigate Richard Mauser's business would be splashed on the front pages of the *Cabot Cove Gazette* and would dominate conversation.

I knew that the so-called good ol' days weren't necessarily as good as we liked to think they were, but I silently wished for a return to them as I closed my book, and my eyes.

Chapter Six

You haven't been posting anything lately and I wonder if you are OK. —Janet

I answered a call from Edwina Wilkerson the following morning as I was putting away the groceries I had ordered. "I just heard from Myriam Wolcott," she said. "She's asked me to visit her."

"Did she say why?"

"She wants to speak with me about her visit to the shelter's office. She asked whether you'd come."

"I barely know her."

"But you were there that night, Jessica. I know you're busy, but I'd really be grateful if you would come with me."

"When are you planning to go?"

"Later this morning, at eleven. I can pick you up."

"All right," I said. "I'll be waiting."

*   *   *

Edwina drove the way she did everything else in life—
fast! You got the feeling that she viewed each day as
possibly her last and intended to cram a lifetime into it.
But I didn't comment as she sped along the road leading out of town and to the community where the Wolcott house was located.

It was a split-level, identical to all the other homes
on the block, the lawn and small flower garden in
front as perfectly maintained as the neighbors' yards.
We pulled up to the curb and I took note of a small
yellow car parked across the street. The sun was in
my eyes and I squinted to see if I recognized the
driver who sat stoically behind the wheel. It was
James Teller, from the *Gazette*. I waved and he returned the gesture.

But it was another vehicle that more fully captured
my attention, a marked Cabot Cove police cruiser containing two officers. One was a familiar face, a deputy
sheriff who'd been with the department for a number
of years, while the second was unfamiliar to me. There
was also a black Lexus sedan with a Maine license plate
parked in the driveway.

Edwina and I got out of her car. A white granular
substance coated a spot in the driveway that I assumed
was there to cover Josh Wolcott's blood. Although the
newspaper article had said that crime scene tape had
been strung, it had been removed, a positive sign where
Myriam was concerned. Teller had told me that she
was considered a "suspect," which I chalked up to his
youthfulness. A "person of interest"—a more neutral
designation and one meant to indicate that many people were being questioned—was the politically correct
term these days and was more likely the way Myriam

was being viewed at that juncture, unless evidence surfaced to make her an official suspect.

Two red bicycles—one a larger boy's model, the other a smaller one meant for a female rider—were piled together in front of the two-car garage. While the lawn and garden were manicured, the house was starting to show some neglect; white paint on the garage door had started peeling, and the trim around the front door was doing the same. A screen on the front window was torn as if someone had put a fist through it.

Edwina rang the bell.

We heard movement before the inside door was cracked open by Myriam, who peered questioningly at us through the screen door.

"Hi, Myriam," Edwina said.

"Yes, hello," Myriam said as she unlatched the door. Warm air enveloped us as we entered. It was dark inside; no lights were on and the drapes were tightly drawn.

"I'm so sorry about Josh," I said, giving her a brief hug.

"Yes," Edwina said. "This is a terribly difficult time for you."

"Thank you for coming," Myriam said weakly. She wore tight-fitting jeans, a white blouse underneath an open brown cardigan, and running shoes.

Myriam led us into the living room. "Please sit down." She flipped a wall switch, and two table lamps came to life. "I don't have much in the house, haven't had a chance to go shopping, but I do have some tea I can make, and there's cookies." She smiled. "My neighbor brought over a plate just now. She said there should always be cookies around with kids in the house."

I was saddened to see how little support Myriam was getting from the community. Had Josh died of a disease or in an accident, the ladies of Cabot Cove would have dropped off more casseroles and cakes and other dishes for the grieving family than they could possibly consume. Thank goodness one neighbor had the compassion to bring something for the children.

The lack of provisions spoke to how ill at ease Myriam's neighbors must be, given the circumstances of her husband's death. But I was willing to give them the benefit of the doubt. Perhaps the presence of a squad car was keeping them away, and when it disappeared (along with Teller's vehicle) the neighborhood would rise to the occasion. At least I hoped so.

"Nothing for me," I said as Edwina and I took chairs on either side of a table on which books and magazines were piled high. Edwina also declined the offer of refreshments.

"Is it cold out?" Myriam asked, pulling her sweater closed. "I haven't been out of the house today."

"It's pretty chilly," I said, "but I tell myself I can smell a breath of spring in the air. Nice weather should be here soon."

Myriam gazed around the room as if she didn't know how to start, her eyes resting briefly on a small dent in the wall that might have been made by an object being thrown. Edwina asked about the children. "How are they doing? Are they here with you now?"

"They're doing okay, I suppose," she said, starting to pace. "I don't think it's really hit home with Ruth. She's the youngest, just twelve. It's hard to read Mark. He's filled with anger. He's over at his friend's house. Thank goodness for that family; they're so understanding."

"Ruth is such a sweet old-fashioned name," Edwina commented. "Is she named in honor of someone?"

Myriam chewed on the inside of her cheek. "She was named after Josh's grandmother. I would have liked something a bit more modern, but Josh insisted, so Ruth it was. I call her Ruthie most of the time. She's such a little girl for such a serious name."

"Where is Ruthie?" I asked.

"She's upstairs with my mother. She'll be down in a moment." She hesitated, then continued. "My mother arrived early this morning. She drove here from Bangor last night."

"It's good that she wasn't too far away," I offered.

Myriam didn't respond.

"And how about you, Myriam?" Edwina asked. "How are you doing?"

Myriam plopped in a chair and exhaled loudly. "Me? What can I say? Josh is gone, shot dead by some crazy person." She shook her head. "I don't know how I'm doing. I don't know what to feel. I still can't believe it."

"Do the police have any leads?" I asked.

"Not that I know of. Of course, there's always me." Her laugh was sardonic. "Our wonderful sheriff grilled me for hours. The kids were questioned, too. How unfair to subject them to such trauma. They'd just lost their father in a horrible way, but the sheriff didn't seem concerned about that."

"I understand how you feel," I said, "but Sheriff Metzger has his job to do."

"He's an insensitive bully," Myriam responded.

Of all the words I might come up with to describe Mort, "bully" wouldn't be on the list. I fought an urge to defend him; it wasn't the appropriate time or place.

"The shelter has a child advocate," Edwina said. "We can arrange for the children to get some counseling, if you like. It would be helpful for them to talk with someone about their father, help them work through their feelings. Will you consider it?"

"I'll think about it," Myriam said.

Footsteps were heard on the stairs, and we all turned to see Myriam's daughter, a thin girl enveloped in a heavy sweater, followed by an older woman. Myriam got to her feet and held her arms out for her daughter. Ruth ran to her embrace, hugging her mother tightly. Myriam turned her around. "This is Ruth," she said to us. "Say hello to the ladies, Ruthie."

Ruth murmured a greeting, never taking her eyes off the floor. She had a pale face with a pink nose, probably from crying. Her long brown hair had been fashioned into two tight braids, a hairstyle more suited to a younger child.

Myriam's mother reached the bottom of the stairs and stood, hands on her hips, her head cocked as though to ask who we were. Myriam was a tall woman, about five feet seven inches, but her mother was taller, at least five-ten. She was immaculately dressed in a pale green sheath. She wore heels, and her jewelry was plentiful and looked expensive. Her hair and makeup had obviously been professionally tended to.

"This is my mother, Mrs. Warren Caldwell. Mother, this is Edwina Wilkerson and Jessica Fletcher. I told you about them."

"Yes, you did," Mrs. Caldwell said. "I know of Jessica Fletcher. She writes."

My vocation had never been described quite so bluntly before. I smiled and nodded.

Myriam asked whether her mother wanted something to drink.

"Thank you, no," Mrs. Caldwell said, and took a seat on a small red-and-blue-flowered couch that showed wear; I envisioned the children jumping up and down on it.

"Ruthie," Myriam said, "Mommy needs to have a conversation with your grandmother and our visitors. Please go down to the playroom. You can watch TV. I'll call you when we're finished."

"She's very sweet," I said as the girl left the room.

"More important, she's very smart," Mrs. Caldwell added.

She perched on the edge of the couch as though to avoid contact with as much of the cushions as possible, her knees tightly pressed together, long, tapered, red-tipped fingers laced on her knees. "I understand that you had a conversation with my daughter a few nights ago," she said, addressing both Edwina and me.

Edwina and I glanced at Myriam to see whether she was distressed by the question. Her privacy was being breached.

"It's all right," Myriam said. "I told her where I went."

"You mean when Myriam visited the women's shelter office?" Edwina said.

"Yes, that is what I'm referring to."

"Myriam was upset," Edwina offered. "She'd . . ."

"Let's face facts. She came because of what her husband did to her," Mrs. Caldwell said flatly.

Edwina nodded slowly.

"It was an ill-advised visit," Myriam's mother continued.

Edwina looked to me before responding, "I was pleased that she sought us out. She needed someone to talk to, someone who would understand what she'd just experienced and who could provide nonjudgmental comfort."

Mrs. Caldwell smiled sweetly, although I suspected that it took effort to do so. "Comfort is what a family is for. She should have come to me," she said.

I sensed Edwina tensing. "But you weren't here and she came to us," she said, working at keeping pique from her voice. "Do you have a problem with that, Mrs. Caldwell?"

"If I did, would it make any difference?" She turned to her daughter. "Would it, Myriam?"

Myriam started to say something but swallowed her words.

"I'm sure that you both are aware that Myriam's marital history with Joshua is an embarrassment."

"There's nothing to be embarrassed about," Edwina said. "Myriam is hardly the first wife to have been abused by her husband. Domestic violence is the greatest source of personal injury to women, causing more than three times as many medical visits as car accidents, more injuries than rapes, auto accidents, and muggings combined. Ten women a day are killed each year by their male partners or ex-partners. As many as four million American women are battered each year by their husbands or partners. That's one every seven or eight seconds. There's no reason at all for Myriam to be *embarrassed*."

Mrs. Caldwell listened patiently as Edwina rattled off her data, a bemused smile on her face. When Edwina was finished, Mrs. Caldwell said, "That's all well and good, but I'm not interested in seeing my daughter lumped into a bunch of statistics. The point is that both you and Mrs. Fletcher have been privy to what is a very private matter, and I insist that it remain just that, a private matter."

I hadn't said anything up to this point, but now I felt compelled to respond. "Mrs. Caldwell, as a volunteer, my only role is to lend an understanding and sensitive ear to a victim of domestic abuse," I said. "Edwina has received considerable professional training in dealing with abused spouses, and in our volunteer classes she has stressed to all of us the importance of discretion and privacy. In fact, it's only because Myriam has given approval that we're discussing this with you. I assure you that all of us who work at the shelter, staff and volunteers alike, never discuss what goes on inside with anyone who isn't specifically involved in the case."

"My daughter is not a 'case,' Mrs. Fletcher," Mrs. Caldwell said coldly.

Edwina jumped in with, "Jessica didn't mean to offend you, Mrs. Caldwell, but her point is valid. What happens at the shelter stays there. I suggested to your daughter that she leave the house that night to avoid any further physical violence, advice she declined to follow—which I fully understood. Frankly, I'm surprised that you even feel the need to raise the privacy issue."

Mrs. Caldwell straightened and lifted her chin as she retorted, "I'm protecting my daughter, who has the misfortune of being considered a suspect in her husband's murder."

There was silence in the room.

I broke it by asking, "Have the authorities used the term 'suspect' in regard to your daughter?"

"They questioned me as though I was," Myriam said.

Her mother chimed in, "Of course she's a suspect. They always consider a family member first." She looked at me. "You must know that, Mrs. Fletcher. After all, you *do* write murder mysteries."

I turned to Myriam. "You aren't saying that Sheriff Metzger actually accused you of having killed your husband, are you?"

"Not in so many words, but he might as well have."

"Did you ask for a lawyer?" I said.

Myriam turned pale. "No! Do . . . do I need one?"

"We'll take care of that when the time comes," Mrs. Caldwell said.

I was tempted to put in a good word for Mort, who was usually pretty sensitive when it came to interviewing recently bereaved family members. But I hadn't been there, and defending him would serve no purpose at this time. Instead I said, "I understand that your brother and his wife were here, Myriam."

Her expression said that she was surprised that I knew. "It was mentioned in the newspaper article," I explained. "Have they left?"

"Yes," Myriam muttered.

"Her brother, Robert, is a very responsible person," Myriam's mother said. "He had business obligations to get back to."

I thought it was a shame that Myriam's brother's business responsibilities trumped his responsibilities as far as his sister was concerned. Given that she had just suffered such a shocking loss, I would have hoped that either he or his wife would have stayed behind to help. But perhaps Mrs. Caldwell had shooed them out, or, just as likely, they had left to escape her domineering rule.

"The press has no right to interfere or report on family matters," Mrs. Caldwell said through a pronounced sneer. "I suppose they've asked for your expert opinion, Mrs. Fletcher."

Although James Teller had called me for a comment, I didn't mention it.

"There's a reporter parked outside the house right now," she said. "Those ghouls!"

"It's not surprising," I said. "There's been a murder, and they have a job to do, too."

She dismissed me with a pointed shake of her carefully coiffed head and addressed her next comment to Edwina. "Let me get to the point of why Myriam has asked you here today. She's still in shock, as you might expect, and can't be depended upon to think clearly."

Myriam's pained expression made me wince.

Her mother continued. "My daughter made a very big mistake going to this shelter that you run, airing her dirty family laundry, and contributing, I'm sure, to your town's gossip mill.

"I . . ."

"Please stop right there," Edwina said sternly, holding up her hand. "Your daughter came because she'd been physically abused by her husband, because she needed a refuge from him, and I'm very proud that Mrs. Fletcher and I were there to provide it. As for this so-called gossip mill, nothing that was said that night ends up in any mill. I apologize if I appear to be argumentative, Mrs. Caldwell, but it's clear to me that you don't understand how a women's shelter operates and why it's important to a community—especially to those who are being abused."

Mrs. Caldwell stood, ran her hands over the front of her dress, and after a prolonged sigh said, "I can see you aren't accustomed to being challenged, Mrs. Wilkerson. Let me leave it at this. If any mention of my daughter's misguided visit to your shelter is made to anyone—and I stress *anyone*—you'll hear from my lawyer." She aimed a tight smile at us. "It was a pleasure meeting you both."

Edwina and I watched her stride across the room and disappear down the stairs to join her granddaughter. Myriam continued to sit on the couch, legs tightly crossed, hands hugging her elbows, head bowed. She looked up and said, "My mother is, well, she's a very intelligent and, I guess you could say, determined woman. Please don't take offense at her way of speaking. It's just that she loves me and the children and wants to protect our name. Reputation is very important to her. Try to understand."

Myriam uncoiled her body and showed us out. She thanked us for coming and closed the door behind us, engaging the lock. I saw that Teller's car was gone; the patrol car remained in place.

"Can you believe it?" Edwina said as her tires screeched away from the curb.

"Take it easy," I said. "Slow down."

"Sorry. Protect the family name and reputation, my foot. By the way, Jessica, mind a bit of advice?"

"Oh dear. Did I talk out of turn?"

"No. Of course not. I'm just steamed at that—that

terrible woman." She pulled the car to the curb, turned off the engine, and looked at me. "You referred to Myriam as a *victim* of domestic abuse."

"Wrong word?"

"It's accurate, of course, but women in that position dislike the term. *Survivor* of abuse is more acceptable, although they aren't crazy about that either."

"Lesson learned."

"Thank you."

Edwina started up the car. After admonishing her to ease up on the accelerator, I commented, "I believe there's more to it than worrying about the family's name and reputation."

She shot a glance at me. "Like what?"

"Like not wanting the authorities to know that her husband was a batterer. If the police hear that, they'll have the perfect motive to assign to Myriam: abused wife who'd taken enough and killed her attacker."

"Won't they find out anyway? The children might already have said something."

"They might have," I said. "And the family that Mark always sought solace with may have spoken with the police, too. And it probably wasn't wise of Mrs. Caldwell to tell Myriam to invite you and me to the house together, given our connection with the shelter. She may have inadvertently informed the police and the press of exactly what she was trying to keep secret."

Edwina stopped at a light. "Myriam's mother is clearly an abusive personality," she mused aloud. "Maybe that's why Myriam chose Josh. It's not an unusual pattern."

The light turned green.

"Do you really think that Myriam might have shot Josh?" she asked.

"I have no idea what happened," I replied, "but the police always first look for a motive, and then for proximity to the murder. Unfortunately, Myriam Wolcott provides both."

Chapter Seven

After years of abuse I left my husband and went to a women's shelter in our hometown. It wasn't an easy decision but it had to be done, otherwise I really think he would have killed me. The people at the shelter were terrific, put me up until they found a nice apartment for me, new phone number, driver's license, everything to hide me from my husband. Do you have a shelter in your town in Maine? If so, check it out. It could save your life. —S.S. in Florida

Edwina and I had errands to run, so we parked in town and agreed to meet back at the car in an hour. It had started to snow and I was glad that I'd thought to wear a jacket with a hood. Hopefully it would be no more than a March snow shower, not enough to coat the roads and make driving treacherous.

I ducked into Charles Department Store, where I hoped to find a replacement plastic card insert for my wallet; the old one was torn and my credit cards threatened to fall out at any moment. The department store had just what I was looking for—they always seem to have what I need—and I was paying when Tim Purdy, Cabot Cove's historian and president of the historical society, came up to me. A tall, distinguished fellow, he was dressed as he often is in a tweed jacket, brown slacks, and a floppy red-and-yellow bow tie. A tan trench coat was casually draped over one arm.

"Hello, Tim."

"Good morning, Jessica." He glanced at a clock on the wall that read a few minutes past noon. " 'Good afternoon' is more appropriate. How are you?"

"Fine. I haven't seen you in a while."

"I've been hibernating, putting the final touches on the revised history, and you're just the person I wanted to see."

Tim is passionate about our town's history and had written a wonderful book about it a few years ago, which he was in the process of updating.

"You've found me," I said pleasantly. "What can I do for you?"

"Two things, Jessica. First, I'm thinking of expanding the section on the river and its meaning to Cabot Cove."

"Oh? You think that's necessary?"

"I wouldn't have, but Dick Mauser's plant and the controversy over whether he's polluting the river change things."

"Do you have any new information about it?" I asked.

"The EPA is sending a team."

"So I've heard."

"In that light, I fear that I shortchanged the river and

its role in the town's development in the first edition and want to beef it up."

"That seems like a good idea, Tim, whether the EPA comes up with anything or not."

"The library found some old photos of the river for me. They're from the thirties. I'll add them to the new edition."

"How nice, but what's that have to do with me?"

"Let's go over there," he said, motioning toward benches in the store's shoe department. Once we were seated, he said in a low voice, "You heard about what happened to Josh Wolcott, of course."

"Yes."

"A terrible tragedy. But you know, Jessica, it started me thinking about the revision I'm working on. Updating the book to include more about the river's impact on the town prompted my thinking about another update that should be considered."

"Which is?"

"A chapter on murders that have taken place in Cabot Cove over the years."

"That again? I thought we discussed that when you were about to write the original book and decided *not* to include *that* sort of history."

"We did decide that at the time, yes, but it occurs to me that you can't really do an honest history of a place without including its less savory aspects. New York had its Son of Sam, Boston the Boston Strangler, Los Angeles its Night Stalker and Hillside Strangler, and Chicago with all its Mafia killings, and—well, after all, Jessica, we have had murders here in Cabot Cove over the years."

"Still . . ."

"And you were involved in them."

I was afraid that he was going to bring that up.

"An unfortunate reality," I said.

"I did mention in the original version that we have a distinguished writer of murder mysteries living in town, namely, one Jessica Fletcher."

I sighed and responded, "Which is fine with me, provided it refers to me only as a *writer* of crime novels. My having played a role in solving a few cases doesn't belong in a Cabot Cove history."

"You're being modest," said Tim, "but the history would benefit from some—how shall I say it?—from including some provocative material. To be honest, I was sort of hoping that you'd agree to write a chapter about murder in Cabot Cove. Everyone views us as being an idyllic, crime-free, picturesque town that never has to deal with the sort of problems other communities have. But that's a whitewashed version of the town's history. The truth is that we're a community of men and women, some of whom do bad things. I got to thinking about it at the council meeting the other night when the debate over the women's shelter erupted. We have domestic violence, just like every other place, and maybe we should own up to it, the way you and Edwina and others are doing with the shelter."

A family came into the store and started browsing shoes.

"I think we'd better let them have our seats," I suggested. We walked outside and stood under a canopy to avoid the last remnants of the big, wet, white flakes.

"I understand what you're saying, Tim, but I really don't think that you should devote a chapter to murders that have occurred here. It isn't as though we had a Lizzie Borden or Jack the Ripper. And as for me writing a chapter like that, I'm afraid the answer is no."

"I sort of figured you'd say that, Jessica," he said, not trying to keep the disappointment from his voice, "but maybe you'll think more about it. Will you?"

"Sure, but please don't count on my changing my mind. Now, you must excuse me. I have a few more errands to run, and I'm meeting my ride home in a half hour. Great seeing you, Tim. Best to Ellen."

I pulled up my hood and darted across the street into the dry cleaner's to pick up a pair of slacks that I'd had altered.

"Hi, Jessica," Jack Wilson said as he paid his bill. "Nasty day."

"Looks like it's already stopping," I said. "How're things with my favorite vet?"

"Busy as usual. I can't believe what happened to Josh Wolcott."

"The whole town's in shock."

"Except the person who killed him. Have you heard anything?"

"Nothing more than anyone else," I said, fudging the truth a little.

"What I hear is that the sheriff and the state investigators are narrowing in on Myriam Wolcott."

I thought of what Jim Teller had said, that Myriam was considered a suspect. At that early stage of the investigation, everyone who ever knew Josh would be under suspicion until the field was culled to those with the greatest motive and the means to have killed him. I just hoped that our sheriff, Mort Metzger, wouldn't rush to judgment and prematurely accuse anyone of the crime, something he was known to have done on occasion.

My final stop was the law office of Cyrus O'Connor, Jr. Cy had moved back to Cabot Cove after graduating from law school and joined his father in a practice that the elder O'Connor had established years ago, a general law firm that handled virtually every legal problem anyone might have with the exception of felony criminal cases. Unfortunately, Cy's father had died of a massive heart attack while representing a client in court, leaving Cy as the firm's sole practitioner. He was a pleasant young man with a sharp mind and an obvious love of the law. I arrived at his office to pick up a codicil I'd had added to my will, and as I walked into the reception area, I was surprised to see Myriam Wolcott's mother, Mrs. Warren Caldwell, seated and reading a magazine. She glanced up at me, gave forth the tiniest of smiles, and returned to her reading. My "hello" elicited another glance, another painful smile, and renewed interest in the magazine.

As I took a chair across the room from her, Cy O'Connor's receptionist, Sharon Bacon, came from his office. Sharon was in her early sixties, a stout woman in all senses of the word. She was a round, resolute, and reliable assistant to her boss. She'd been Cy Senior's receptionist and legal aide since her graduation from secretarial school, and although she possessed no degree, her knowledge of the law and her understanding of its arcane language had been of considerable help to both father and now son.

"Hi, Jessica. He'll be with you in a minute."

"I have time," I replied, although I wondered how long it would be if Mrs. Caldwell met with him before

I did. That question was answered when Cy poked his head into the waiting area and said, "Come on in, Jessica." He said to Mrs. Caldwell, "Mrs. Fletcher and I will only be a few minutes."

He shook my hand, closed the door, and went behind his desk, where he picked up a manila envelope. "Here it is, the codicil you wanted. I think it's in perfect order." He withdrew the paper from the envelope. "You can sign it now and I'll notarize your signature." He buzzed for Sharon, who entered the office. "Need you to witness Mrs. Fletcher's signature," he said.

With the formalities out of the way, O'Connor said, "I can't believe what happened at the Wolcott house."

"Everyone would prefer not to believe it," I said. "I see that Myriam's mother, Mrs. Caldwell, is in your waiting room."

"You know her?"

"I met her this morning. She drove down from Bangor to be with her daughter and grandchildren."

"She called earlier and said it was urgent that she speak with me. My father had done some legal work for the family years ago, although I can't imagine what she'd want from me."

I shrugged.

"Josh was a client of mine," he said. "In fact, I met with him the day before he was killed." He made a tsking noise. "What a thing. What's the world coming to?"

"Did he seem upset?" I asked.

"No more than usual. He was a tightly strung sort of guy, a real type A." He hesitated as though to decide whether to say what he was thinking. "You have any thoughts on what might have happened?"

I shook my head. "Obviously someone who was angry with him—very angry—let that anger dictate his or her need for revenge."

"Do you know Josh's wife, Myriam?"

"I've met her on a few occasions," I said carefully.

"The poor kids. She has a son and a daughter."

"So I understand."

"Sharon's cousin Beth had the boy in her biology class. Sharon said Beth told her Mark got into a lot of scuffles. Of course, that's probably par for the course at his age."

"I'd better be going, Cy, or I'll miss my ride back home."

"Oh, sure. Good seeing you."

"Thanks for the good work on the codicil. Just send the bill."

"Shall do."

When I walked into the reception area, Mrs. Caldwell looked up and nodded. I returned the non-verbal gesture and left the building. Edwina was waiting in her car.

"Get everything done?" she asked.

"Yes. I just left Cy O'Connor's office. Mrs. Caldwell was there waiting to see him."

"Really?"

"He said that she'd called earlier today to set up an appointment."

"Cy doesn't handle criminal cases," Edwina said as she revved the engine.

"I don't know if that's why she was there. He told me that his father had done legal work for the family and that Josh Wolcott had been a client. Maybe she's there to talk about a will or other family matters."

"Pretty quick to be doing that, isn't it?" Edwina said

as she headed for my house. "The body's not even cold yet."

"I have a feeling that when she decides to do something, Mrs. Caldwell doesn't let anything get in her way, not even her son-in-law's murder."

"Cold as ice," Edwina summed up.

As I was getting out of the car in my driveway, Edwina said, "I wish Myriam hadn't come to the shelter."

"Why?"

"It's just that someone like Dick Mauser will use Josh's murder to smear the shelter again."

"How will he find out about Myriam's visit?" I asked.

"You know Cabot Cove. I'm afraid someone will say something somewhere. And Mauser will pick it up."

"If he does, it can't be helped," I said. I looked up into the pewter sky and smiled. "Looks like it might snow again. Thanks for the lift, Edwina. I have a sudden need to get lost in my kitchen and cook something to help get my mind off things like March snow squalls—and murder."

Chapter Eight

We're still here for you if you need to vent. All of us have walked in your shoes. Come back whenever you want. We're here to help. —Elaine in Tucson

Two days after I'd visited Myriam's house and been introduced to her overbearing mother, Evelyn Phillips called me and imparted the following information: The Wolcott family computer had been taken from the house by Sheriff Metzger and his deputies, its contents to be analyzed by a forensic computer expert from the state's crime lab. I knew from an Authors Guild seminar I'd once attended how even files that have been deleted by the user can be resurrected. In this day and age, one's private life is anything but private, and I hoped that Myriam hadn't written anything on her computer that would prove embarrassing—or in this case injurious.

"The word about town is that Sheriff Metzger is getting closer to charging her with Josh's murder."

"Until he actually does, I'd prefer to think that he won't," I said.

"Well," Evelyn said, "she *is* retaining Cy O'Connor as her attorney."

"Retaining a lawyer is probably a wise move," I said. "I've seen it too many times. Someone says the wrong thing and ends up being falsely accused. An attorney can head that off. But why Cy O'Connor? As far as I know, he doesn't do criminal law."

"I thought you might know of a reason."

"I haven't any idea, Evelyn. That's a matter for Myriam to deal with."

I'd no sooner hung up when Mort Metzger called.

"Morning, Mrs. F."

"Good morning, Mort. Good hearing from you."

"I've been all drove up lately, to use one of your Maine expressions, with the Josh Wolcott murder. Busy as a tire changer in the left lane of the West Side Highway."

"Yes, I imagine you are, Mort. How is your investigation proceeding?"

"Making progress. I need to talk to you, Mrs. F."

"That's never been difficult."

"I'd prefer not to talk on the phone. Think you can swing by headquarters later today?"

"That shouldn't be a problem."

"Say right after lunch?"

"I'll be there at one."

I hung up and pondered the reason for his call. Not that it was unusual to hear from our sheriff. I'd become good friends with Mort and his wife, Maureen, and circumstances had led me to help him out on occasion. That he wanted me to come to his office indicated that it was something serious, and I couldn't help but wonder whether it had to do with the murder of Josh Wolcott. I hoped not. I'd had my fill of becoming involved in real murders over the years, and each experience left me with a bad taste in my mouth, not to mention physically and emotionally drained.

Writing about murder is different. I'm able to sit at my computer, play out my fantasies, and give my imagination full rein. At the end I bring the bad guy to justice, ensure that good triumphs over evil, and establish a sense of order that we don't always find in real life.

Until my conversation with Tim Purdy about including a chapter in the Cabot Cove history chronicling the town's murderers, those nasty episodes had receded into my past, stashed away in a separate and secure compartment of my brain. But I'd been thinking about some of them ever since bumping into Tim at Charles Department Store, and as hard as I tried to stow them away again in my memory trunk, I couldn't quite close the lid. The ones that coincided with holidays or special occasions were most vivid in my memory.

There was the Christmas when a popular citizen, Rory Brent, a jovial 250-pound man with flowing white hair and beard—he played Santa Claus every year at the town party—was shot to death, presumably by a neighbor known for his nasty temper. I ended up digging into the two families' lives and staving off a miscarriage of justice.

One Thanksgiving, a drifter, Hubert Billups, arrived in town, and his constant presence on the road outside my house had set me on edge. I hosted a dinner that

Thanksgiving; the guest list included my dear friend from London, Scotland Yard inspector George Sutherland, a number of friends from Cabot Cove, and at the last minute Mr. Billups. He was found stabbed to death a few hours after dessert, and because he had been a guest, I was drawn into the investigation, with George at my side.

Then there was the murder of a local lobster broker just prior to our annual lobster festival, when I was not only immersed in finding the killer, but also a target myself.

The most memorable murderous moment occurred leading up to Halloween. Tim Purdy conducted an annual Halloween ghost tour, the highlight of which was a recounting of the "Legend of Cabot Cove." Her name was Hepzibah Cabot. Her husband, a sailor, who was away for extended periods, had had a fling with another woman while on a trip. Hepzibah learned about it, confronted him when he returned home, chopped off his head, and committed suicide by throwing herself into the sea. She became a legend because over the decades people reported seeing her in various places, Cabot Cove's own resident witch. On this particular Halloween a strange woman, Matilda Swift, rented a cottage on an estate owned by a friend of mine, and her otherworldly behavior had tongues wagging. She was found murdered in her cottage while the annual Halloween costume ball at the estate was under way, and I ended up looking behind the costumes worn by the people at the party—and at their motives—to help identify the killer.

Maybe Tim was right. Maybe the town's history should include its less illustrious moments, just as long as I wasn't the one writing about them. Recalling them was unsettling enough.

The weather had cleared and the temperature had risen, a welcome harbinger of the spring that would follow. I rode my bike into town, parked it in front of police headquarters, and went to Mort's office in the relatively new building. He was meeting with a deputy when I arrived and I waited out front until he was free.

"Thanks for stopping by, Mrs. F. Sorry I couldn't send a car for you. All my deputies are out on the Wolcott case."

"No problem, Mort. I enjoyed the ride into town."

"One of these days you should get yourself a driver's license."

"Maybe I will," I said, "but it isn't high on my priority list."

He chuckled and went to the coffee machine that sat on a shelf behind his desk. "Coffee? Tea?"

"Neither, thank you."

He poured himself a coffee, resumed his seat behind the desk, leaned forward, and said, "So, you know all about the problems Mrs. Wolcott had with her husband."

My raised eyebrows and cocked head reflected my surprise.

"The women's shelter," he said. "I'm told that you were there when she came in after her hubby beat her up."

"Mind if I ask who told you that?"

"Don't mind at all. In questioning a neighbor of the Wolcotts, one of my deputies picked up that she'd gone to the shelter. Not sure if it was the wife, Mrs. Wolcott, or one of the kids who told the neighbor. And I got it that you were there from someone else closer to the scene. But it's true, right? You were there?"

I did a quick calculation about whether admitting I'd been present violated the rules of privacy at the shelter. I decided that even if it did, I couldn't lie to the police, and said, "Yes, I was there, Mort. Why do you ask?"

"Well, Mrs. F., knowing that Wolcott beat up on his wife is kind of an important thing to know, wouldn't you say?"

"It certainly is for his wife."

"What did she tell you that night?"

"Now, Mort," I said, "you know that you're treading on a sensitive issue. Women who come to the shelter are assured that what transpires there is privileged information."

His frown said that he didn't buy it.

"That's all well and good, Mrs. F., but I'm dealing with a murder here. Seems to me—and the county DA agrees—that when there's a murder involved, all bets are off. It also seems to me that the relationship between the Wolcotts is darned important. I'm sure it won't surprise you that we're looking at Mrs. Wolcott as a suspect."

"It doesn't surprise me at all," I concurred. "And I know what's behind you wanting to know what happened that night at the shelter. If Josh Wolcott was a wife batterer, it provides Myriam Wolcott with the motive to have killed him."

He started to say something, but I continued.

"Be that as it may," I added, "I don't think it's appropriate for me to be telling tales out of school, in this case tales out of the women's shelter."

Mort held up his hand. "Take it easy, Mrs. F. I just thought that we could get this over with, have a pleasant chat about it." His voice took on a more conspiratorial tone. "The DA and the state and county investigators will just have to subpoena you and Ms. Wilkerson, do the same with the shelter's records."

"Then I'll wait for that, Mort. I'm not trying to be difficult, but I take very seriously the pledge of confidentiality I took when I started volunteering at the shelter. I'm sure you can understand that."

"Of course I do, and I admire you for it. It's just that I'd like to save the town and the county some money, gather up evidence without having to go the legal route. Besides, I've always been up front with you, haven't I?"

"Yes, you have, Mort, and I've always appreciated it. But in this case . . ."

"Yeah, yeah. I know, I know, you gave your word and you mean to keep it."

"Thank you for understanding. May I ask you a question now?"

His eyebrows went up. "You can ask."

"Have you been contacted by the attorney Cyrus O'Connor?"

"Got a call from him first thing this morning. Sounds to me like you know more than you're telling me."

"Just responding to a rumor around town, Mort, that Myriam Wolcott might be retaining him as her lawyer."

"I don't pay much attention to rumors, Mrs. F., but in this case it's true. It surprised me, too. Never knew the man to take on criminal cases."

"Has he agreed to represent her?"

"Seems so. He put a stop to questioning her unless she's charged. Typical lawyer's first move."

I stood and glanced out the window. "Spring is in the air," I said.

"Can't come soon enough."

"Mort."

"Yeah?"

"Who told you I was there when Myriam Wolcott came to the women's shelter?"

He winced.

"I think I'm entitled to know. After all, it appears that I'll now become involved in a very direct way."

"Her brother," he said flatly.

"Myriam's brother?"

"Right. Seems that she called him the night she came to the shelter. I had him in here yesterday for questioning, and he told me about the call."

"Her mother will not be pleased," I said.

"You know her?"

"We've recently met."

"Tough old bird."

"That's one way of putting it. Are we finished?"

"I am if you are." He rose and walked me outside.

"If I'm subpoenaed about that night at the shelter, I'll naturally comply."

"Sorry, Mrs. F."

"I know you have a job to do. Please send my love to Maureen. Has she been cooking up exotic dishes lately?"

Another wince. "Let's not discuss that, Mrs. F. Thanks for coming by."

I couldn't help but laugh as I pedaled away from his office. Maureen Metzger was a dear soul, full of life, one of the town's real doers. She was also one of Cabot Cove's most adventuresome—and least successful—cooks.

My cell phone started ringing and vibrating while I was riding home. I stopped and checked the screen to see who was calling. Seeing the name Josh Wolcott caused me to flinch. I answered and heard Myriam Wolcott say, "Jessica Fletcher?"

"Yes. Myriam?"

"Yes, it's me. Have I caught you at a bad time?"

"I'm just riding my bike home, but I'm happy for the break. I admit that I was startled to see Josh's name on my screen."

"I haven't changed the phone yet."

"How are you?" I asked.

"Oh, I'm all right, I suppose, all things considered. Mrs. Fletcher, um, Jessica, I was wondering whether you could spare me a few minutes."

"Of course."

"I have some time this afternoon. Will you be home?"

"I should arrive in fifteen minutes, and I plan to stay there for the rest of the day."

"I could come around three," she said. "I can't stay long because—well, because it's been so hectic, and with the children and all, I . . ."

"Come at three," I said, "and stay as long as you wish."

Her call dominated my thoughts for the rest of the trip home. Once there, I put up a pot of coffee, defrosted some cinnamon buns from Sassi's Bakery, and awaited her arrival. I heard the car pull into my short driveway and opened the door. Myriam looked more put together than when I'd last seen her, although the lines on her young face reflected the strain she was obviously under. She managed a smile at my greeting and said, "Thanks for seeing me."

"It's no trouble at all," I said. "Coffee's made, and I have some absolutely wonderful pastries from Sassi's. Come in and we can talk."

But Myriam found it difficult to express herself. Once inside, she demonstrated her state of anxiety by pacing my living room floor and rubbing her hands together. I invited her to sit several times, which she ignored, and she didn't take me up on my offer of something to drink and eat. I'd begun to wonder whether she'd ever get around to telling me why she'd come when she finally sank onto my couch and said, "I just don't know what to do, Mrs. Fletcher."

I sat next to her and said, "I don't wonder that you'd be confused, Myriam. And please, it's Jessica."

"They think that I killed Josh. Every day someone else wants to talk to me. I'm afraid I'll go mad if I have to answer the same questions again."

"I understand that you've retained Cyrus O'Connor to represent you. Hasn't he put a stop to the questioning, at least for the moment?"

"You know that?"

I wasn't about to tell her that I learned the news from our sheriff. Instead I said, "Your mother was in Cy O'Connor's waiting room when I stopped into his office the other day. I assumed that she was discussing your representation with him."

"I suppose so," she said through an exasperated sigh.

I was puzzled at her reply, and my expression mirrored it.

"Mother hired him."

"Cy's not a criminal attorney, you know."

"She knew that."

"Then why . . . ?"

Myriam raised her hands as if to say something, then dropped them in her lap with a sigh. "You don't know my mother, Jessica."

I held back what my initial impression of her mother had been.

"She's a very strong-willed woman," Myriam said. "She wants a young attorney she can control. I'm sure of it."

"That's not a very smart way to go," I offered. "It's like being one's own attorney, and you know what they say about that. Or choosing a doctor because you can dictate your treatment. There are some very skilled criminal attorneys in the area who I'm sure would be glad to take your case—if you think you're going to be charged with a crime."

She fell silent.

"I'm sitting here, Myriam, wondering why you wanted to see me today."

"How can I say it?"

"Just say it, that's how."

"I need someone to stand up for me," she said in almost a whisper.

"I'm not sure I understand."

"Stand up for me with my mother and others once

I'm charged with Josh's murder. You're highly respected in town, and I know that you've helped people in the past who were falsely accused of killing someone."

"You say you need someone to stand up for you with your mother? It's true I don't know her well, but she's obviously very much in your corner. And Cy O'Connor is a bright and capable young attorney, even if he's not experienced in handling criminal cases."

"He told Mother that he wasn't the right kind of lawyer to take my case, but she insisted. I suppose the money she offered helped sway him. My father left Mother a sizable sum when he died. She can afford to buy who she wants."

I somehow doubted whether O'Connor would inject himself into a legal matter with which he was unfamiliar simply for money, but he may have been responding to an appeal for help. Then again, while I knew the father, I didn't really know the son. Perhaps he had another reason for taking a case that was outside his area of expertise.

"Although Mr. O'Connor isn't a criminal attorney," I said, "I'm sure he's qualified to handle things at this early stage. If—well, if your legal requirements become more serious, you can always bring in an experienced criminal attorney."

"Tell that to Mother." She jumped up and began pacing again.

I formulated my response in my mind before saying it. "Myriam, I'm sure your mother only wants to help you navigate this difficult situation, and that must be comforting, but I can't help but feel that since you're the one directly involved, you should be the one making the decisions. After all, it's your life and your children's lives that are at stake."

As diplomatic as I attempted to be, my words caused her to stiffen. "I don't want to give you the wrong impression about Mother," she said. "She's a wonderful, very intelligent woman who knows about such things, things that I don't know anything about. Who else can I trust?"

I realized that it would not be productive to argue the point. Her lack of self-esteem was painfully evident when she came to the shelter, and she continued to demonstrate it.

"I'm sure whatever decisions you and your mother make will be the right ones, Myriam. But let's get back to what you want of me. You say that you want me to stand up for you. I'm not sure what that entails. We aren't really familiar with each other, but I'm certainly concerned for you and your family. Beyond that . . ."

"You do believe me, don't you?"

"About what?"

"That I didn't kill Josh."

"I have no reason not to," I said, failing to add that my belief in her innocence might change should evidence surface to the contrary.

"It's important that you believe me, Jessica. You're well respected in town and are friends with the sheriff and . . ."

"Let me think this over," I said, interrupting her by standing and removing the plate of pastries to the kitchen. Her comment about my being friends with Sheriff Metzger shed light on the reason she was there. She hoped that I'd put in a good word for her with

Mort, which I would not do. Standing up for her as a friend, really more of an acquaintance, was one thing; injecting myself into the investigation was another.

Myriam followed me into the kitchen. "I have to get home," she said. "Mother took Ruthie out for the afternoon and doesn't know I came here. She'd be upset if she knew. Thanks for being here for me, Jessica. I really appreciate it."

I watched her drive off, poured myself a cup of coffee, and settled in my office. Like it or not, I was being dragged into the Josh Wolcott murder, something I'd promised myself wouldn't happen. I could hear Seth Hazlitt: *"There you go again, Jessica, gettin' yourself all bound up in another murder. When will you learn?"*

And I wouldn't have an answer for him.

Chapter Nine

"Wife Charged in Wolcott Murder."

The headline stared up at me from the front page of the *Cabot Cove Gazette* as it sat on my front step the following morning. But it wasn't news to me. I'd already heard about it via an earlier phone call from Seth Hazlitt.

"Thought I'd give you a heads-up, Jessica," he said. "They've brought in Mrs. Wolcott and they're going to charge her with killin' her husband."

"When did this happen?" I asked. "She was here with me yesterday afternoon."

"Was she, now? What brought that about?"

"She said she needed to talk. Nothing much came out of it except that she was understandably nervous and upset. Perhaps she knew this was coming. Where did you hear about her arrest?"

"Over at Mara's. I was there for breakfast bright and early and got talkin' with that fella Evelyn Phillips has hired at the paper, Teller. Said to call him Jimmy. Nice chap. He'd just come from police headquarters and had all the inside dirt. Said he was there last night when they brought her in. Showed me the pictures he took on his digital camera. Feel a mite sorry for that Mrs. Wolcott, having those pictures goin' in the paper, but I suppose there's nothing she can do about it."

Good old Mara's Luncheonette, I thought. If you wanted to know what was happening in Cabot Cove, you stopped in there and cocked an ear toward the myriad conversations taking place.

"What about the Wolcott children?" I asked.

"Her mother is tending to them is what I hear."

"Oh dear, I just realized that it's Friday."

"What's Friday got to do with anything?"

"The courthouse is closed." One of Mayor Shevlin's cost-saving measures in his efforts to conserve funds and stave off having to let go any public service employees was to close all municipal offices on Fridays, including the courts. "There's no chance to appeal for bail because they won't be able to arraign Myriam until Monday. She'll be stuck in jail all weekend."

"That's tough luck," Seth said.

I thanked him for his call, picked up the paper, and began reading. Evelyn and her assistant didn't offer much more in the way of details than I'd received from Seth, although they did quote Mort Metzger. Our sheriff stated, "Based upon evidence collected, we are charging Myriam Wolcott with the shooting death of her husband, Joshua Wolcott. We continue to investigate the circumstances surrounding this tragic event and will have more to report later on."

Cy O'Connor, whose photo also accompanied the article, was quoted as saying, "My client, Myriam Wolcott, denies the charges against her, and I'm confident that she will be vindicated."

I busied myself around the house for the remainder of the morning and waited for the phone to ring again. It did as I was about to leave for a lunch date at Peppino's with Tim Purdy. The taxi had just arrived and I motioned for the driver to wait.

"Mrs. Fletcher?"

"Yes."

"This is Mitchell Quaid. I'm sure you don't remember me, but we've met at a few civic functions."

"I remember," I said.

"I'm calling because—well, do you have a minute?"

"I'm afraid I'm just on my way out the door."

"Then I'll make it brief. I'm sure you're aware of Josh Wolcott's murder."

"It would be hard not to be," I said.

"I'm calling because I was a client of Wolcott's."

"Yes?"

"I became a client because he seemed to have a pretty impressive roster of other clients who'd entrusted their money to him."

I wondered where this was going.

"To cut to the chase, Mrs. Fletcher, I signed up with him and took a bath. I lost three-quarters of what I gave him to invest."

"I'm terribly sorry to hear that, Mr. Quaid, but why are you telling *me* this?"

"Because one of the clients he bragged about representing was you."

"What? That's absolutely untrue. He offered his financial services to me a long time ago, but I declined. I cannot tell you how angry it makes me to hear that he used my name falsely to attract clients."

"Well then, all I can say is that you made a wise decision. I thought that if you'd been a client and lost money, too, you might be interested in launching some sort of a class action suit against whatever money was left in his hands when he died."

"That's obviously out of the question," I said, "and I'm awfully sorry to hear of your misfortune. I don't mean to cut this short, Mr. Quaid, but I am running late."

"That's all I had to say, Mrs. Fletcher. I'm sorry to bother you."

"No, that's quite all right. You didn't bother me at all. Well, that's not exactly accurate. What you told me is very bothersome indeed."

It took me until I arrived at the restaurant to calm down a bit from the indignation I felt at having had my name used fraudulently by Josh Wolcott. How dared he tell anyone that I'd become one of his financial services clients? If my previous suspicions about him needed any bolstering, this incident certainly served the purpose.

"I hope that expression on your face doesn't mean you're upset with me," Tim said after we'd been seated.

I told him about the phone call from Mr. Quaid.

"It doesn't surprise me," was his response.

"It *doesn't*?"

"No. Do you know Mrs. Judson? She's a friend of Elsie Fricket."

"Vaguely."

"Josh Wolcott convinced her to turn over the money

her husband had left her when he died. It was a disaster. Most of it disappeared, including money she received from remortgaging her house. It was almost paid off, as I understand it, but he convinced her to take out a home equity loan on the promise of big profits. He wiped her out. She had to go live with her daughter."

"Then the man was an out-and-out thief. Did she bring charges against him?"

"I believe she complained to whoever licenses financial planners, but it was already too late to recoup any of her savings. Anyway, later they determined that he operated within the law, but probably only barely."

I fell silent.

"Jessica?"

"What? Oh, sorry. I was thinking about what you just told me and the phone call I received."

"Hate to sound crass, but at least Wolcott won't be scamming anyone again."

"You read about his wife being charged in his death."

"Sure."

"It occurs to me that there are probably more than a few people with a motive to have killed him."

"If Mrs. Judson and Mr. Quaid are any example, Jessica, you may be right."

"I'm sure they're not the only ones."

We shifted conversational gears for the rest of lunch. As we stood outside Peppino's, Tim asked whether I'd had second thoughts about writing a new chapter for the town history.

"Afraid not, Tim."

"Even with this new case? Might not be the wife, you know. You already have another possible motive."

"That someone Josh Wolcott cheated might have

gotten revenge? I don't know, but it's a possibility. I'll have to think more about it."

Which turned out to be an understatement. It seemed that there was nothing else I could think of as the day progressed. I took a walk around town to work off the shrimp scampi and ended up in front of police headquarters. Should I drop in on Mort Metzger and see whether he was interested in the thoughts I'd been having about the Wolcott murder?

Sure. Why not? Mort has always been gracious when I deliver my two cents about an ongoing case, although there have been times when he's become what I suppose could be termed "pleasantly testy."

Trusting that he was in a good mood, I went inside, told the deputy at the desk I wished to see the sheriff, and waited for Mort to respond to his call.

"To what do I owe this visit, Mrs. F.?" Mort asked as I entered his office.

"Just thought I'd stop by and say hello," I replied. "Hope it's not an inconvenient time."

"Oh, no, not at all, Mrs. F. I'm just sitting around doing crossword puzzles and reading magazines."

His sarcasm wasn't lost on me. I smiled, sat in the only chair without papers piled on it, and said, "Mort, I know you're up to your neck with the Wolcott murder, but that's why I'm here. You've charged Myriam Wolcott with the murder?"

"Yup."

"Mind if I ask what you're basing it on?"

"I never mind when you ask anything, Mrs. F., so long as you don't mind if I don't answer."

"I never have minded. Mort, I know that the fact that Myriam was an abused wife gives you a motive."

He nodded.

"And?" I said.

"And what?"

"Is that all you have—the motive?"

"You really know how to hurt a guy, Mrs. F. You don't really think that I'd accuse someone of murder if all I had was the motive, do you?"

"I apologize," I said, "and I realize that you aren't about to tell me what other evidence you have. But I'd like to offer a suggestion where motive is concerned."

"Always glad to have your input."

"I've come to learn that Josh Wolcott angered a number of people over the years because of harm he'd done them as their financial adviser."

Mort's expression was noncommittal.

"So," I said, "I just thought I'd let you know what I've learned."

"And I appreciate it, Mrs. F. Hope your feelings aren't hurt that I already knew about Mr. Wolcott's financial consulting business and that he'd conned some people."

"Then you're way ahead of me."

"Yup," Mort said, leaned back in his chair, and folded his arms across his chest, a Cheshire cat's grin on his broad face. "I've already started looking into those folks who might have carried a grudge against Wolcott. Of course, that's sort of a wild-goose chase. As far as I'm concerned, he hit his wife one too many times, and she got even."

"You haven't found the weapon, have you?" I said.

"Nope, but the lab just finished examining the bullet that killed him."

"I understand that Wolcott was an avid hunter and had an extensive gun collection in the house."

"But all the weapons are accounted for. He had them registered."

"Including his handguns?"

"How would you know about that?"

I hesitated before saying, "His wife told me. She said he'd lately been leaving one of them lying around in various rooms in the house."

Mort came forward and made a note on a yellow legal pad. "What else did she tell you?"

"That she hated hunting."

"He wasn't shot with a handgun."

"No?"

"It was a .308 Winchester bullet, popular with deer hunters."

"How can you be sure that he registered every gun he owned, Mort?"

"I'd say that chances of him not registering one is small, real small. He was a model gun owner."

I withheld a satisfied smile. What was occurring with Mort followed a pattern that I'd enjoyed before. Once you engaged him in a conversation about a case, his initial rigidity melted away and he became more talkative, asking questions of me as well as answering my questions of him. As long as I had him in a chatty mood, I intended to keep it going.

"Has the state forensics lab finished analyzing what was on the computer taken from the house?" I asked.

"You know about that, too, huh?"

"Just scuttlebutt."

"Yeah, well, they're working on it as we speak. Two computers."

"Two? That, I didn't know."

"One the wife and kids used; the other he had in his office."

"His office computer could provide you with other suspects, people whose money he may have mishandled."

"That's possible, Mrs. F., only don't put too much faith in that. What's on the computer Mrs. Wolcott used is more likely to be important."

I waited for him to say more. I had the feeling that he'd been made aware of something on the personal computer that wasn't exculpatory for Myriam but chose not to elaborate. His silence confirmed it for me.

Our give-and-take ended when Mort received a call and had to leave the office.

"Thanks for your time, Mort," I said.

"My pleasure, Mrs. F. If you come up with any other information, you'll let me know."

"Of course," I replied.

On my way out, I asked whether I could see Myriam Wolcott.

"I guess so," Mort said, "provided you get an okay from her attorney."

"I'll check with Cy," I said.

"And provided she wants to see *you*."

Chapter Ten

A car I hadn't seen before was parked directly in front of my house. As I groped in my shoulder bag for my key, the driver, an older man wearing a suit and tie, got out and waited for me at the foot of my driveway.

"Jessica Fletcher?" he asked.

"Yes."

"This is for you, ma'am," he said as he handed me an envelope.

"What is this?"

"A subpoena, ma'am."

As I inserted the key in the door, I heard the phone ring. By the time I got to it, my answering machine had kicked in and Edwina Wilkerson's voice said, "Jessica, it's Edwina. I need to talk to you. I just received . . ."

I picked up the phone, which stopped the machine's recording. "Hello, Edwina," I said. "It's Jessica. I just came through the door."

"I'm so glad you're there. I received a subpoena a half hour ago and—"

"I just received mine," I said. "I haven't had a chance to look at it yet."

"It's from the county DA. She wants to depose me in the Wolcott case."

I thought back to what Mort had said about the possibility of being subpoenaed.

"Mine must say the same thing."

"What should we do?"

"Comply with it."

"It's not right. What happened that night with Myriam should remain private."

"I agree with you in general, Edwina, but she's now been charged with murdering her husband, and we've been issued subpoenas. That changes things."

"They'll use it to say that she had a motive to kill him."

"I'm sure you're right."

"We should get together and discuss what we'll say."

"That's not a good idea," I said. "We don't want to make it seem that we collaborated on our statements. The district attorney could make an issue of it."

She sighed deeply and audibly. "I suppose you're right," she said. "Have you had any contact with Myriam?"

"No, I haven't, but I intend to ask her attorney for permission to visit her in jail."

"Poor thing. She didn't kill Josh. She didn't kill anyone. She was an abused woman, that's all."

I didn't say anything to indicate that I agreed with her. I wanted to believe what she'd said, but there was nothing tangible to prove that Myriam was innocent of the crime. Until there was . . .

I'd been opening my envelope while talking with

Edwina and saw that the subpoena directed that I make myself available at the district attorney's office Monday at ten a.m.; Edwina's deposition was scheduled for eleven that same morning.

"I just had a thought," she said. "Maybe Myriam's lawyer can fight our subpoenas."

"I doubt that he could, Edwina. Look, let's just do what we're legally required to do and leave it at that."

"I still think that . . ."

I hurried Edwina off the phone with a promise to check with Myriam's lawyer and settled at my desk to call Cy O'Connor's office. Sharon Bacon answered.

"Hi, Sharon. It's Jessica Fletcher. Is he in?"

She lowered her voice. "He's here but he's in conference."

"Mrs. Caldwell, Myriam Wolcott's mother?"

"Yes. How did you know?"

"Purely a guess. I'd like to speak with him about permission to visit Myriam in jail. Could you pass that request along and ask that he call me?"

"Shall do."

O'Connor called back fifteen minutes later.

"Did Sharon tell you why I'd called?" I asked.

"Yeah, she did. Mind if I ask why you want to see Myriam?"

I told him of the visit Myriam paid me the day before she was arrested. "She said she needed support, Cy, and I feel that the least I can do is provide it."

"There's no doubt that she can use *someone's* support. Sure, I'll arrange for you to visit anytime you wish, within prescribed hours, of course. Give me a call whenever you want to see her and I'll set it up."

"How about tomorrow?"

He seemed to hesitate. "I guess that would work. While we're on the topic, Jessica, would you be available to meet with me after you've visited her?"

"I don't see why not."

"Good. There are a few things I'd like to discuss with you. Give me fifteen minutes to call the sheriff's office to set it up, and I'll get back to you."

Cy's request that we get together after I'd visited his client in prison gave me something else to ponder. He and I didn't have any pending legal matters, so he likely wanted to discuss Myriam's case. The question was why. Maybe it had to do with the subpoena I'd received. Was he aware that it had been issued and delivered? Did he want to discuss what I would say during the deposition?

My musings reminded me of a day I'd spent with a British judge during a trip to London. Despite the fact that the American system of jurisprudence is based upon the British system, there are major differences. This particular judge was appalled that American lawyers were allowed to prep witnesses prior to their testimony or depositions. A British lawyer would find him- or herself in serious trouble should he or she do that. I was similarly surprised that this same judge, and all others in the British system, routinely sum up evidence for the jurors as they interpret it prior to the jury going into its deliberations. Not wanting to offend him and possibly end our informative discussion by expressing my discomfort with this practice, I simply tucked the knowledge away for use in a future book. As they say, we speak the same language as our British cousins—or do we?

Cy was as good as his word. The phone rang fifteen minutes later.

"Done," he said. "Sheriff Metzger is expecting you at ten."

When I arrived at police headquarters the next morning, O'Connor was waiting for me.

"I didn't expect to see you until later," I said.

"I thought Myriam might be more comfortable if I tagged along. You don't mind, do you?"

"Of course not."

"We have a few minutes before they bring her to an interview room," he said. "Let's go outside and talk."

We stood beneath an overhang in front of the building.

"First," he said, "I want to thank you for taking an interest in Myriam and her case."

"No thanks are necessary," I said. "She's suffering and asked for my help. I feel it's the least I can do."

"She's mentioned you a number of times during our conversations and told me about the night she spoke with you and Ms. Wilkerson at the shelter."

"That was a privileged conversation, but since Edwina and I both have been subpoenaed, I'm afraid the details of that night will be made public."

"I'll be present during your deposition," he said. "Standard procedure."

"Mind if I ask a question before we go in?" I said.

"Shoot."

"Why did you take this case?"

He broke into a boyish grin. "I know why you're asking. Criminal law isn't my specialty. But I'm afraid that to answer that I'll have to delve deeply into my psyche."

"Digging into psyches is something I do with regularity in my books."

"We don't have time for a full-scale excavation at the moment," he said, glancing at his watch again. "But if you're free for dinner tonight . . . ?"

"As a matter of fact, I am."

"I won't keep you out late. I want you rested up for your deposition."

"It's not until Monday."

"And I'll be there to make sure the DA doesn't go over the line."

"Then we'll all have to be on our toes. Let's go see your client."

Chapter Eleven

A haggard Myriam Wolcott was led into the room where Cy and I had already taken seats. The deputy who delivered her indicated that she was to take a chair on the opposite side of the table from us. "Please don't touch the prisoner," she instructed.

I saw Myriam shiver.

"Hello, dear," I said. "I hope it's all right with you that I've come to visit."

She muttered something and nodded. I'd expected that she'd be dressed in some sort of prison garb, but she wore gray slacks, a pale blue sweatshirt, and sneakers.

O'Connor took his seat and said, "Mrs. Fletcher asked me for permission to see you, Myriam. I was sure that you'd agree to it."

Another nod from her.

"When you visited me at my house," I said, "you said that you needed some support. Well, that's why I'm here. Are they treating you all right?"

"They don't beat me, if that's what you mean."

"That's good to hear," said O'Connor through a forced laugh.

Until that moment, Myriam appeared to have been in a fugue state. She suddenly came forward in her chair and exclaimed to me, "I didn't kill Josh! You have to believe me."

Before I could reply, O'Connor leaned in and said, "I'm sure Mrs. Fletcher knows that you're innocent. What's important is that we convince a jury."

His words caused her to shake. She sat back, folded her arms about herself, and sniffled. "A jury?" she said. "A trial?" She came forward again. "I don't want that. I don't deserve that. I didn't kill anyone. Why won't they let me out? What's happening with my children? No one will tell me anything."

I began to question my decision to visit. Rather than contribute comfort and support, my presence seemed to be upsetting her. I shifted in my chair and pondered how to leave gracefully.

"You have to keep up your spirits, Myriam," O'Connor said, "stay optimistic. I know it's hard for you to do that sitting here in jail, but it's important. I already explained that the courts are closed and until they open, you can't be officially charged and we can't ask for bail. But I have confidence we'll have you out of here soon. I've only just started putting together your case and—"

"And what do you know about putting together a murder case?" she growled, her expression stern.

I watched O'Connor's face. If her pointed question stung him, it didn't show. He smiled easily and said, "Don't you worry. I know my job. But as I've told you, anytime you want to bring in another lawyer, all you have to do is let me know. Until then, if you'll write down your questions"—he slid a piece of paper and a pen in front of her—"I'll do my best to find the answers for you."

Myriam looked at the blank sheet and sighed. She picked up the pen and wrote "1" and put a circle around it. Then she wrote "Children?" Tears filled her eyes and she put down the pen to press them away with her fingers. A gamut of emotions raced across her face as she scribbled on the page. Finally, she pulled into herself and seemed to shrivel in the chair. "I don't know what to do," she said softly.

"My best advice at this juncture," said O'Connor, "is to keep that chin up and think positive thoughts. Being incarcerated isn't pleasant. I know that. But it's early in the investigation. I'm bringing in a private investigator tomorrow to work on your behalf. He's top-notch. And with friends like Mrs. Fletcher—and you have legions of friends and supporters, I'm sure— things will work out for you." He pulled her paper away, folded it in quarters, and tucked it in his breast pocket.

I forced myself to participate in the conversation. "Myriam, is there anyone you'd like me to call for you? Do you have what you need here? Can I bring you anything? Toiletries? Something to read? I can check with Sheriff Metzger as to what's allowed."

She answered each question with a nod—no, yes, no, no, no—as if too exhausted to talk.

There was a knock on the door and the deputy opened it. "There's another visitor," she said. "The prisoner's mother."

Before we could say anything, Mrs. Caldwell pushed past the deputy and stood in the doorway, arms crossed over her bosom, anger etched on her face.

"Madam, you have to wait your turn," the deputy said.

"Hello, Mrs. Caldwell," O'Connor said, standing. He waved at the deputy. "It's all right. Let her in."

Mrs. Caldwell pointed at me. "Why is this woman here?"

O'Connor looked at me; I suppose that my puzzled expression matched his.

"You may leave now, Myriam," her mother said. "Tell the deputy to take you back inside. This meeting is over." She glared at O'Connor. "I'll be at your office in twenty minutes, and I expect to see you there."

Cy's face was flushed, and I waited for him to say something in defense of our being with his client. But he held his tongue, and Mrs. Caldwell stormed out.

Myriam slowly pushed out of her chair and shuffled over to the deputy, holding out her wrists so the officer could cuff her before returning her to her cell.

"I don't believe what just happened," I said, watching as a demoralized Myriam was led away.

O'Connor sat grim faced, his fingers rolling rhythmically on the tabletop.

"Do you have an explanation for what occurred?" I asked.

"Probably, but it will take a while to put it in plain words."

"I have all the time in the world."

He managed a tight smile and shook his head. "Are we still on for dinner?"

"Yes."

He stood, closed his briefcase, and said, "I'll pick you up at seven? I know you don't drive."

"Seven will be fine," I replied.

He left me alone in a room filled with questions.

Chapter Twelve

Cy O'Connor arrived at my house at the stroke of seven, bounded from his racing green sports car, and rang the bell.

"Right on time," I said.

"A family trait," he said. "My father was a stickler for being prompt, claimed that people who ran late were just looking for attention."

"He makes a good point," I said. "Where are we going to dinner?"

"The Katahdin Club, if it's all right with you."

"That's fine," I said. "You're a member?"

"Yeah. Dad was. When he died, his membership passed to me. I've kept it up. Good for business."

The Katahdin Country Club was named after Maine's Mount Katahdin, the state's highest peak, the centerpiece of Baxter State Park. Henry David Thoreau once climbed the 5,268-foot-high mountain and wrote about it in a chapter from *The Maine Woods*, although he spelled it "Ktaadn." Regardless of the spelling, the club was the second of two golf clubs to open in Cabot Cove once the town had begun to experience growth.

Its development was not without controversy. Many people in town objected to a pristine tract of land along the coast being developed for the privileged few, and they fought vigorously against it. It was eventually decided, however, that the area needed such a facility, and the plans were approved—but with a provision written at the last minute. In order for the private Katahdin Club to open and for its wealthy members to enjoy an eighteen-hole golf course designed by a leading architect, the developers were obliged to create a second eighteen-hole golf course on an adjacent tract of land that would be open to the public. That seemed to satisfy both sides, and the two facilities have flourished ever since.

A young man in a valet's uniform took the car from O'Connor, and we entered the club beneath a long red canopy that stretched from the door to the circular drive. O'Connor, beautifully dressed in a gray suit, blue shirt, and multicolored tie, walked quickly and with a spring in his step, and I had to hasten my pace to keep up with him. He was greeted by other club members as we approached the maître d', who led us to a table in the dining room with floor-to-ceiling windows overlooking the sea.

"You a golfer, Jessica?" O'Connor asked after we'd been seated.

"I have played, but I wouldn't call myself a golfer. I'm not very good at it. I take it that you play."

"I hack away. Not my favorite way to spend time, but it's good for my practice."

The dining room was large and nicely lit. Tables were adorned with starched white tablecloths and glistening silverware; a vase of fresh red and purple flowers was on each table, and a pianist sat in a far corner at a white baby grand playing familiar show tunes.

"Is this your first time at the club?" he asked, taking menus from the waiter.

"No. I've been to a few functions here, not many."

"Maybe you ought to join," he suggested. "I'll be happy to be your sponsor."

"Thank you, but no. I'm afraid I'm not the country-club type."

"I think I know what you mean," he said through a smile. "Drink?"

"White wine would be nice."

As the waiter took our order, I looked beyond him to another side of the room, where I spotted Richard Mauser standing with a group of men. They each held a glass and laughed heartily at something he'd said. O'Connor noted my interest in the group.

"Dick Mauser," he said. "He's the club president."

A good reason not to take O'Connor up on his offer to sponsor me as a member.

"He spends a lot of time here."

"I suppose he would, being president," I said.

"Not the most simpatico of people."

I avoided adding my verbal agreement.

"What appeals?" he asked, indicating the menu, which I hadn't looked at yet. I picked it up, glanced at the entrees, and said, "Poached salmon and a salad would be fine."

"I'm a hopeless carnivore," he said. "Never met a steak I didn't like."

Our orders placed, I asked what he'd had on his mind when he issued the dinner invitation.

"Myriam Wolcott, of course," he replied. "I need help."

My first thought was that he was about to discuss not having any experience with criminal law. Instead he said, "You've met Mrs. Caldwell."

I couldn't help but laugh.

He grinned and nodded. "She's a piece of work, isn't she?"

"I—I don't know what she is, except that she isn't especially pleasant. I gather from what I've seen that she's very much involved in her daughter's defense."

"Your turn for an understatement, Jessica. She's hired me to be her daughter's counsel."

"Which brings up a question."

"And I know what it is. Why would she choose me to handle a murder case, considering that it'll be my first?"

"It's a reasonable question, isn't it?"

"Sure it is, and I've been hearing it asked around town every day. Why would I be retained when there are a dozen good criminal attorneys ready and willing to defend her?"

I didn't have to encourage his answer.

"I'll level with you, Jessica. When I decided to go to law school and follow in my father's footsteps, my goal was always to practice criminal law." His chuckle was self-effacing.

"What kept you from doing it?"

"Dad. He was sort of a crusty guy who considered criminal law to be—well, to be not exactly clean. Certainly not the field for his fair-haired boy. As far as he was concerned, criminal lawyers had to wallow in the same sties as their clients. He considered them the bottom of the legal barrel."

"That isn't true," I said. "I've known many criminal lawyers who were fine men and women who believed that every person, even criminals, is entitled to a defense."

"Yeah, I know, and I agree with you. But Dad could be persuasive. I was his only kid, and he'd envisioned me being in practice with him as far back as I can remember. Anyway, when I graduated from law school and passed the Maine bar, he didn't leave any doubt that I'd join him here in Cabot Cove. He was very successful, as you know, had a crackerjack legal mind when it came to corporate and estate law. I broached the subject of wanting to practice criminal law someplace, maybe even open a criminal division within his practice, but he wouldn't hear of it. When it came down to it, I knew that Dad needed help. He'd been slowing down ever since my mother died, and I couldn't just walk away. Soooo—here I am."

"So you gave up your dream," I said, hoping he wouldn't be offended.

"Until now."

"And now you're going to be a criminal lawyer?"

"Looks that way."

"Which still leaves the question of why Mrs. Caldwell has retained you to defend her daughter."

He started to reply, smiled instead of speaking, and then said, "That's something you'll have to ask her, Jessica."

Which left me to continue pondering the same question. I certainly didn't expect to be able to pose it to the formidable Mrs. Caldwell.

Over salads, I mentioned that he'd said he needed help from me and asked what he was seeking.

"I'm not sure how to put it," he said. "I suppose you could call it running interference."

"With?"

"With Myriam. You saw how her mother can pose a problem. She's an extremely domineering woman, Jessica, wants to call the shots at every turn, make every decision concerning Myriam's defense. I can't let her do it."

I wasn't surprised to hear that. Although I couldn't have known for sure, watching the staunch Mrs. Caldwell in action certainly didn't butt heads with that evaluation of her. I was taken aback by the way she'd talked to O'Connor when she cut short our meeting with Myriam, and her daughter literally cowered in her presence.

Our entrees were served and we chatted about other things. I wanted to explore further why Cy'd agreed to represent Myriam. His desire to practice criminal law, one that had been thwarted by his father, explained his decision only up to a point, but there had to be another dynamic at play. Was it money? Myriam had speculated that gain might have been influencing him, and although he didn't seem like the sort of young man who would sell out for a payday, I had to consider the possibility.

I reintroduced the topic of Josh Wolcott's murder after coffee had been served, along with rice pudding that O'Connor claimed was a specialty of the club. "What did you mean by running interference?" I asked.

"I need someone to keep Myriam in check, to keep her on an even keel, and to understand that the legal moves I make on her behalf are necessary." He signaled to the waiter for our check.

"Has she questioned your moves so far?"

"You were there when she challenged me today. I keep telling her she can change lawyers. I want her to understand the choice is hers, but she never takes me up on it. Look, let me be straight with you. The problem is that . . ."

We both looked up at Richard Mauser, who'd come up to the table and was hovering over us. He slapped O'Connor on the back and said, "Looking for Mrs. Fletcher here to write a best seller about how you defended Wolcott's killer?"

O'Connor and I looked at him quizzically. Mauser's face was florid, and he was perspiring despite the cool air in the room. His tight shirt collar forced his naturally fleshy face to puff out, giving him the look of a red toad.

"Hello, Richard," O'Connor said.

Mauser looked down at me. "Haven't seen you here before. Join me for a drink?" he asked, his alcohol-laced breath causing me to sit back.

"Thank you, no," I said, managing to keep pique from my voice. "We were just leaving."

Ignoring my reply, he dragged over a chair from an unoccupied table and plopped down next to me. He put his hand on top of mine, which I quickly withdrew.

"You ought to come here more often," he crooned, "get a taste of real life instead of those murder mysteries you make up." He said to O'Connor, "I bet you two are conjuring up a way to get the town's favorite husband killer off." He laughed at his own words.

"Cy, we really have to leave," I said.

"Yes, of course," said O'Connor, who pushed back his chair and stood.

"You seeing things differently now?" Mauser said, squinting at me. "I was right, wasn't I?"

I ignored him, folded my napkin, and set it on the table.

He gripped my wrist, preventing me from standing. "Know what I'm going to do, Mrs. Fletcher?" Mauser asked. "I'm going to make the case at the town council that funding your damn women's shelter has to stop. See what it did? Josh Wolcott's wife gets herself in a snit, goes to your shelter, gets her head full of feminist nonsense, goes home, and shoots her hubby. How the hell can you and that woman Wilkerson sleep at night?"

I wrenched my arm away and stood. "We sleep very well, Mr. Mauser," I said. "I might also suggest that you would do better to withhold your opinions until you are no longer drunk and obnoxious. Good evening."

Mauser called after us, "Careful who you hang out with, Counselor. Your father wouldn't put up with the likes of her."

O'Connor spun around and was about to go back to the table, but I grabbed his sleeve and kept him moving in the direction of the door. We stood outside, both of us breathing heavily, our breath steaming into the chilled March night air.

"I apologize for him, Jessica," he said as he handed the valet the parking ticket.

"You didn't do anything," I said. "He's an insufferable boor to begin with, and the drinking only makes him worse."

The ride home was awkward, with O'Connor continuously apologizing for Mauser's behavior. When he pulled into my driveway, I said, "Please, let's forget about Mr. Mauser. Up until his appearance, I had a lovely time."

"He insulted you. And I'm offended on your behalf."

"I appreciate your concern, but I've been insulted by better men than this one," I said. "Thanks for dinner."

"Wish it had turned out more pleasant."

He came around and opened the door for me.

"About your deposition on Monday," he said. "Swing by the office at nine thirty and we'll go to the DA together."

"Shall do," I said. "Before I go in, you'd started to say something when he arrived at the table. You said you wanted to be straight with me. About what?"

"About Myriam and her mother. Mrs. Caldwell wants me to plead Myriam guilty and use a claim of self-defense to get her off."

"I—I don't understand," I said. "Is she saying that Myriam actually killed Josh?"

His silence was chilling.

Chapter Thirteen

Following a Sunday spent worrying the day away, I arrived at Cy O'Connor's office Monday morning at nine thirty, ready to beard the lion in his den. What could he be thinking, having Myriam plead guilty? She had sworn up and down she was innocent, that she had not killed her husband, Josh. Now Cy was going to have her turn around and say she hadn't told the truth, that she *had* killed him, but that it was in self-defense? Would those who'd believed her before still believe her now?

Cy's indispensable aide, Sharon Bacon, intercepted me as I came through the door and ushered me back into the hallway.

"What's going on?" I asked.

"I wish I knew. Ever since Mrs. Wolcott's mother retained Cy, he—" She stopped as O'Connor poked his head through the open doorway.

"Ready, Jessica?" he asked.

"I suppose I'd better be," I replied.

He disappeared back into the reception area.

"Jessica, would you be free after the deposition so we can talk? Cy's got a lunch appointment and we won't be disturbed back here at the office."

"I assume I'll be. I hope it won't take longer than an hour. Cy did say he wanted to get together with me today. But I can put him off until after lunch. How's that?"

"I'd really appreciate it. I made an extra sandwich just in case you were available. You're welcome to it. I didn't want to intrude on your lunchtime without feeding you. Do you like chicken salad?"

"That was very thoughtful, Sharon. I love chicken salad."

Cy and I drove to the DA's office, where the district attorney, Diane Cirilli, and a stenographer waited. I'd met Ms. Cirilli a number of times before. She was a short, slender woman with a dusky complexion and a head full of tight blond curls, and she was dressed today in a nicely tailored gray suit and white blouse. She introduced me to the stenographer, who sat ready to repeat our conversation into a tape recorder through a mask that she would hold to her mouth.

"Thanks for being early," the DA said. "I'm running a bit behind this morning."

The deposition didn't take very long. It focused on what had occurred that night at the women's shelter's office when Myriam Wolcott arrived and told us that she'd been attacked by her husband. After establishing that the meeting had, in fact, taken place, Ms. Cirilli prompted me to repeat what Myriam had said that night. I answered as best I could, recounting what had transpired between Myriam, Edwina Wilkerson, and me.

"And so you're certain that Mrs. Wolcott said that her husband had physically injured her?"

"Yes. That's why she came. She was shaken."

"Did she indicate that this wasn't the first time that he'd attacked her?"

"Yes, she did."

"And what did she say about the Wolcott children?"

"Oh, she said a number of things. She eventually started talking about how well they did in school, how personable they were, things like that."

"Had the children witnessed their father's attack on her?"

"Yes. She said that their daughter—her name is Ruth; she's twelve—became upset and ran upstairs. Their son, Mark, went to a friend's house."

After another fifteen minutes, the DA said, "We're about ready to wrap this up, but one last question. Did Mrs. Wolcott say anything about weapons in the house?"

I nodded.

"You'll have to speak your reply, Jessica," she said, indicating at the stenographer.

"Oh, yes, of course. Sorry. Yes, she said that her husband was a hunter and that he had a collection of weapons. She also said that he'd lately been leaving a handgun in different rooms in the house."

Ms. Cirilli paused and ran her teeth over her upper lip before asking, "Did she ever say during your meeting with her that night that she wanted to kill her husband?"

"No," I said. "I don't recall her saying anything like

that. In fact, she said she loved her husband and that he loved her. She ended up excusing his behavior, which Ms. Wilkerson told me is common with abused spouses. They assign blame to themselves instead of where it's due, the abusing spouse."

"Is that it?" O'Connor asked.

"I think so," the DA replied. "Thank you, Jessica. It was a pleasure seeing you again."

"I assume that her interest in whether Myriam said that she wanted to kill her husband feeds into the motive they're looking for," I said as we left the building.

"Exactly."

"But what if she *had* said that?" I asked. "People say things like that all the time about someone they're angry at or fighting with. They don't really mean it. It's just a way of venting their emotions."

"Tell that to a jury. Would you like to join me for lunch? I've hired a private investigator and I'd really like you to meet this guy," he said.

"I'd be happy to meet him another time," I said, walking with him to where he'd parked his car. "Before you go, I have a question."

"Shoot."

"The other night you said that Mrs. Caldwell wants Myriam to plead guilty but claim self-defense. That kept me up half the night and had my mind churning all day yesterday."

His laugh was boyish. "I shouldn't have dropped that on you at the last second. Can we meet back at my office at, say, two? I'll have the investigator with me, and we can talk about Mrs. Caldwell's request."

"Surely you aren't considering doing it," I said.

He patted me on the arm and said, "I really have to run, Jessica. See you at two."

I took a taxi to his office building, where Sharon busily typed on her computer.

"I'm confused," I said.

Her laugh was rueful. "Join the club," she said.

"He intends to . . ." I stopped in midsentence in case she wasn't aware that Mrs. Caldwell wanted to have her daughter plead guilty to murder.

"Listen," Sharon said, taking some pages from the printer and sliding them into a manila envelope. "I have to deliver these to a client in the next building. Would you mind terribly waiting here for me? I promise I won't be long."

"Take your time," I said, picking up a copy of *The Week* magazine from the coffee table and choosing a comfortable chair. "I'm free until two." But I never opened the magazine's cover. Instead I began thinking about Cy's receptionist and wondering what she thought important enough to ask me for a private meeting.

Sharon Bacon had started working for Cy O'Connor's father as a young woman and had remained with the law firm to this day. The elder O'Connor viewed his chunky, rosy-cheeked right-hand woman with Shirley Temple–like reddish curls as the daughter he'd never had and treated her with great deference and love. In return she was fiercely loyal to her employer and surrogate father, and ran his office as though it were her own home, paying meticulous attention to detail and creating a warm, welcoming atmosphere for his many clients.

She'd never married. "The law office is my spouse," she often said. "It doesn't talk back to me or leave dirty socks on the floor." If she regretted not having married, it never showed in her demeanor. She was unfailingly upbeat and pleasant, with a hearty laugh to accompany a sometimes naughty sense of humor and keen mind.

I was well aware of her personality since I'd known her for all these years. That was why the dejected expression on her face when she returned from her errand and invited me into Cy's conference room concerned me.

We sat at the large walnut table surrounded by tall bookcases filled with leather-bound legal volumes. Sharon set out our sandwiches on two paper plates. "Is water okay?" she asked.

"Just fine."

She took two bottles from the small fridge at the back of the room and placed two glasses by our plates. "If I didn't have to work this afternoon, I'd go raid Cy's liquor cabinet and have a real drink," she said, "a double."

I laughed. "Judging from that scowl on your face, I'd say it might be in order."

She managed a smile. "Who am I kidding?" she said. "You know I don't drink. Anyway, thanks for making time for us to get together."

"It's my pleasure. This sandwich is delicious."

"My mother always insisted that my sisters and I know how to make chicken salad. She said it was her fallback recipe. When all else fails, fall back on chicken salad. Everyone loves it."

After we'd eaten and I'd poured water into my glass, I sat back and looked at Sharon. Signs of whatever strain she was under were still in her face. "You said you needed to talk," I said.

She exhaled, closed her eyes, opened them, and said, "I'm thinking of resigning."

"Oh my! Is this a last-minute decision, or have you been thinking about it for a while?"

"I've been considering it ever since—ever since the elder Mr. O'Connor died."

"That long? I'm sure his son is pleased that you decided to stay."

"I suppose he is." She reached across the table and placed her hand on mine. "You know how they say that the apple doesn't fall far from the tree when a son or daughter is like a parent? Well, in the case of the young Mr. O'Connor, the apple fell a mile away."

I wasn't quite sure how to respond. As far as I knew, Cy O'Connor had done a good job since taking over the firm. Apparently, I was about to hear a different interpretation.

"I wouldn't want this to get back to Cy," Sharon said.

"That you're thinking of leaving? I certainly won't mention it to anyone. But we all reach a point where retirement is appealing."

"That's not the case with me, Jessica. Oh, I could retire. Cy's father set up a very generous retirement plan for me, enough to see me through the rest of my life. But retirement isn't on my mind. I think I might go mad not having the office to come to every day."

"Then why . . . ?"

"Let me be blunt," she said. "I can't stand by while I watch Cy destroy everything his father worked so hard for. Mr. O'Connor must be turning over in his grave."

"It's that bad?"

She answered with a solemn nod.

"I've only had a few legal dealings with Cy, and I haven't had any reason to be dissatisfied."

"Don't get me wrong," Sharon said. "He's a bright and capable attorney. The problem is that he has these delusions of what the law and lawyers should be. His dad knew that law, the *real* practice of law, doesn't involve courtroom theatrics and flamboyant arguments. He knew that it meant drafting ironclad agreements, forging reasonable resolutions of disputes, and setting up estates that were in the best interests of his clients. It may not be exciting, but it's important."

"Yes, it is."

"Young Cy is—well, he's watched too many courtroom dramas on TV. He kept urging his father to set up a criminal defense office so that he could defend criminals. His father steadfastly refused, and I give him credit for that."

"But now?" I asked, trying to see where Sharon was going with this.

"I think Cy is bored, and some of his legal work reflects that. I've heard him tell friends how tiring it is to draft agreements and research case law, but that's the nuts and bolts of being an attorney. I've had to correct simple mistakes he's made. Not that he didn't know better, but he's just too busy tooling around in his fancy sports car and hanging out at the club and chasing women and . . ."

"He's young," I said.

"Young and foolish. His father left him a lucrative practice, and I'm watching him squander it. This business with Myriam Wolcott is the straw that broke this camel's back."

I'd been waiting for her to get around to that.

"When he told me that he was going to defend her I did something I seldom do. I challenged the wisdom of it, asked him to reconsider. He didn't take kindly to my butting in."

"That decision he made has raised a question with a lot of people in town," I said.

"And for good reason." Her face tightened. "That woman!"

"Who?" I asked, although I already knew.

"Mrs. Wolcott's mother, Mrs. Caldwell. She treats Cy and me as though she owns us, as though it's her firm, laying down the law, making demands, telling Cy what to do."

"Like pleading Myriam guilty?"

Her expression changed to one of surprise. "You know about that?"

"Yes. Cy told me after we had dinner together at his club Saturday."

"His club," she said scornfully. "Do you know what he recently told a mutual friend? He told her that he wants to land some big-money cases, enough to close down the office here in Cabot Cove and go to Boston or New York to practice criminal law."

"Again, Sharon, he's young, perhaps immature. A big city naturally appeals to him. But let's get back to Myriam Wolcott pleading guilty. How can that be? As far as I know, she's denied having killed Josh at every turn. Why would she possibly agree to such a thing?"

Sharon hesitated before answering, and I could almost see the gears turning in her brain—how much should she tell me? I decided that I wouldn't press her for further information, but I didn't have to.

"I don't know how well you know Mrs. Wolcott," she said, "but she's an incredibly malleable woman, the sort who believes whatever the last person who talks to her says. Her mother has convinced Cy—and she's evidently working on her daughter—that Myriam will never be found innocent by a jury here in Cabot Cove. I think she's wrong—I *know* she's wrong—but Cy has bought it."

I sat back and let what she'd said sink in. Was Cy's dream of practicing criminal law so strong that he'd take on a case in which the accused, his client, would agree to pleading guilty to a murder she hadn't committed because of pressure from her mother? Had Myriam been right, that the lure of a big payday swayed what would otherwise have been a more rational decision?

It occurred to me as I sat there that Myriam might not be the only malleable one. No matter how much money was involved, no matter how fervently he wanted to practice criminal law, Cy O'Connor was making a mistake. Could he be a man who was so easily manipulated that it was possible that he would sell out his client in order to satisfy his own needs? If that was the case, his father might well be twisting in his grave.

Sharon wasn't finished venting.

"Mrs. Wolcott's mother is using her daughter's visit to the women's shelter as the basis for her self-defense plea."

"I knew that her visit would provide a motive for

the DA," I said, "but I hadn't considered it being used as a defense. Frankly, Sharon, this is all very upsetting."

As we cleaned up after our luncheon, I mentioned that I was supposed to meet with Cy and the private investigator he'd hired. "Why is he bothering to hire a private detective if he intends to plead her guilty?" I asked.

"Probably for show," was Sharon's reply.

"What's his name?" I asked.

"He's from Boston. His name is Harlan McGraw. Cy says that his father had worked with him before."

"Wait a minute," I said. "Harlan McGraw? *Harry* McGraw?"

"Cy called him Harlan."

"Oh, my," I said. "Harry McGraw."

"You know him?"

"I certainly do."

Chapter Fourteen

I'd met Harry McGraw when I was researching background for one of my novels. I'd hired another Boston detective, Archie Miles, to look into a twenty-five-year-old murder case. When Archie was killed on his way to Maine to interview a witness, his partner, Harry McGraw, entered the picture. We became friends despite our different approach to life. Harry is—well, Harry marches to his own drummer, always in some sort of personal jam, but he is a good detective. He's a straight talker, sometimes to his own detriment. I'd lost contact with him a few years ago, but now we were going to become reacquainted.

"If you know this guy, maybe you can have him talk some sense into Cy," Sharon said as we returned to the reception area of the law office.

"I don't know if I have that much influence, but if I have the opportunity, I'll raise it with him. I'm sorry things aren't going well for you at the firm."

"It felt good to get it off my chest, Jessica. Thanks for being my sounding board."

It was still early for my meeting with Cy and his newest recruit in the Wolcott murder case, Harry McGraw. While Sharon returned to her desk, I walked over to Charles Department Store to browse their selection of teakettles. After forty years, mine had whistled its last, and it was time for a new one. When I arrived back at O'Connor's office carrying my purchase in a shopping bag, Harry McGraw was hanging around the reception area talking with Sharon. He turned as I entered, extended his arms, gave me a bear hug, and said, "Jessica Fletcher! Look at you. How come you haven't aged a day?"

"Getting through harsh Maine winters keeps you young," I said. "And how are you?"

"Me? I get older every hour. Must be all those harsh Boston winters that keep me chained inside my favorite bar. It's great seeing you, Jess."

"And I'm glad that you're here," I said, smiling broadly. Harry always made me smile.

He looked older, but not due to the passing of years. McGraw's lifestyle undoubtedly played a larger role. He'd always believed in living fast and hard, making decisions in his personal life that sometimes backfired and worked against his self-interest. His handsome albeit hangdog face had sagged slightly, giving him an even more world-weary look. His clothes, a navy blue jacket, pale yellow button-down shirt, and skinny red tie, hung loosely from his angular frame. I suppose you could describe his looks as nondescript, but that was a useful image in his line of work.

Cy O'Connor joined us. "Come on in," he said.

We settled in chairs around the same table Sharon and I had recently deserted.

"So you two know each other," he said.

"We sure do," McGraw said. "Jessica bailed out my bacon a few times. I was so impressed, I offered her a job in my agency."

"Which I promptly turned down," I said lightly.

"Maybe you can help Harry with this case," O'Connor suggested.

"Maybe you'd like to explain just what it is you want me to do, Mr. O'Connor," McGraw interjected.

"Happy to, but it's Cy. Let's drop the formality. Look, the reason Jessica is here is that she witnessed my client's visit to this women's shelter we have in Cabot Cove and was told by my client that her husband beat her with regularity."

"So she offed her old man," Harry said.

"I wouldn't have phrased it quite that way," I inserted.

"Afraid so," O'Connor said.

I held up my hand and said, "As long as I've been invited into this discussion, I have a few questions, Cy."

"Go on."

"As far as I know, Myriam Wolcott has repeatedly proclaimed her innocence."

"Right."

"So why would she plead guilty?"

"Let's be a little more accurate, Jessica," said O'Connor. "Myriam will admit that she killed her husband but will plead not guilty, using self-defense as her reason for doing it. It's done all the time. It's not anything revolutionary."

I could feel my ire rise at his condescension. "That still doesn't answer my question, Cy. She has claimed all along that she *didn't* do it. Josh Wolcott was a financial adviser with questionable ethics, no question about that. He bilked more than one client out of his or her savings. It's possible that one of them killed him to exact revenge. Until I hear Myriam tell me that she actually killed Josh, I refuse to believe this scenario that you and . . ." I hesitated before saying, "That you and Myriam's mother have concocted."

O'Connor's face turned red and he glared at me. "You think I've 'concocted' something with Mrs. Caldwell? You don't know what you're talking about, Jessica."

I was tempted to repeat what Sharon had said at lunch but knew that it would be inappropriate. I also knew that despite having been drawn into the case, I wasn't directly involved with Myriam's defense. I was judging it as an outsider who hadn't been made privy to what decisions O'Connor and Myriam's mother had made jointly. But I was sickened at the thought of Myriam being turned into a pawn for one man's ambition and whatever her mother's motives might possibly be.

"Well now, let's not get into a hassle over this," McGraw put in, evidently sensing a need to lower the heat. "Either she is or isn't guilty. It doesn't matter to me. All I need to know is what you have in mind for me to do, Counselor. I didn't come all the way up here to enjoy the spring weather, such as it is. I'm assuming you have something you want me to do."

"I want you to find others who'll testify that my client had been abused by her husband. The more people who'll corroborate that claim, the better our chances of getting her off the hook with a self-defense plea."

"Finding others who know about Myriam's abuse, aside from me and Edwina Wilkerson, won't be easy," I said. "Myriam did what most abused women do— kept it to herself."

O'Connor, whose expression mirrored the anger that he was feeling, forced a smile and said, "I'm sure someone with Harry's experience will prove you wrong, Jessica." His smile slipped. "I'm surprised and, frankly, annoyed with your attitude." He pulled a sheet of paper from a folder on the table and handed it to McGraw. "It's a simple agreement that spells out what we agreed to on the phone, Harry. I'm pleased to have you on the case."

I'd grown increasingly impatient and decided that staying would only increase my negative reaction to what I'd been hearing that day, not only from O'Connor but from Sharon Bacon. "I really have to leave," I said.

"Are you free for dinner?" O'Connor said to Mc-Graw, turning his back to me.

"I'm always free for dinner," Harry said.

"Good." O'Connor stood and slapped him on the back. "You're staying at the Thomases' B and B?"

"Yeah. Nice room, nice people."

"Craig and Jill are good friends," I put in.

"I'll pick you up at seven," Cy said, shaking hands with McGraw. "We'll go to my club."

I hadn't wanted to share another meal with Cy, especially at his club, but I felt the invitation extended to Harry in front of me was pointed in its exclusion of me.

Cy finally turned to me. "Thanks for stopping by, Jessica."

"Don't mention it."

McGraw and I left the office together. Sharon smiled at me, but when Cy stopped at her desk, she busied herself at her computer.

"Why do I get the feeling, Jessica, that you and the counselor don't get along?" Harry asked as we stood on the sidewalk.

"We did until now," I said.

"Need a lift?" he asked. "My car's parked over there."

"I'd appreciate that," I said. "Got a spare hour for me?"

"For you I've always got time."

"Great. There's something I'd like to run by you."

Chapter Fifteen

McGraw had visited my home on a number of occasions back when we worked together, and he immediately made himself at home, discarding his jacket, loosening his tie, and sprawling on the living room couch. I made a pot of coffee and joined him.

"Like old home week," he commented as he scooped several spoonfuls of sugar into his cup.

"I must say that I'm delighted to see you, Harry. Of course, things have changed in Cabot Cove since you were here last."

"It got bigger," he said.

"But not necessarily better," I said. "What did you think of the meeting with Cy O'Connor?"

His raised eyebrows provided a partial answer. "I don't get it," he said. "Hey, I'm not arguing. I can use the money. But if this Myriam Wolcott says she didn't kill her old man, why would O'Connor plead her guilty—or as he said, she'll admit to the crime but try to get off pleading self-defense. And what's with this mother of hers?"

I filled him in as best I could about Myriam's visit to the women's shelter—the death of her husband, her mother's emergence on the scene, and her decision to hire O'Connor to defend Myriam despite his not having any criminal law experience. When I was finished, Harry said, "Is this O'Connor on the up-and-up?"

"As far as I know."

"I did some work for his father. Nice old guy, a straight arrow, all business, no nonsense, not like too many other lawyers I've worked for. You say his kid doesn't defend criminals. So what's he in this case for, the money?"

"Perhaps. The mother is calling the shots."

"And she wants her kid to say she did the deed even if she didn't?"

"From what I gather, Myriam's mother and Cy O'Connor don't trust a Cabot Cove jury to find her not guilty."

"So change the venue."

"I assume Cy has considered that." I winced. "Or maybe he hasn't. At any rate, I don't believe for a second that a jury here wouldn't be fair and impartial."

Harry stood and looked out the window. "Looks like snow," he muttered.

"It's forecast for tonight."

He turned and faced me. "What's this about the victim being a financial scam artist?"

I told him about the call from Mr. Quaid, Tim Purdy's tale of the older woman whose savings were wiped out, and the experience Seth Hazlitt and I had had with Josh.

"Doc Hazlitt," McGraw said, laughing. "How is the irascible old coot?"

"I won't tell him that you said that, Harry," I said, laughing, too. "Seth is fine, and yes, he's as irascible as ever."

"Hope to get to see him while I'm in town. About these people who lost money through the victim. Seems to me that one of them had as much a reason to pop the hubby as his wife."

"My thought exactly. Maybe you should look into that."

"That's not what I'm getting paid for."

"If you're being paid to look for people who know that Myriam Wolcott was abused by her husband, you might as well stay in bed. I seriously doubt whether anyone knows that except for me, the woman who established the women's shelter, and Myriam's family."

"Come on, now, Jessica. Someone always talks."

I thought about that for a minute. "You might start with neighbors of Myriam Wolcott, the Hanley family. The Wolcott son, Mark, evidently spends a lot of time there when things get heated at his own home. I don't know how much the Hanleys know about Josh Wolcott's abuse of his wife, but the boy might have indicated something to them."

"I'll give it a shot," McGraw said as he finished his coffee with a flourish, smacked his lips, and said, "You always made good coffee, Jess."

"Thank you."

"Is that sheriff still around? Metzger, wasn't it?"

"Mort is still here."

"Maybe I'll stop in and say hello, see what his take is."

"That's a fine idea."

I walked him to his car in my driveway.

"You really don't believe that your friend Myriam killed her husband, do you?" he said as he got behind the wheel.

"No, I don't, but it's only my *belief*, as you put it."

"Your *beliefs* have usually panned out, Jessica. I'll stay in touch."

McGraw called at six that evening while I was preparing dinner. Background noise said that he was in a public place, most likely a bar.

"I'm on my cell," he said.

"Where are you?"

"A place called Peppino's. Must be new."

"New to you. It's been here a while."

"Thought I'd pass along some info. I stopped in to see your sheriff. Nice guy. I told him I was working for O'Connor on the Wolcott case. According to him, Mrs. Wolcott admitted just hours before I got there that she killed her husband."

I suffered a momentary shortness of breath before saying, "According to plan."

"I don't know about that, but thought you'd want to know."

"I appreciate it."

"I also eavesdropped on a conversation at the bar, a habit of mine. Anyway, it's a busy bar, lots of happy chitchat. There were three business types sucking on drinks and talking about the victim. The gist of what I heard was that one of their buddies must be tickled that Wolcott's out of the picture. They were laughing about it. One of 'em said that this buddy of theirs,

Mauser or Hauser, not quite sure, must be throwing himself a party, celebrating that Wolcott got it."

"Mauser," I said.

"You know him?"

"Yes."

"Well, anyway, thought I'd pass it along. You learn a lot hanging out in bars. At least I always do."

"Thanks, Harry."

"I'd better get back to my room and dress for dinner with O'Connor. Don't want to look out of place at a country club."

I couldn't help but smile. No matter what Harry Mc-Graw wore, he would look out of place at any country club, including the Katahdin.

So had Richard Mauser also invested through Josh Wolcott and lost money? I pondered. *How many others like him had seen their finances dwindle because of Josh's malfeasance or downright dishonest dealings?* That question was one that I decided had to be answered.

Chapter Sixteen

"Is it true?" Evelyn Phillips asked without even a pre-liminary hello.

"Is *what* true?" I replied, the phone propped on my shoulder as I poured myself a bowl of cereal.

"That Myriam has admitted killing Josh?"

I hated being put in that position. I certainly wasn't about to confirm what she'd said, and that meant having to lie. I knew it was true because Mort Metzger had told Harry McGraw, and Harry had told me, but I did what I often do when I find myself in that situation: I avoided answering by asking my own question.

"Why do you say that?" I asked.

"It's a rumor, Jessica. I'm going crazy trying to con-firm it. Mort Metzger won't return my phone calls. The same with Cy O'Connor. Even someone inside the sheriff's department who I can usually wheedle infor-mation out of is avoiding me."

"What makes you think that I'd know anything about it?" I asked.

"Because you have your ear to the ground, especially when it involves murder."

"That's some reputation to have."

"But it's true. You do know a lot. So, Jessica Fletcher, I put it to you straight: Did Myriam Wolcott admit that she killed her husband?"

"If Mort isn't returning your calls, it's probably because . . ."

"That's it! You could call Mort for me. I know that he'll return *your* calls."

"I can't do that, Evelyn. Why don't you . . . ?"

I heard a phone ring on her end. "Sorry, Jessica. Have to run. Another call. Maybe it's Mort. Bye."

Saved by the bell, or at least the ring.

I puttered around the house for most of the morning. It wasn't so much that there were things that had to be done. It was more a matter of trying to occupy my mind and forget about the Wolcott murder. While I managed to accomplish a few things, my mind-control efforts weren't successful and I decided at a few minutes before noon to call O'Connor to see whether I could arrange for another visit with Myriam.

"He's out playing golf," Sharon Bacon told me.

"When will he be back?"

"Any minute now. I'll tell him you called."

"Thanks. Oh, Sharon, I heard this morning that Myriam Wolcott has admitted that she shot Josh."

"Not a good time for that discussion, Jessica. He's just come through the door. I'll tell him you're on the line."

O'Connor picked up the phone.

"I'd like to set up another meeting with Myriam," I said.

"No can do."

"It was all right the other day."

"Right, but things have changed. Better that Myriam's contact with others not connected with the case be kept to a minimum."

I was about to suggest that I certainly had become "connected" with the case through no fault of my own but decided not to, at least at that moment.

"Your old buddy McGraw is quite a character," O'Connor said. "He's a real fan of yours, told me about some cases that you'd worked on together."

"He's a good detective."

"He also told me that you suggested that he look into the possibility that someone else might have killed Josh Wolcott, somebody whose investments went bad."

"Which makes sense to me."

"That's not what I'm paying him for. You see—"

"I know. Myriam has now admitted to shooting her husband."

"Can't anything be kept a secret in this town for even a few hours?"

"Afraid not, Cy. You're saying that you won't pursue that possibility, which I find puzzling. You have Harry on your payroll. Why not set him loose investigating that angle?"

"That's a job for the police."

"Are they doing it?"

"I don't know. Ask your pal the sheriff. All I know is that I have a client who needs a rock-solid defense."

"But she says she's guilty."

"Sure, guilty of pulling the trigger, but she had a legal right to shoot him. The guy was a monster who threatened her life and the life of her kids. Her own mother knew it for years and pleaded with her daughter to leave the guy. She should have, but that's water over the dam. Myriam did what any caring mother would have done considering the circumstances. The fact that she shot him is one thing. Getting a judge and jury to accept the self-defense plea and find her not guilty is what's more important right now. Her admission that she pulled the trigger works in her favor. She's an honest woman. Being battered by her husband is now public knowledge. Everyone chosen for the jury will have been made aware of that. That's what I want McGraw to do—not only find others who knew about her being abused, but at the same time spread the word around town."

"And how will you account for the missing gun?" I asked.

"Jessica, do you have a law degree?"

"No."

"Then I'd appreciate it if you wouldn't second-guess me."

"If Myriam Wolcott did indeed shoot her husband, then I'm sure that your self-defense defense is the best way to proceed. But what if she's lying? As an officer of the court, I'd think that your finding out who really killed Josh Wolcott would not only exonerate Myriam; it would bring the true murderer to justice."

A deep, audible sigh came through the phone. "Sorry about not being able to accommodate you this time," he said. "I don't need Myriam hearing conflicting bits of advice at this point. Thanks for calling."

I replaced my phone in its cradle, sat back, rubbed my eyes, and allowed the sting of his criticism to abate. He was right, of course. I was invading his area of expertise, the law, and doing it without benefit of education or license. On the other hand, a degree doesn't necessarily ensure that lawyers make good decisions. Here was one who was decidedly making a wrong one.

Up until that day I'd been operating on my belief that Myriam Wolcott hadn't shot her husband. After all, she'd proclaimed her innocence, not only to me but to Mort Metzger and others in law enforcement. Why the sudden turnaround?

Her confession clearly changed Cy's strategy for the defense.

Still, there was something inside of me that didn't buy it. Even while Myriam was still declaring her innocence, her mother and Cy O'Connor were preparing to have her admit to the crime in hopes a plea of self-defense would sway a judge and jury.

How did they convince her to change her mind?

Couldn't get a fair trial in Cabot Cove?

Nonsense!

What was going on?

I was determined to find out.

I stopped in to see Seth Hazlitt that afternoon, but his nurse said he was backed up with patients.

"Why don't you come by for dinner?" he said when he poked his head into the waiting room between office visits.

I mentioned that Harry McGraw was in town, and Seth suggested that I bring him along.

I called Harry at the B and B and told him of Seth's invitation.

"Sounds good to me," Harry said. "Maybe the doc can tell me how to get rid of the pain in my back."

"I'm sure he'll be happy to do that, Harry. Pick me up?"

"Always at your service, Jessica. Shall I bring the town car or the stretch limo?"

"Bring a bike and we can pedal there together."

"My stretch limo is in for service. Have to be my rented wreck. See ya."

To my surprise, Seth had also invited Mort and Maureen Metzger. Seth pulled me aside in the kitchen right after I arrived at his house and said, "I managed to talk Maureen out of bringing some newfangled noodle dish she's been experimenting with, but she insisted on providing dessert. Said she had to practice for the Blueberry Festival."

"That's months away," I said, "but thanks for the warning."

Seth had prepared a chateaubriand, fingerling potatoes, a salad, and French bread straight from Sassi's Bakery. He's an excellent cook when he finds the time, his menus usually treading heavily on beef, as well as dishes high in fat and calories. A dietician he's not. We'd barely sat down when he raised the Wolcott murder.

"I understand you're working for Mrs. Wolcott's defense team," he said to McGraw.

"That's what they tell me," Harry replied. "I'm looking for people to back up her story about being abused. She'd tried to keep it secret and she was pretty successful. No luck so far."

"Must be awkward asking about such things," Seth said.

"Not really," was Harry's response. "Everybody's talking about the murder anyway, so I just say that I hear that the wife had been beaten up by her husband. Everybody knows the rumors, but nobody chimes in about having direct knowledge, at least not yet."

"Did you get to speak with the Hanley family?" I asked.

"Oh, right. Almost forgot. Yeah, I found their house and stopped by. Nice folks. I got the husband aside and asked whether the Wolcott kid ever talked about his mother being abused by his father. The husband, he says that he and the missus knew things weren't copacetic at the Wolcott house but that the kid never said anything directly. 'You know how teenagers are,' he says. 'They don't talk, just glue themselves to the computer.' The wife says that Mark seemed upset sometimes and that she asked him what was wrong, but he always managed a smile, according to her, never used words like 'abuse' or 'battering' or anything like that."

"I'm glad you tried," I said.

"Nothing ventured . . ."

As the discussion of the Wolcott murder continued, I noticed that Mort Metzger remained uncharacteristically quiet. Our sheriff was someone who had opinions about many things and was seldom reticent about expressing them. But he offered little, listening to each person's comments, nodding a few times, and looking as though he preferred to be elsewhere. I chalked it up to not wanting to say something about the case that might be inappropriate, and on a few occasions I tried to change the subject. But Seth, who'd been instrumental in getting the women's shelter established, seemed anxious to hammer home the point that domestic abuse should not be swept under a rug; it was a serious matter that had to be given attention.

"Happens every day," he said, "that somebody gets killed. Of course usually it's the abused partner, but in this case the victim fought back."

"Assuming that she did it," I said.

"She said she did," Maureen said. "Isn't that right, sweetheart?"

"Yup," said Mort. His laugh was forced. "I expected her lawyer, the young Mr. O'Connor, to claim her confession had been coerced, you know, beaten out of her with a rubber hose like on TV."

"What caused her to confess?" I asked him.

Mort shrugged. "She just spat it out. She sat down, said, 'I killed him,' and started to cry. We asked her to give us the details, but she clammed up, wouldn't say another word."

"Had her mother been in to see her prior to that?" I asked.

"Mrs. Caldwell? Seems like she's there all the time. Sure she was there. So was her brother."

"I asked to visit Myriam this morning," I said. "Cy O'Connor refused my request."

"Not unusual," Mort said. "Lawyers like to keep their clients, the guilty ones anyway, sequestered best as possible."

"Except for her mother and brother," I said.

"That's family," said Maureen.

"Besides," Mort added, "you're a writer. Maybe O'Connor's afraid that you'll write about her."

"I still find it strange," I said. "He wants me and Edwina Wilkerson to testify that Myriam was abused, supposedly to bolster her self-defense claim."

" 'Supposedly?' " Seth said. "Sounds like you have reservations about Mr. O'Connor."

"Forget I said that," I muttered. "I'm not sure what I mean."

We drifted into less serious topics and the mood

lightened palpably. It was when coffee and Maureen's dessert—a runny blueberry cobbler with a soggy topping—were served that Mort received a phone call, which he took in another room. We all looked up when he returned.

"That was Gladys at headquarters," he said.

"And?" Seth asked, spooning a pile of whipped cream over his cobbler.

"Looks like Cabot Cove is finally on the map," Mort said as he retook his chair.

"Meaning what?" Seth asked.

"Meaning that we're about to have visitors from Bangor," Mort replied.

"Stop playing games, Mort," Seth said, pique in his tone. "*What* visitors from Bangor?"

"*The Hour*," Mort said. "The Wolcott murder got somebody's attention at that TV show that's on Sundays. From what they told Gladys, they're doing a report on domestic violence and how it can lead to murder."

The Hour was a Maine TV fixture. It was patterned after *60 Minutes* but specialized in stories unique to our state. It was always well-done and had broadcast some important exposés about misdeeds in government and industry.

"How did they know about the Wolcott murder?" Maureen asked.

"Those guys must scour all the local papers," Mort replied. "All I know is that there's a whole contingent arriving day after tomorrow. They want to interview me."

"I wish it was *60 Minutes*," Maureen said. "I'd love to meet Scott Pelley or Lesley Stahl or Anderson Cooper. Will they be interviewing you at the house, sweetheart?" she asked. "Maybe I could bake them something—"

Mort interrupted her. "I don't think they'll want to film at our house, hon." He turned to me. "They'll probably want to interview you, too, Mrs. F., you and Ms. Wilkerson, seeing how you two were the ones at the shelter the night Mrs. Wolcott came in all battered and bruised."

"Myriam's confidentiality has already been badly breached," I said, pushing my spoon around the dessert plate to make it appear as if I'd eaten more. "I don't want to be a party to contributing to that on TV. We'll never get another victim—er, survivor—to come in again if we make such public appearances."

The discussion moved on to a comparison of *The Hour* with *60 Minutes* and some of the wonderful programs they'd aired over the years. When that topic had been exhausted, we called it a night and McGraw drove me home. I invited him in for a nightcap, and we settled in my living room, a glass of single-barrel bourbon in his hand, pomegranate juice in mine.

"Tell me more about what you heard at the bar at Peppino's," I said.

"Just what I told you. Buddies of his were laughing about how Mauser wasn't going to mourn the loss of Wolcott."

"Did they indicate he'd lost money with Josh?"

"No. Who is this Mauser anyway?"

I explained.

"Sounds like a pain in the neck."

"Yes, he is that. Cy O'Connor seemed angry that I asked you to look into other possible suspects."

"Yeah, he was a little uptight about it."

"Will you?"

"See if anybody lost enough money to have wanted to kill the guy? Sure. For you, Jess, anything."

"I'll be doing a little snooping of my own, too."

Harry laughed. "Why am I not surprised?"

Chapter Seventeen

Myriam Wolcott was arraigned the following morning at the courthouse, Judge Ralph Mackin, an old friend of mine, presiding. I'd debated attending but decided not to, although Harry McGraw did go and reported back to me.

According to Harry, Myriam was there with her attorney, her mother, and her brother. "She looked like an overcooked strand of spaghetti," was the way Harry described her. "I thought she'd collapse any minute, but O'Connor and her brother were at her side and propped her up."

"Did she say anything?" I asked.

"Just said 'not guilty' when the judge asked how she pleaded. That was it, not another word. The judge did bring up that she admitted to shooting her husband and asked O'Connor what the not-guilty plea was based on. O'Connor says that she acted in self-defense, that she'd been abused by the guy and shot him to protect herself and the kids."

"What did Judge Mackin say to that?"

"Nothing. He just made a few notes. The DA and some of her people were there, too. O'Connor asked that the judge release her on bail, made the point that she had roots in the town, had two kids who needed her, wasn't a flight risk, upstanding citizen, all the usual."

"How did he respond?"

"He denied it but said that O'Connor could give him a written motion. I had the feeling that this judge is a pretty cool guy and might let her out on bail, house arrest, slap a monitor on her ankle."

"That would be good for her and the children," I said.

"I guess."

"Did her mother or brother say anything to the judge?" I asked.

"Nope. That mother is one tough-looking lady."

"So I've noticed. Harry, there's a special town meeting this evening that I'll be attending. The Richard Mauser you've heard about is a member of the town council. He's called the meeting to try to stop funding of the women's shelter. He's been against it from the beginning, and the Wolcott murder has evidently gotten him fired up again. If you're not doing anything tonight, you might be interested in coming with me to see the fireworks."

"Sounds like a good way to kill an evening. There's not a lot to do in this town. Not that I'm complaining. The money O'Connor's paying is good, but I wish I had something to report back to him. Nobody seems to know firsthand that Mrs. Wolcott was abused by her old man. Sure I'll come."

"It'll give you a chance to see Richard Mauser. I'd love to know what his connection to the Wolcotts is, and if he lost money by investing with Josh Wolcott."

McGraw laughed and said, "What do you want me to do, get up during the meeting and ask him?"

"Nothing that direct, but you might have an opportunity to speak with him. You've always been good at getting people to say things they might not say to someone else. Besides, it'll give you a chance to see how a small town council works."

"Count me in."

Harry and I drove into the town hall parking lot that evening and pulled into a parking space adjacent to the one occupied by Richard Mauser's black Cadillac. On the rear was a bumper sticker that read "I'd Rather Be Hunting." Mauser waved as he climbed out of his car, but when he realized who I was, his smile turned into a scowl and without a word he headed for the building.

"That's Richard Mauser," I told Harry as we exited the car.

"Big guy," Harry commented.

"A heavy in several senses of the word," I said. "You'll get a better look once we're inside."

I expected a fairly sparse crowd that night because of the last-minute nature of the meeting, but I was wrong. People filed in one after another, and I wondered whether they were there out of a sincere interest in the fate of the women's shelter or because the shelter, however tangentially, involved Josh Wolcott's murder. No matter why, they kept arriving, and soon all the spectator seats were filled. Harry and I sat with Seth Hazlitt and Edwina Wilkerson. I saw Mort and Maureen Metzger on the opposite side of the room. That Mort was there surprised me. He seldom attended council meetings unless the sheriff's department was on the agenda.

"Mauser's the one on the left," I told McGraw, nodding toward the florid-faced, heavyset man in a suit and tie at the council members' table.

"Looks like a pet pig one of my ex-wives used to have."

"Be nice, Harry," I murmured.

"I am being nice. I loved that pig."

There was a buzz in the room. I heard a woman behind us say, "She admitted she shot him. At least that's what they're saying."

"I heard that Wolcott was a con man," her companion, presumably her husband, replied.

"So what?" the woman said. "She killed him. She said she did."

"Maybe she had a good reason."

"There's never a good reason to shoot someone."

Their debate was interrupted by Mayor Shevlin, who tapped his gavel to start the proceedings, as other members of the council joined Mauser at the table.

"I've called this special meeting," Shevlin said, donning his reading glasses, "because one of our members, Dick Mauser, is invoking a clause in our charter that allows for special meetings to be called when"—he read from the charter—"'when a financial issue demanding immediate attention and that threatens to impact the city's financial stability is brought to the council's attention by a member.'" The mayor put down his papers and removed his glasses. "Dick has made the point that our funding for the women's shelter falls under this clause. Now, I admit that although the amount we allocate to the shelter each year is only a small part of our overall budget, Dick has the right to bring it up again at this special meeting. Since we're here because of him, he has the floor."

Mauser got to his feet, ran his index finger beneath his restrictive shirt collar, and looked around the room with a satisfied smile. "First I want to thank you all for coming here tonight. Don't you believe what the mayor says about this bein' a small part of the budget. Every dollar counts in this economy, and to see even a tiny portion squandered on *unnecessary* services is gravel in my craw. It should be for you, too.

"There's people in this country working hard, people who run businesses, businesses that support the economy. And are they asking for a government handout? They are not. And we're giving more attention to a bunch of whiny women who can't get along with their husbands. Well, tell them to grow up; tell them to work harder like the rest of us.

"My question is when are we going to wake up? When are we going to see through what the backers of the women's shelter claim, that they *help* women? Truth is, if Mrs. Joshua Wolcott hadn't visited the shelter a few nights before she shot her husband dead, he'd still be alive today."

Edwina jumped to her feet. "Untrue! How can you make statements like that?" she said loudly. She appealed to the mayor. "This man has no idea what he's talking about. He's presenting his opinion as if it's a fact and it's not."

The mayor pounded his gavel a few times on the wooden table and asked her to take her seat. "There will be time for you to have your say, Ms. Wilkerson. Right now Councilman Mauser has the floor."

Mauser glared at Edwina before continuing. "The truth hurts," he said. "It always does. But the reality is, Mrs. Wolcott went to the shelter and complained about the way her husband was treating her. Nobody even knows whether she was telling the truth or not."

"This is insufferable," Edwina piped up from where she sat.

"Please, Edwina," the mayor said.

"Sorry," she sang out, clearly not sorry at all. Edwina leaned over and whispered to me, "I tell you, Jessica, that man is lucky I don't carry a gun."

"Edwina!" I whispered back, frowning at her.

"Point is," Mauser continued, "claiming to be abused by her husband gave her the excuse to kill him. That's what she's gonna argue in court. You've all heard about it, I'm sure. 'Self-defense,' she says. I say, bull hockey! You better believe me: You keep pumping taxpayer money into that so-called shelter and you're supporting a place that gives people an excuse for taking the law into their own hands. I move that we cease funding the shelter, effective immediately."

I was surprised that Mauser received a smattering of applause from some in attendance. To me, his argument was absurd; how could any thinking person support what he was suggesting? But I reminded myself that in a democracy, people of various viewpoints and beliefs are free to express themselves, and to vote the way they see things, as skewed as their visions may be.

Two other members of the council spoke after Mauser, a man and a woman, each expressing support for the shelter, before the mayor threw open the floor for public statements. Edwina, who'd been fairly bouncing in her seat, was first to approach the microphone in the center aisle. She cited statistics both statewide and local to bolster her arguments that Cabot Cove needed such a service. She surprised the attendees by saying that women were not the only ones in town to use the shelter's services, that men could be victims of abuse as well. Finally, she read from a study that concluded that municipalities that aggressively addressed domestic abuse prevented violence and were able to lower their crime rate and realize a financial savings overall.

A smattering of citizens followed Edwina and expressed their views, all of them positive about continuing funding, with one exception—a muscular young man wearing a tight T-shirt and jeans who said that he agreed with Mauser. He didn't give a reason for his opinion, simply said, "Councilman Mauser is right," and left.

"Who's that?" Edwina asked me.

"I don't recognize him," I replied. "Perhaps he's new to town."

A vote was taken, and again Mauser was the only council member voting to rescind funding for the shelter. Most people left the room following the vote, but a few dozen of us moved into an adjoining room where coffee, tea, soft drinks, and cookies from Sassi's Bakery were available, a tradition established years ago. I expected that Mauser would quickly depart, but he didn't. He took a position at the end of the table holding the refreshments and continued his diatribe about the shelter with anyone who would listen. Seth and I had served ourselves and joined Mort and Maureen

Metzger at the other end of the table. Harry McGraw had accompanied us but now shifted in Mauser's direction. He stood behind a couple who were arguing with the councilman until they walked away. I sidled closer to hear what Harry was about to say.

"Mr. Mauser, Harry McGraw," he said, extending his hand. Mauser took it. "I'm a private detective working for Cy O'Connor."

"Is that so?" Mauser said. "Working to get the murderer off, you mean."

Harry smiled. "You might put it that way, Mr. Mauser, only it seems to me that she had a right to do what she did."

Mauser's already red face darkened a shade or two. "Nobody has a right to kill another person," he said.

"I agree," said Harry, "only sometimes a person's driven to it, you know, takes enough abuse—" He paused. "Or gets scammed by a guy who takes your money, a guy like her husband."

Mauser paused and cocked his head.

"You know what I mean," McGraw continued. "I mean, this Wolcott guy took a lot of people for a ride, the way he did you."

"What are you talking about?" Mauser said. "I don't know where you get your information."

"Part of my job is to see whether there might be other people in this lovely town who had a motive to kill Wolcott."

"Are you suggesting that . . . ?" Mauser sputtered to a halt.

"I'm not suggesting anything," said McGraw. "But you're a leading citizen in Cabot Cove, on the council and all. I'm sure you'd want to see justice done, *real* justice." When Mauser didn't respond, Harry said, "Am I right?"

It was apparent from my vantage point that Mauser struggled to get himself under control. When he had reined in his temper, he said in a voice that passed for moderation, "Mrs. Wolcott shot and killed her husband. The women's shelter implanted in her the evil notion that it was all right to pull the trigger. End of story, Mr. . . . ?"

"McGraw. Harry McGraw. Pleasure meeting you, Councilman. Maybe we can get together sometime and talk about how Wolcott ripped people off. By the way, how much did he take you for?"

"Good night, Mr. McGraw," Mauser said, and lumbered away, hunched forward, his briefcase under his arm. Harry picked up a cookie, took a large bite, and came to us.

"Well, that was certainly direct," I said, although I wasn't entirely surprised. Bluntness was among McGraw's many personality quirks. He would not have made a good diplomat.

"Just wanted to give him a chance to back off on his stance about the murder and the shelter. Did you watch him? He didn't say it, but everything about him tells me that he was ripped off by Wolcott."

"You didn't really expect him to admit it, did you?" I asked, laughing.

Mort Metzger, who'd stood by quietly while witnessing the exchange, finally said, "What was that all about?"

"Harry was fishing to see whether Mr. Mauser was another of Josh Wolcott's victims of financial malfeasance."

Mort's expression was a melding of confusion and discomfort. He took my elbow and moved me away from the others. "Look, Mrs. F.," he said, "I know that you have this notion that somebody else killed Josh Wolcott, somebody who he cheated."

I started to say something, but he cut me off with, "Mind a word of advice?"

"When have I ever said no to you, Mort?"

"Fair enough. I've always appreciated it when you've come up with information that helped me out with a case, but I really think you should butt out of this one."

"I'm listening."

"Okay, let me tell you why," he said. "One, Myriam Wolcott has admitted that she killed her husband. That alone should be reason enough. But I'll give you another. For your friend to confront Dick Mauser like that was pretty darn rude, if you ask me. Yeah, I know he's a difficult guy, a bully even, but he's an important member of the community. There's nothing to be gained by getting him all riled up."

"What if Myriam was pressured to confess?" I asked. "What if she's lying?"

Mort looked at me as though I'd lost my mind. "What reason would she have to do that, Mrs. F.? Why would anybody say they killed somebody if they didn't?"

"Come on, Mort. As a policeman, you know there have been lots of people who've made false confessions to crimes. They all have their reasons for doing what they do, even if we don't know what they are."

And I intend to keep looking for Myriam's reason until I'm proved wrong, I thought.

"Be that as it may, this is not the big city, and Myriam Wolcott is not one of those crazies who confess to crimes they didn't commit," Mort said. "She even told us where she threw the gun. I've got my guys checking out that part of the river."

"And when did she have time to throw the gun in the river?" I asked. "Before or after she was on the phone with nine-one-one saying that someone had shot her husband?"

Mort gave me an exasperated look. "My suggestion is that you back off and accept what looks to me like an open-and-shut case. She claims that she did it in self-defense, and that's good enough for me. The jury will decide if she was justified. For me, the case is closed and I'd appreciate it if you'd not muddy the waters."

"You've made your point, Mort."

"Yeah, but did I get through to you?"

"Loud and clear."

"Good. No offense?" He cocked his head and gave me a charming smile to show there were no hard feelings.

"Of course not."

"One more piece of advice?"

"Mmmmm?" I hummed noncommittally.

"Call off your buddy McGraw. Let him do whatever work he's supposed to do for Cy O'Connor and go back to Boston."

"I'll pass along your recommendation," I said.

"Good. Now that that's settled, how about coming to the house for dinner day after tomorrow? Maureen's got a new recipe for scallops. It's pretty good."

"Thanks, Mort. I'll check my schedule and call."

I recounted our conversation to McGraw as he drove me home.

"Maybe he's right," McGraw said.

"And maybe he's not. I'm not the one who hired you," I said, "but I'm still convinced that Josh Wolcott might have been killed by someone other than his wife."

"I don't know whether you're right or not," he said as he pulled into my driveway, "but as long as I'm here, I'll keep nosing around."

"Cy won't like it," I said as I opened the door.

"No reason for him to know," McGraw said, shrugging his shoulders. "Hey, what are friends for? Anyway, I have a hunch *I* want to follow."

"What's that?"

"I think that this Mauser character really wants Mrs. Wolcott to be convicted of the murder."

"Why would he want that?" I asked.

"Maybe because he knows that she didn't do it and wants to protect somebody else."

"Such as who? Himself?"

"Just a thought," Harry said, grinning. "Catch up with you tomorrow."

Chapter Eighteen

It snowed overnight, coating everything in white. I'd checked the weather on TV before going to bed and was told that the forecast was for ample sun and moderating temperatures. I assume that the meteorologist pushed the wrong button and was referring to Miami or Phoenix.

An unexpected snowfall wasn't the only surprise that morning.

A headline in the morning newspaper trumpeted, "Bail Granted." A report by Evelyn Phillips and James Teller revealed that Cy O'Connor had submitted a motion to Judge Mackin to grant bail for Myriam Wolcott, and the judge had agreed—provided she wore an ankle bracelet, was restricted to her home with the exception of medical emergencies and visits with her attorney, and turned over her passport, which was a moot point since she didn't have one. The article said the district attorney had protested, claiming that since Myriam had already killed once, she posed a threat to her family and neighbors. Judge Mackin ignored the DA and ordered Myriam released. The news pleased me. At least Myriam would be in her own house and with her children until her trial, which the paper informed me would commence months from now, in August.

A less official bit of news came from Edwina Wilkerson.

"They're here," she said breathlessly when I picked up the phone.

"Who's here?"

"The EPA inspectors. They're about to test the river near Mauser's factory." She sounded gleeful. "I can't wait for them to nail that miserable excuse for a human being, fine him ten million dollars, and put him out of business."

I knew that Edwina had been keeping tabs on the arrival of the EPA people. I also knew that her loathing for Richard Mauser now exceeded rational boundaries.

"I'll buy the whole town a drink when he's run out of town," she told Mara at her dockside luncheonette, according to others who were there.

"They haven't found anything yet," I told her.

"Oh, but they will," she countered.

I realized that it was impossible at that moment to have a reasonable conversation with her about Mauser and changed the subject to the latest about Myriam.

"I didn't know that," she said. "That's wonderful news. I'll bet Mauser is tearing his hair out."

So much for changing the subject.

I'd no sooner ended that conversation when Harry McGraw called.

"Good morning," I said.

"No, it isn't. I came out this morning to find two of my tires slashed."

"Oh, Harry, that's terrible. Who could have done such a thing?"

"Beats me. Remember that young guy who stood up and said he agreed with Mauser about the shelter?"

"Yes. I'd never seen him before. Why?"

"When we came out of the meeting, I saw him hanging around my car, like he was looking it over."

"Why didn't you say something?"

"No crime in what he was doing. I've got a guy from a local garage bringing over two new tires. Hey, I didn't think people did stuff like this in Cabot Cove."

"We're not without our problems."

"Last time I was here you were bragging about how little crime there is, but you've got a woman who shoots her husband, a flimflam financial adviser who steals widows' pensions, and a guy who gets his jollies cutting up tires."

"Have you called the sheriff's office?" I asked.

"No, but I will. What's on your plate today?"

"I haven't put it together yet. Do you have a suggestion?"

"I may have some news for you if you're going to be around."

"Tell me."

"I've got this friend in Boston with the Better Business Bureau. I called her yesterday and she put me in touch with somebody in Bangor who handles Maine. I asked her for a list of people who filed complaints against Wolcott. She's supposed to get back to me in an hour."

"Please let me know, Harry. I'll be here all morning."

He called back a little after eleven.

"Did you get a list?"

"Yeah. Not many on it, just four—a guy named Quaid, a woman named Judson, and two other guys, a Peter Zeweski and somebody Caldwell . . . Robert Caldwell. No Mauser on the list, though. Of course, just because he didn't go on record doesn't mean he wasn't taken for a ride."

"Did you say one of the names was Caldwell?"

"Yeah. That mean something to you?"

"His first name was Robert?"

"Uh-huh."

I was certain that Myriam's mother had mentioned that Myriam's brother's first name was Robert.

"Do you have an address for Robert Caldwell?"

"Yeah. Some town called Gorbyville."

"Gorbyville," I repeated. "That's about sixty miles from Cabot Cove."

"Sounds like a place Stephen King would like. Take out the *b* and you've got Goryville. Why the interest in this guy?"

"Unless I'm mistaken, Robert Caldwell is Myriam Wolcott's brother."

"Caldwell. That's the mother's name?"

"Right."

"So if this Robert Caldwell is Myriam Wolcott's brother, it means the vic was fleecing his own brother-in-law."

"It looks that way," I said.

"I have to go in a minute; the guy with the tires just pulled in. One last thing. This gal at the Better Business Bureau told me that they checked with the organization that certifies financial planners, you know, gives them a bunch of letters to use after their names."

"Certified Financial Planner," I said. "Hold on." I fetched the card that Josh Wolcott had given me and came back on the line. "Wolcott had the letters *CFP* after his name on his business card," I told Harry.

"My best new old friend at the Better Business Bureau says that when they checked they found that Wolcott used to be certified," McGraw said, "but after too many complaints the regulators took it away from him."

"When?"

"Two years ago."

Long before he gave me his card and was still representing himself as a CFP.

"This is all interesting, Harry. I'll let you go to get your car fixed."

"If you're free, let me take you to lunch and we can bat this around."

"I'm free. Pick me up at noon?"

"On the dot, provided this guy knows how to change a tire."

As promised, Harry pulled up to my house at noon and we drove to the waterfront for lunch at Mara's. Harry remembered it from his last visit to Cabot Cove.

"Like an office watercooler," he said as we entered. "All the latest gossip."

I laughed. "There are no secrets in Cabot Cove," I said lightly, "especially not in Mara's."

Mara recognized Harry and gave him a hearty greeting as she escorted us to a booth at a window overlooking the harbor and dock. The temperature had managed to nudge above freezing, and much of the snow had melted.

"How's that British friend of yours?" Harry asked after we'd been handed menus.

"George Sutherland? He's fine. We don't get to see much of each other."

"He's Scotland Yard, right?"

"Yes. A chief inspector."

"I got the feeling that Doc Hazlitt isn't his biggest fan."

"Oh, that's not true. Seth is—well, Seth is overly protective of me."

"Or nuts about you."

"Don't be silly."

"Hey, don't kid a kidder. I pick up on those things."

Mara came to the table to take our order. She leaned closer to me and said, "Those folks from the Environmental Protection Agency are in town. They had breakfast here this morning."

"So I've heard," I said, "not about breakfast but that they were here."

"Mr. O'Connor brought them in."

"Cy did?" I said. "Is he involved with them in some way?"

"Beats me, Jessica. Nice that Mrs. Wolcott gets to go home, at least for a few months. Nice lady. He really must have pushed her to do what she—"

"Last time I was here I had blueberry pancakes," McGraw said, interrupting her. "Best I ever had."

"House specialty," Mara said. "Served all day."

Our orders delivered—the pancakes and a side of sausage for him, a salad and dry English muffin for me—McGraw became silent as he looked out the window.

"What are you thinking?" I asked.

He turned to me. "The more I learn about this guy Wolcott and his shady business dealings, the more I agree with you, that maybe it was one of his victims who blew him away, not the wife."

"My feelings about that are summarily dismissed," I said, "because she's admitted to the murder."

"Yeah, except she wouldn't be the first person to admit to a crime she didn't commit. Maybe she's shielding somebody else, like this brother-in-law who got taken to the cleaners by Wolcott."

"Her brother was there the night of the shooting," I said. "The newspaper said she'd called him right after she discovered the body and that he and his wife rushed there."

"Maybe he was there earlier than that."

"It would put another light on the case if it were true."

"I got an idea. What say we take a ride over to this Goryville after lunch?"

"Gorbyville."

"Whatever. Let's take a look at this brother of hers up close."

Gorbyville, Maine, is one of many towns that sprung up around the logging industry, one of the state's major industries. Based upon what Myriam Wolcott's mother had said, I had wondered if her son Robert held some sort of important executive position with one of the companies there, but it turned out that Robert Caldwell was the owner of an insurance agency in Gorbyville, with an office in a strip mall in the center of the small town. McGraw had also gotten the address of the house where Caldwell and his wife, Stephanie, resided. We decided to stop in at his office first.

"Is Mr. Caldwell in?" I asked the pretty young blond woman in the firm's outer office.

"Do you have an appointment?"

"No, we don't," I said. "I'm Jessica Fletcher. This is Harry McGraw. He's a private detective working for Myriam Wolcott's attorney."

The receptionist seemed unsure of what to say or do next.

"We won't take much of his time," McGraw said. "Just a coupla questions."

She wrote down our names and with a "please wait here" disappeared into an office at the rear. We could hear her and a man's voice but couldn't make out what they were saying. Finally she emerged and said, "Mr. Caldwell is very busy, but he says he can see you for a few minutes."

Caldwell appeared from the back office. He was a good-looking man, solidly built, with an old-fashioned crew cut. He wore a white shirt, no tie, gray slacks, and moccasins.

"What can I do for you?" he asked.

After introducing ourselves, I said, "Mr. McGraw is working on behalf of your sister. Cyrus O'Connor has hired him to help in her defense."

Caldwell ignored Harry and said to me, "And you're Jessica Fletcher, the writer. My mother mentioned you to me."

"I am a writer, Mr. Caldwell, but that's not why I'm here." I looked around before asking, "Could we sit down with you for a few minutes, somewhere more private?"

His receptionist looked annoyed but said nothing.

"Yeah, I suppose so," Caldwell said, "but I can only give you a few minutes. It's a very busy day. I have a lot of appointments."

We followed him to his office, which was cramped

and messy. File folders and papers were piled everywhere. I noticed that the yellow-and-brown shag rug was badly worn in spots. Color travel posters hung crookedly, more befitting a travel agency than an insurance firm. There were two photographs on the wall behind the desk. One depicted Caldwell dressed in camouflage clothing, holding a rifle, and standing proudly over the carcass of a deer he'd evidently just shot. The second was of him and a woman I assumed was his wife. It had been taken on a sunny beach, possibly in the Caribbean.

Caldwell stood with his hands on the back of the chair behind the desk and pointed to the only other available seat, which I declined.

"Okay," he said, "why have you come to see me?"

I glanced at Harry before replying, "We're trying— no, *I'm* the one who's trying to determine whether someone else might have shot your brother-in-law."

His expression was blank.

"I know your sister," I continued. "I was at the Cabot Cove women's shelter the night she came in, her face bruised, her self-esteem shattered. To cut to the chase, Mr. Caldwell, I have my doubts about what really happened that night in her driveway."

He dismissed me with a crooked smile and a slow shaking of his head. "I don't know whether you read the papers, Mrs. Fletcher, but my sister has confessed to killing Josh."

"I'm well aware of that," I said. "I also know that people confessing to crimes they haven't committed isn't as rare as you might think."

"Why would she admit to killing Josh if she didn't do it?" Caldwell asked.

"I thought you might have some thoughts on that subject," I said. "You were the first one she called."

"You think she's crazy?" he said through a sneer.

"Hardly," I said. "Is she protecting someone?"

"Like who?"

I didn't respond, nor did Harry say anything.

Caldwell looked at his watch. "Time's up," he said, pointing to the door.

"You mind one more question?" Harry asked.

Caldwell sighed.

"Your brother-in-law, Josh, was quite an operator," Harry said.

"Meaning?"

"Meaning that he was a so-called financial adviser whose advice took some people to the cleaners."

"I wouldn't know about that," said Caldwell.

"Sure you would," Harry countered. "How much did he fleece from you?"

For a moment I thought that Caldwell might physically lash out at Harry. His fists were clenched and his mouth drew into a tight, angry line.

I quickly said, "The point is, Mr. Caldwell, that the people your brother-in-law stole from might have had reason to want him dead. We know that you invested with him and that . . ."

Caldwell came around the desk, opened his door, and said, "I have nothing more to say to you." He put on a forced smile. "Have a nice day."

We walked past him and the receptionist's desk and went outside.

"The guy's got a temper, huh?" Harry commented.

"You did take him by surprise," I said.

"Always the best way. We know one thing."

"Which is?"

"His brother-in-law sure as the devil must've taken him for a bundle if Caldwell was willing to file a complaint. Not exactly good for family relations."

"Neither is financial malfeasance," I said.

"You see his face when I said he was fleeced?"

"I certainly did."

"Let's head back."

We turned to see Caldwell climb into an older-model yellow Toyota in front of his office and drive away.

"I have a better idea," I said. "As long as we're already here, let's go by his house before he calls his wife to warn her about us."

McGraw smiled. "You're on the scent, huh?" he said.

"I just hate to waste an opportunity, Harry. Game?"

"Always."

I didn't mention that not only did I want to take advantage of already being in Gorbyville; I wanted to make good use of the time I had with Harry. His official capacity as investigator for Myriam Wolcott's defense gave me—us—an explainable reason for seeking out people and asking questions. As long as he was willing to join me in trying to find a different explanation for Josh Wolcott's murder, I intended to benefit from it. He wasn't being paid by Cy O'Connor to chase down my theory, however, and his doing so would probably anger the lawyer. He was being a good guy, which he'd always been.

The Caldwell home was only a mile or so from Robert Caldwell's insurance office in a cluster of small houses on a lake. They might once have been summer vacation bungalows but now had been converted into year-round houses. A few teenagers played soccer in the street, and an elderly woman walked a dog on a leash. We parked across from the house and took it in.

"Hate to make judgments," McGraw said, "but I'd say his company isn't setting the insurance world on fire."

"It is a little run-down," I said. "Let's see if she's home. Her name is Stephanie."

"I hope the guy didn't call her from his car."

"Nothing we can do about it if he did," I said.

Stephanie Caldwell opened her front door as we approached and stepped outside onto a marred concrete slab that served as a front step. She stood with her arms crossed over her chest, hip cocked, her posture and expression asking who we were and why we were there. She had a rough, somewhat crude look to her; her skin was sallow, features coarse—nose, lips, jaw—and beneath her tired eyes were faint dark circles. She struck me as a woman who'd gone through some rough times and had aged beyond her chronological years. Her clothing was nondescript, drab tan slacks and sweater that matched her hair.

"Mrs. Caldwell," I said.

"Yes. Who are you?"

"I'm Jessica Fletcher. This is Harry McGraw, a private detective. We're from Cabot Cove and . . ."

"What do you want?"

"Just a few minutes of your time, ma'am," Harry replied.

"About what?"

"About Josh Wolcott's murder."

"Why do you want to talk to me? My husband and I weren't anywhere near Cabot Cove when Josh was killed. We had nothing to do with it."

"We understand that," I said, "but we do have some questions, the answers to which might help your sister-in-law."

It was impossible to tell whether the snort from her was directed at our reason for being there or at the mention of Myriam.

"I know we're barging in," I said, "but we would appreciate if you would grant us a few minutes."

"Why don't you talk to Robert?" she asked.

I hesitated admitting that we had, but Harry said, "We will but don't want to bother him at work. Being in the insurance business must keep him busy."

The woman we'd seen walking the dog stopped at the curb in front of Stephanie's house and waved to her. Stephanie raised a hand halfheartedly in return and turned to the door. "I don't want to give the neighbors anything to talk about," she said. "You'd better come in."

The inside of the house was small and dingy. The front entrance led straight into the living room. A slat on a venetian blind was broken and dangled from the cord. A dirty plate and a half-empty bottle of water sat on a coffee table in front of a TV set on which a soap opera played silently. We could see two other rooms off the main one. Access to the kitchen was on the back wall, and to the right was the door to the bedroom, through which the unmade bed was visible. Stephanie walked to the bedroom door, shut it, and returned to us.

"All right, get to it," she said as the three of us stood awkwardly in the center of the room.

"You and your husband rushed to Myriam's home the night Josh was shot," I began.

"So? What's wrong with that?"

"Nothing at all," I said. "I'm sure that you and your

husband were a source of much-needed comfort for Myriam."

My comment was met with a chilly silence, her stance the same as when we'd first met her in front of the house.

"Myriam reached out to you even before calling nine-one-one, so am I correct in supposing that you and your husband had a good relationship with Myriam and Josh?"

"Robert and Myriam get along," she replied.

"What about Josh? Did you have a good relationship with him as well?"

That question caused a change in her posture. She sank down in one of two stained white swivel club chairs and swung back and forth, a twisted smile on her face. "What are you trying to get at? He was our brother-in-law. He was Myriam's problem, not ours."

McGraw, who stood next to me, his eyes taking in everything, said, "Yet your husband must have been pretty upset the way his brother-in-law handled his finances."

Stephanie got to her feet. "You know about that?"

"Yeah," Harry said. "It's pretty common knowledge."

What she said next came as a surprise, both in content and in tone. "That phony con artist screwed us royally!"

"That must have been terrible for you," I said.

"How much did he take you for?" Harry asked.

She didn't answer. Playing for time, she picked up a T-shirt that was draped over the arm of her chair, balled it up, opened the door to the bedroom, and threw it on the bed.

I took the chair that was a match to hers, my mind

going in two different directions. I couldn't help but wonder how this woman's staunch, patrician mother-in-law reacted to her daughter-in-law's lifestyle and language. At the same time, I wanted to learn more about the relationship between this family and Josh and Myriam Wolcott. "You weren't the only ones that your brother-in-law scammed, Mrs. Caldwell," I said.

"Seems he had a habit of stealing from his clients," McGraw added. "There are plenty of them in Cabot Cove."

"He was a swine," Stephanie said, nearly spitting with disgust. She paced the room. "He almost wiped us out. Robert took all the money his father left him when he died and handed it over to his big college-man brother-in-law to invest." She almost growled as she said it. "His father had left us a beautiful vacation home in Calais. We were in seventh heaven. Robert's agency was never that profitable, and we were always scraping to make ends meet." She grabbed the water bottle from the table, unscrewed the cap, and took a swig. "Robert sold the place and gave Josh the money. I pleaded with him not to, but he's stubborn . . ." She paused before adding, "And not too bright. Josh blew every cent of it, every last cent. I could have died when Robert finally got up the courage to tell me that the investments Josh put us in had collapsed, were worth nothing." She became more animated. "I hated him."

"Josh?"

"Yeah, Josh. And Robert, too."

"I'm so sorry," I said.

"It ruined the marriage; that's what it did," she said, her eyes flaming. "I don't know why I even stay here." She threw herself into the chair opposite mine.

"Did Myriam say anything the night that you and your husband drove to her house, anything to indicate that she'd shot Josh?"

"Myriam is a wimp. But she did it, right? She confessed."

"Did she confess to you that night?"

"Not to me, but we were never close. I just felt sorry for the kids. They were both crying. I stayed with them while Robert talked to Myriam."

"Did Robert tell you that Myriam confessed to him?"

"No, but she told the cops. Isn't that enough?"

"Yes," I said, "but there's some doubt in my mind whether she's telling the truth."

"Why? The guy beat her up, didn't he? We knew it. If Robert ever did that to me, I'd . . ."

I thought she might begin to cry, but instead she drained the last of her water and sat sullenly, eyes directed at the empty bottle held on her lap in both hands.

"I know this is upsetting to you," I said, "and we won't stay much longer. But by any chance had you and Robert been to Myriam's house earlier that evening, before Josh was killed?"

"What are you getting at?" she snapped.

"Had he, or possibly the both of you, been there earlier?" I pressed.

She fixed me with a threatening stare as she said, "Are you suggesting that maybe *we* shot him?"

"I'm not suggesting anything, only asking a question."

Harry sensed that I'd moved the conversation into a controversial area and said, "Like Mrs. Fletcher says, I'm a detective working for Myriam Wolcott's lawyer. I'm trying to get everybody's timeline straight, that's all. If you weren't there earlier, you weren't there, pure and simple. I suppose you've got people who'll testify that you were home until Mrs. Wolcott called."

"Get out!" Stephanie barked.

Harry held up his hands and said, "Hey. Take it easy. Just asking a simple question. It'll come up in court."

"Out!" Stephanie shouted.

"Thanks for your time," McGraw said, ushering me toward the exit.

Stephanie pushed ahead of us to the front door and flung it open, only to have Robert Caldwell step into the room.

"What are you doing here?" he asked, anger written on his face.

"Just leaving," Harry said, smiling.

"What did you tell them?" Robert yelled at his wife.

"Nothing, just what a loser you are and how you blew everything we had. I'm glad he's dead."

"These people are strangers. Just keep your mouth shut. Are you going to broadcast the news all over the neighborhood? It's none of their business."

"Well, it's true, isn't it?"

McGraw and I left and walked quickly to his car, their combative voices carrying clearly across the street. Harry pulled away and headed back in the direction of Cabot Cove.

"Man," he said, "that guy Wolcott sure fouled up a lot of people, even in his own family."

"He certainly did," I said. "I keep thinking about the mother. She has a daughter who married a wife beater and scam artist who hurt many people including his own in-laws, and a son who isn't very successful in his business, who squandered money, and who is married to a woman who's angry and resentful. I can't say that I like Mrs. Caldwell, but I understand a little better why she's so committed to the facade she puts on."

"You always see the best in people, don't you, Jessica?"

"I'm not sure that's true, Harry. It's just that as I get older, I'm more respectful of the human dilemma, our failures and foibles and the hurdles we're called upon to face from time to time."

"Know what I think?" he asked.

"Tell me."

"I think Mrs. Wolcott is lucky to have somebody like Jessica Fletcher on her side and looking for the truth."

"Somehow I don't think she'll see it that way."

Chapter Nineteen

I'd promised Harry a home-cooked meal as a thank-you for his assistance, but first he wanted to stop in to see Sheriff Metzger to report his slashed tires. The deputy at the desk told us that the sheriff was being interviewed. I thought that someone from the *Gazette* might be with him, but the deputy said, "Those TV folks from *The Hour* are here."

"Do you think they'll be much longer?" I asked.

"Shouldn't be," he replied. "They've been in there for more than an hour already, and . . ."

The door opened and a four-person film crew preceded Mort into the waiting area.

"Hi, Mrs. F.," Mort said. "McGraw."

"Hello, Mort. Will you have a minute when these folks leave?"

"Jessica?"

I turned to see a familiar face, Clay Dawkins. I'd met Clay in New York years earlier when he was a TV producer for one of the networks. He'd produced a documentary on the popularity of murder mysteries, and I was one of the authors interviewed for the show. We'd kept in touch until he announced one day that he was leaving New York City for a job with a TV station in Burlington, Vermont, and we'd lost contact.

"Hello, Clay," I said. "What a pleasant surprise."

"A pleasant surprise and a timely one," he said. "I intended to call you later today." He ushered me away from the others. "Your sheriff is a great guy. I let it drop that I knew you, and he told me that you're involved in some way with the murder investigation."

I stole a glance at Mort, who was talking with Mc-Graw.

"Not officially," I said, "but I've been looking into it."

"For a book?"

"Not this time. I happen to know the accused, Myriam Wolcott." I hesitated before whispering, "I have some doubts about her having killed her husband."

"She confessed, didn't she?"

"Yes, she did," I said, and left it at that. "But tell me about you. The last I heard, you were headed for Vermont. I didn't know that you'd ended up in Bangor with *The Hour*."

"I'm new to the production, moved to Bangor just a month ago. It's a fine show. But, Jessica, you changed the subject, and now you've piqued my interest."

"How so?"

"The documentary we're doing is about domestic abuse, which seems to be reaching epidemic proportions, if the statistics are accurate."

"The statistics are likely to be inaccurate," I said, "since so many cases go unreported."

"In this case it ended up with the murder of the

abusing spouse. As far as I know, there's no question that she shot her husband, but you say there is."

"There's always a question in cases like these. It's just my opinion. I don't have a lot to go on, and I can't claim many who agree with me."

"I'd like to know more."

"How long will you be in town?"

"About four days. Depends on how the interviews go. I just had an idea. How about an on-camera interview with you?"

"Oh no! Thanks, but no."

"Okay, but I'd really like to pick your brain about your theory that the accused might not be guilty. It could add an interesting dimension to the story."

"Happy to share whatever I know," I said, meaning it. I decided on the spot that I needed all the assistance I could muster if I was to get to the bottom of things. Harry McGraw was proving to be a help, but having a savvy TV producer asking his own set of questions around town certainly couldn't hurt.

"What are you doing for dinner?" I asked.

"No plans yet. Find a local spot to eat with the crew."

"I can't invite the whole crew," I said, "but you're welcome to come for a home-cooked meal. What do you think?"

"Sounds appealing."

"Good." I gave him my address and asked him to be there at seven.

While Clay and I talked, Harry filed a report with Mort regarding the damage done to his car, after which we left.

"What did the sheriff say about your tires?" I asked

Harry once we were in my kitchen and I'd started preparations for dinner.

"He took the report but said he doubted whether the guy would ever be caught."

I gave Harry a bourbon and soda and left him to watch TV in my office while I fussed in the kitchen—salmon filets, mashed potatoes, green beans, and a salad were on the menu for the evening. Clay arrived promptly at seven, and after he'd been served a drink we settled in my living room.

"Must be an interesting life being a private eye," Clay told Harry.

"Can be," Harry said, "only most of the time it means hanging around watching some straying husband or wife, or watching bartenders rip off the house. So you're doing a show on the murder that happened here in good old peaceful Cabot Cove, Maine." He checked me for a negative reaction but didn't receive one.

"The murder's a big part of it, but it's not the main story," Clay said. "We're using it as a jumping-off point to look into domestic abuse in general. It's a big topic these days. I'd like to interview people involved with your women's shelter, which I understand is controversial."

"The only controversy," I said, "is whether the town should continue funding it. You should speak with Edwina Wilkerson. She's the shelter's director. And Dr. Seth Hazlitt. He was the one who originally proposed that a shelter be established here."

"I have those names on my list," Dawkins said. "What about this guy Richard Mauser?"

"He's a member of the town council and is against providing funding. He's quite vehement about it."

"Then I could get the other side of the story from him."

"I'm sure he'd be happy to oblige."

"I'll see if I can set up an interview with Mr. Mauser tomorrow," Clay said.

"He could be too busy these days," I said. "The EPA is investigating whether his factory has been polluting the Cabot Cove River. A team from the agency has arrived in town."

"Never a dull moment in Cabot Cove, huh?"

"Afraid not," I said.

"How about coming along with us when we do the interview, Jessica?"

"I don't think Mr. Mauser would appreciate that."

"Shouldn't be a problem," Clay said. "I'll make you one of the crew. Take notes, look official."

"If you think it would be okay."

"I do," said Clay. "I have a feeling that you're going to help us come up with an even better documentary than we'd planned."

Over dinner, Clay asked me to explain my doubts that Myriam Wolcott had shot her husband, and I filled him in on everything that had happened, as well as what was behind my reasoning. After I'd laid out all my arguments, I wasn't sure if my theory was as strong as my hunch and said so.

Harry was quick to back me up, however. "I've worked cases with Jessica before, and her hunches were always on the money."

"And money could well be the motive," I added.

*   *   *

Clay called the following morning to report that he'd set up an interview with Edwina Wilkerson at eleven and with Richard Mauser at two. I agreed to come along for both tapings and asked McGraw to join us. He picked me up at ten thirty, and we drove to the women's shelter, where Edwina waited. I'd seldom seen her in a dress, but the one she wore this day was lovely, and she'd obviously taken great pains with her makeup and hair. I complimented her.

"Wanted to look good for my adoring fans," she joked.

"You look terrific," I said as the cameraman situated her in a chair and the soundman attached a discreet microphone beneath the folds of her dress. Clay, who was also anchoring the interview, sat in a chair out of camera range and directly across from her. They started filming, and for the first half hour, everything went well. But when Clay raised a question about Richard Mauser and his antagonism toward the women's shelter, I saw Edwina's face turn red. She began talking about Mauser, and the more she talked, the angrier she became.

Clay seemed startled and sat back, amused. Fortunately, at that point the cameraman needed to insert a new disk. When Clay called for a break, I pulled Edwina aside and said, "I know how passionately you feel about the shelter, Edwina, and how upset Richard Mauser's opposition makes you, but this is a good opportunity to extol the virtues of the services Cabot Cove provides for those who need them. You don't want the television focus to be on Mauser's arguments or to give him any more attention than he deserves."

Edwina rolled her eyes. "Oh my goodness. Was I do-

ing that? Thank you, Jessica. I do go off half-cocked
when the subject of that man is raised. I promise I'll
stick to the topic at hand. Just the shelter. That's all I'll
comment on."

I smiled. "You were wonderful when you were doing that."

My advice seemed to sober her, and for the rest of
the session she hewed closely to the facts and the reasons why Cabot Cove's shelter was such a boon for the
community.

"That was terrific," I told her as the crew began to
break down their equipment.

"You were right to tell me to forget about you-know-
who." She shook her head. "It's just that . . ."

"I know," I said, patting her on the arm. I was not
eager to generate another diatribe about the shelter's
avowed enemy. And later, as we stood on the sidewalk,
I could have choked McGraw when he mentioned that
we would be attending the interview with Mauser.

"*You're* going to be there?" Edwina said to me.

"Yes. Clay Dawkins invited me, and—"

"I want to be there, too," she said.

"I don't think that would be wise, Edwina," I said.

"If he's going to slander me and the shelter, I want
to be there to defend myself."

"Edwina," I said, "having you there will only com-
plicate things for Clay and his crew. I'll call you when
it's finished and tell you what he said."

"As if I didn't know all his false statements already,"
she said angrily, and stalked away.

I was sorry to have upset her again.

McGraw shrugged. "You should have given me a
good nudge or told me not to say anything."

"Can't be helped," I said. "Edwina is so knowledge-able and calm and in control when clients come to the shelter office. She knows all the right things to say and all the wrong things to stay away from. Just her as-sured presence goes a long way to soothing the jitters of an abused woman struggling with problems at home. Nothing rattles Edwina there. But say the name 'Richard Mauser,' and it's like waving a red cape in front of a bull. She puts her horns down and charges ahead."

Before heading for Richard Mauser's metal-fabricating plant, where his interview was scheduled to take place, Clay called a lunch break, and McGraw and I joined the crew for pizza at Peppino's.

"How did your interview go with Mort Metzger yesterday?" I asked when our food was served. "Did you get what you need for the show?"

"I liked him," Clay said. "I have a feeling that inves-tigating a murder is not his favorite thing to do, but he seems on top of things. However, Jessica, I hate to dis-appoint you. As far as he's concerned, the case is open-and-shut. No doubt in his mind that Mrs. Wolcott killed her husband."

"Did he get specific about what he's based that on?" I asked.

"What else could it be? I suppose her confession is the main thing," Clay replied. "He said he didn't want to try the case in the press but was willing to talk in general about motives. He said it's not unusual for a battered wife to crack and strike back at her abuser. Oh, and he added that it's a lot easier when guns are available—and apparently there were plenty of guns in the Wolcott house and the wife had access to them. That last is my interpretation."

"They never did find the murder weapon," I said.

"Yeah, I asked the sheriff about that and he confirmed it." Clay finished the last bite of pizza on his plate. "And there are the Internet posts," he added as he pushed back his chair. "That pizza was terrific."

"What Internet posts?" I asked.

"From her computer. The sheriff mentioned that the forensic report on her computer found that she participated in some kind of message board for abused women and wrote a lot about her situation with her husband, how badly he treated her, her anger at him. According to the sheriff, she even said she wanted to kill him." Clay gave a dismissive sniff. "You'd think people would realize how public the Internet is. They post things thinking it's like an old-fashioned diary where you can reveal your most private thoughts in anonymity. It's not private at all."

I was surprised that Mort Metzger would have spoken so openly about evidence in the case on a television program. Clay evidently read my thoughts. "He told me this off-camera, Jessica," he said. "We stuck to the subject of domestic abuse in general for the show."

"What else did he say about the Internet posts?"

"Not much. Seems there were a number of people, mostly other women, he assumes, who sympathized with her. There is one person, though, that the sheriff is looking into."

My eyebrows rose. "Who's that?" I asked.

"He didn't mention a name. According to him, some guy—oh, and he's only assuming that it was a man—

sent the accused a series of messages encouraging her to shoot her husband."

"That's—that's horrible," I said. "Is there a way they can trace back the origins of those messages?"

Clay grinned. "Everything is traceable, Jessica. In fact, my researchers tell me that Internet-savvy abusers keep track of their victims' whereabouts by following their activity on the computer. Your sheriff says that the state forensic people are working on where the posts came from."

I'd never been to Mauser's place of business before and wondered whether the EPA inspectors would be on hand examining the plant and the river for signs of pollution. The parking lot overlooked the river, and McGraw and I walked to its banks while the crew unloaded gear from its rented van. No one was down near the water, and I went to the river's edge and scooped up water with my hand, smelled it, touched it with my tongue, and dumped back what was left in my palm.

"Polluted?" McGraw asked.

I shrugged. "It doesn't smell awful, but I'm not sure I'd drink a glass of it."

We joined the others as they entered the building, a two-story concrete structure with a sign over the front door, MAUSER INDUSTRIES. A woman at the front desk greeted us and said, "Mr. Mauser is expecting you."

We fell in line behind her as she went through a door leading to a stairway. "Sorry about the stairs," she said, eyeing the equipment. "We don't have an elevator."

We went down a corridor at the top of the stairs to a large office at the end. Mauser was on the phone behind his desk and waved us in. Ceiling-to-floor windows behind him afforded a view of the factory, which took up most of the first floor. As I stepped inside, I was surprised to see Cy O'Connor seated at a small round table. His expression indicated that he was surprised to see me, too. Mauser hung up the phone and stood. Because I was behind the crew, he didn't see me at first. But as he shook hands with Clay, I saw recognition bloom on his face and he growled, "What's *she* doing here?"

Clay turned to me, then back to Mauser. "She's helping me with the documentary, Mr. Mauser. We've worked together before."

"And what about *him*?" Mauser said, indicating McGraw.

"He's also helping us," Clay replied.

"I don't like this," Mauser said. "I thought you were doing a fair and balanced story about this ridiculous women's shelter, not stacking the deck in its favor. I'm not interested in participating in a whitewash."

"I assure you we're not stacking anyone's deck," Clay said. "We're here to get your reasons for not wanting to fund the shelter. We like to present both sides, and I assure you that your views will be fully represented."

Mauser cocked his head at O'Connor, who came to us. "Mr. Mauser just wants to be certain that his side will be fairly represented," he said.

Was O'Connor there in an official capacity? I wondered.

I decided to ask.

"Yes, I'm Dick's attorney," he said.

Of course it was only my viewpoint to date, but as

far as I was concerned, Mauser was a potential suspect in Josh Wolcott's murder. Everyone who'd been fleeced by Josh was on my list of suspects. True, it was only speculation on my part, but since O'Connor was representing Myriam in her husband's murder case, it seemed to me to be a potential conflict of interest for him to represent Mauser, even if the cases were not the same. Perhaps it wasn't a literal conflict of interest, but it was enough to raise the issue in my mind.

"No offense, Jessica," O'Connor said, "but my client prefers that you not be here during the taping. The same goes for you, Harry." O'Connor didn't try to mask his annoyance at seeing the private detective with me.

Clay started to defend our being there, but I said, "We'll leave."

McGraw and I exited the office and returned to the parking lot. I looked back at the factory. A young man, the same one who'd expressed his terse agreement with Mauser at the town meeting, stood there, arms folded across his chest, his gaze on us.

"That's the guy who said he agreed with your Mr. Mauser," Harry said.

"He's not *my* Mr. Mauser, but yes, that's the fellow who spoke."

"And the same one who was eyeing my car that night."

"Is he?"

"He must work for him."

"Looks that way."

The young man disappeared inside.

"I think I just lost my gig with O'Connor," Harry said.

"Because of me," I said. "I'm sorry."

Besides regretting being responsible for his loss of a payday, it also meant that I'd be losing him, too.

"I suppose you'll be heading back to Boston," I said.

"Not right away," he said. "I'd kind of like to see what happens."

"But you won't be getting paid," I said.

"That's okay, at least for a while. Hanging out with you is always interesting, Jessica. So what's our next move?"

"I don't know. You have ideas?"

"I'd like to find out more about this O'Connor. Something doesn't set right with me. I liked his old man, a real straight shooter. Not sure the son is."

"I think I can find out more about him," I said, thinking of Sharon Bacon, O'Connor's assistant. "The funny thing is that when I had dinner with Cy at his club, he and Mauser didn't appear to get along well at all. Now he's Mauser's attorney."

"Probably being paid a classic buck."

Sharon had said that O'Connor had told people that he was looking for a big payday so that he could shut down the practice and move to a larger city. Was Mauser providing that payday, along with Myriam Wolcott's mother? I was deep in that contemplation when Clay and his crew emerged from the building and came to the parking lot accompanied by Cy O'Connor, who came directly to me.

"My apologies if I offended you, Jessica," he said tersely. "It's just that Mr. Mauser was upset, and as his attorney I have an obligation to protect him."

"I wasn't aware that he had become your client."

"He's having a skirmish with the EPA," Cy responded, "a typical example of big government interfering with an honest businessman's ability to make a profit."

O'Connor turned to McGraw. "I don't think I'll need you any longer," he said. "You haven't turned up anyone to corroborate that my client was abused by her husband. Stop by the office tomorrow and my assistant will give you a check for what's owed."

As O'Connor walked away, I called after him, "Is Myriam Wolcott home yet?"

He said over his shoulder, "As we speak."

"I'd like to see her again."

"No can do," he called back at me as he climbed into his sports car and sped away.

McGraw looked at me, grinned, shrugged, and said, "McGraw and Fletcher. Nice name for a private detective agency."

I laughed. "How about Fletcher and McGraw?"

"Whatever you say, Jessica. What say we find out what's really going on in this peaceful little town of yours."

Chapter Twenty

McGraw dropped me at home and said he had things to do for the rest of the afternoon and evening. I'd not responded to Mort Metzger's dinner invitation, which was for that night, and called to see whether it was too late to accept.

"Of course not, Jessica," Maureen said. "I always make enough for an army."

Which was true. Maureen Metzger always cooked in great quantities. She was the eternal optimist, assuming that her culinary efforts would be so enjoyed by her guests that they'd ask for seconds, or even thirds. It didn't always turn out that way: "Bad for my diet" or "I'm stuffed as it is" or "My stomach's been acting up lately." I'd heard all those reasons for declining second helpings, and I'd used a few myself. Maureen never seemed offended, and their freezer was undoubtedly packed with leftovers, probably to Mort's chagrin.

Maureen was busy in the kitchen when I arrived, and shouted a welcome from there. Mort ushered me in, and I joined Seth Hazlitt, Jack and Tobé Wilson, the Kosers, and Tim and Ellen Purdy in their basement rec room, where Tim had already taken over the pool table, and Jack Wilson was showing photos of their latest African safari; Jack and Tobé go on two safaris each year armed with expensive cameras.

Everyone was in good spirits, even Seth, who could on occasion be grumpy, depending on how his day had gone in the office. I fell into the swing of the conversation, which included Richard Koser telling a long, complicated joke that had everyone laughing. Maureen eventually joined us and said that dinner would be served shortly—the entrée was a recipe for sauerbraten she'd gotten from someone's food blog. "It's cooked Chinese style," she proudly announced, "a true meeting of East and West."

I glanced at Seth, who said with a straight face, "Sounds delicious."

It turned out to be a lovely evening—the sauerbraten was different but not bad—just the tonic for what had been a stressful week. Seth offered to drive me home, but I declined. "I'll stay and help Maureen and Mort with the cleanup," I said. "Besides, I'm wide-awake."

Actually, I wanted to spend some time alone with Mort on the off chance that he might share some information about the Wolcott case. As it turned out, it was Maureen who offered an interesting tidbit. We were in the process of wrapping leftovers when she brought up Myriam Wolcott.

"Poor Mort," she said. "That murder case has him all worked up. I've never seen him so tense, so short-tempered."

"He's under a lot of strain," I said. "Did he have anything to say about the interview *The Hour* did with him?"

Maureen laughed. "My handsome movie-star husband," she said. "He told me that the fellow who interviewed him, Clay Dawkins, was really nice, made him feel right at home."

"Yes," I said, "Clay is a true professional."

"Oh, that's right, you knew him back in New York."

"I was also with him when he interviewed Edwina Wilkerson and when he met Richard Mauser."

Maureen put down the dishcloth she was using to dry a large pot and said, "I didn't know that." She glanced through the door to see whether Mort was coming up from the basement where he'd been putting away folding chairs. "Did you know, Jess, that Mrs. Wolcott received e-mails from a man encouraging her to kill her husband?" Maureen asked in a low voice.

"I did hear something about that," I said.

"And . . ."

"Maureen," Mort said from where he stood in the kitchen door.

"Hi, hon."

"I don't think you ought to be telling Mrs. F. things like that."

I jumped in to defend her. "She wasn't telling me anything I didn't already know," I said.

"Still."

"You told Clay Dawkins about it," I said. "Has the forensics lab traced those messages yet?"

His silence told me that the topic was off-limits.

"Hon, maybe Mrs. F. and I ought to have a little talk, in private," Mort said.

"What's so important that I can't hear it?" asked Maureen.

"Just a few things Mrs. F. ought to know." Mort kissed Maureen on the cheek and led me from the kitchen to a glassed-in porch at the rear of the house.

"Don't think poorly of Maureen," I told him. "You like to keep the specifics of an investigation under wraps, but you know how things are in town. It's hard to keep a secret no matter how hard you try."

"I'm not concerned about keeping secrets, Mrs. F. It's just that when you poke your nose into the Wolcott matter, it makes my job tougher."

"Which I certainly never intended," I said. "But I can't help but feel that something is being overlooked."

"By me?"

"By everyone involved."

"Know what happened this afternoon, Mrs. F.?"

"You make it sound ominous."

"Dick Mauser called me after the crew from *The Hour* left. He says that you and that private eye, McGraw, went there with the producer."

"Yes, that's true."

"He says that you and McGraw have been hounding him about what happened between him and Josh Wolcott."

"'Hounding him'? That's not true. Do I think that people who were ripped off financially by Josh should be investigated more closely as to a possible motive? I plead guilty to that."

"You're entitled to your opinion, Mrs. F., but best that you keep it just that, your opinion. The Wolcott case is over as far as my investigation is concerned, case closed. I wish they were all that easy. Mrs. Wolcott has admitted that she shot her husband but claims it was in self-defense. Her attorney, Cy O'Connor, will do everything he can to get a jury to see it his way and find her not guilty. What the jury does is not my concern— or yours."

I started to respond, but he cut me off.

"I don't need people like Dick Mauser calling and complaining that you're prying into his affairs. He's on the town council, and the council funds my department. Don't get me wrong, Mrs. F. I appreciate the help you've given me in the past, but this case is over, a slam dunk."

"I feel as though I'm being scolded like a student in one of the classes I used to teach."

"Don't mean to sound that way, and please don't take this wrong," he said. "My suggestion is that you get back to what you do best, writing about murders, and leave the real thing to me."

I didn't argue, nor did I agree. I thanked him for being honest with me and returned to the kitchen, where Maureen was finishing up.

"Have your talk?" she asked, obviously annoyed at being excluded.

"Yes. I think I've intruded enough on Mort's territory. He has a good point. My job is to *write* about murder. His is to deal with the real thing."

Mort offered to drive me home, and I took him up on it. There were no hard feelings. I'd been complaining about people who assumed that I was involved with his cases—the editorial staff of the *Gazette*, for instance— and it was time to butt out and do what I do best. Once secure in my house and in pajamas, robe, and slippers, I sat at my computer, opened a notebook in which I'd outlined my next novel, and typed "Chapter One."

Part Two

Chapter Twenty-one

It turned out to be a soggy spring in Cabot Cove. We had more rain than usual, and the river overflowed twice, closing a few roads. But as we edged into summer, the rain stopped, the no-see-ums, mosquitoes, and black flies multiplied—thanks to the wet spring—and the town became busy welcoming tourists, including the many fly fishermen who flock to the area's fishing camps. We were also gearing up for the annual Blueberry Festival, which takes place over an August weekend.

I'd been surprisingly successful in blotting out what had become an obsession with the Wolcott case despite regular e-mails from Harry McGraw asking for updates. Harry had hung around town for a few days, but once I'd decided to divorce myself from the case, he'd headed home to Boston, where he had new business to attend to. He'd repeated in each message, however, his willingness to return if I decided to pursue the investigation again.

Notwithstanding Harry's reminders and the temptations provided by Myriam's release on bail, I had gotten a good start on my new novel. Since Sheriff Metzger had dressed me down in March, I'd focused on my writing and had become almost a hermit in my home office, declining many social invitations that I might otherwise have accepted, eating most of my meals at home, even curtailing the time I volunteered at the shelter's office. Instead, I immersed myself in the plot that my imagination had conjured.

After several months of virtual seclusion, I finally felt freed up enough to rejoin the world, which included taking part in plans for the festival as a member of its organizing committee.

The Blueberry Festival was a highlight of Cabot Cove's many yearly celebrations, and I loved being involved. While Maine is widely known for its lobsters (Cabot Cove's annual lobster festival draws visitors from miles around), our blueberry crop—both wild and cultivated—is also synonymous with the state. In fact, ninety-eight percent of the country's wild blueberries come from Maine. I had ordered a few pints of Blue Crop blueberries from my local market, intending to bake up an entry for the festival, and I was not alone. I could swear that the aroma of fresh-baked blueberry pies wafting around town drifted into my bedroom one hot, humid morning as I awoke to the sound of a dog barking and a low-flying plane coming in for a landing at our local airport.

August had developed into a scorcher. The temperature had hovered near ninety for the last few days, and the humidity pressed down on the town like a moist blanket. I had to laugh because some old-timers still resisted installing an air conditioner, refusing to believe that Maine had hot summers despite the perspiration running down their cheeks. Old beliefs die hard. However, the meeting of the Blueberry Festival committee took place in the senior center, where recent renovations thankfully included the installation of central air-conditioning.

The event was only weeks away, and according to the committee's report, things were falling into place. There would be the usual parade following two foot races—a one-mile fun run and a five-mile course for the more physically fit. Live music would entertain the two nights of the festival, and the town's theatrical troupe would put on an original play written by its director and featuring local thespian talent. A popular event was the blueberry quilt raffle, in which quilts featuring a blueberry theme would be auctioned. While the Blueberry Festival has never equaled our annual Lobster Fest in terms of drawing visitors, it's gotten bigger each year and was poised to match the attendance of that other tribute, to Maine's sumptuous crustaceans.

But while all these events were important, no one denied that it was the blueberry pie bake-off and the pie-eating contest that whetted most people's appetites, figuratively and literally. Tobé Wilson had filled out her judging roster, letting me off the hook, and I was mulling whether to enter one of the competitions. Last year's festival featured forty-seven pies entered in the contest, as well as competition for the best blueberry cobblers, blueberry cheesecake, and blueberry muffins. The pie-eating contest had been won by a teenager who'd announced that he was defending his title this year. It was all good fun, and proceeds from entry fees, auction pledges, and purchases went to fund local charities, the women's shelter now among them.

As the meeting was breaking up, one of the organizers approached me. "We haven't received your entry form yet, Jessica. Aren't you going to enter a pie this year?"

"I was thinking about it," I said, "but I haven't formally declared my intention."

"Better get your entry slip and fee in by tomorrow," she said.

"I'll do it right now," I said. She handed me an entry form, which I filled out, and I wrote her a check for fifteen dollars.

"Good luck," she said. "I loved your pie last year. There's a good chance you can move up this time with Mabel Atkins retiring from the competition."

"I won't count on it," I said. "I enjoy baking, but I wouldn't place it high on my list of accomplishments."

"You're a better baker than you think, Jessica," she said.

As I left the building, Seth Hazlitt was coming out of Sassi's Bakery carrying a bag.

"Morning, Jessica."

"Good morning, Seth."

"Good to see you out and about at last."

"It's good to be out and about after so much time spent with my computer. I see you have some goodies from Sassi's. Something blueberry, I assume."

"Ayuh. Blueberry donuts." He cocked his head and squinted at me. "Lookin' forward to testifying at the Wolcott trial?"

Edwina Wilkerson and I were scheduled to appear for the defense, speaking about Myriam's visit to the shelter and bolstering her claim of having been abused.

"I'm trying not to think about it," I said. "Will you be there?"

"I might stop in, offer you some moral support."

"Thank you. I'd appreciate that."

The truth was that I hadn't been especially successful in not thinking about the trial and my upcoming testimony. I'd assiduously avoided conversations about the trial over the preceding months, pretty much confining myself to reading about it in the *Gazette*. Evelyn Phillips had called occasionally to discuss new developments, which weren't many.

Whenever I saw Mort, I refrained from asking any questions, and he never offered any comments.

It was better that way.

Myriam Wolcott hadn't been seen by anyone I knew since her release on bail in March, and it was only from Evelyn's reporting that I knew that Cy O'Connor was expressing confidence that his client would be acquitted based on her plea of self-defense. The murder weapon had never been found despite an assiduous search by the police along the river into which Myriam had supposedly thrown the gun. The Wolcott children, sixteen-year-old Mark and his younger sister, Ruth, had been pulled out of school following their father's murder and spent the rest of the term with a tutor, according to those who knew something about the family. It must have been brutally traumatic not only to have lost a father to violence, but also to be living under the menace of losing their mother to a possible lifetime sentence in prison.

When I reflected back on the night Myriam came to the shelter office, I never would have dreamed that her life and that of her family would take such a drastic and destructive turn, or that I would be drawn into it.

While I'd been hibernating, Richard Mauser's hostility toward the women's shelter persisted unabated, as did Edwina's obsession with fighting him. He had written an op-ed piece for the *Gazette* in which he reiterated his arguments against the shelter and the town's funding of "fripperies." Edwina responded with a rebuttal to his piece, which delighted Evelyn Phillips. "I'd love to persuade them to debate issues in the paper every week," she'd said in one of her calls. "My circulation's up and the advertising manager is tickled pink."

Apparently their messages also sparked heated discussions within the community, although I wasn't privy to them because of my self-imposed isolation.

Aside from his onetime diatribe on the op-ed page, little else had been heard from Richard Mauser, although I was told by Sharon Bacon, who'd apparently made her own peace with young Cy's ambitions, that O'Connor had successfully reached a deal with the EPA.

"Cy negotiated the charges down, provided Mauser makes upgrades to his equipment," she'd confided in me. "He got Mauser off with a minimal fine. Of course, Cy's fee made up for it. Between that and the bills I keep sending to Myriam's mother, the firm is doing very well. Cy even hired an assistant for me."

I did watch when *The Hour* aired its program in June. It was skillfully produced and presented a balanced look at the scope of domestic violence in America, and in Maine in particular. Josh Wolcott's murder was highlighted as an example of how such abuse could, and often did, escalate with deadly results. Of course, it was on the air prior to Myriam's trial, so it couldn't provide an ending to that aspect of the story: "The trial of Myriam Wolcott is scheduled at a future date," was Clay Dawkins's final line to conclude his segment of the show. Before the next commercial break, the telephone number for the National Domestic Violence Hotline was flashed on the screen.

I just wanted the trial and everything having to do with it to be over.

I dug out blueberry pie recipes that I'd collected over the years and perused them. Some were appealing, but I knew that I'd have to come up with a special version of the classic favorite if I were to have an outside chance of winning a ribbon, not that I expected even to be in the running. Cabot Cove boasts a number of master bakers, mostly women but also a few men, who seemed to win every baking and cooking contest year after year. Mabel Atkins had been one of them, having won twice over the last five years. Even so, the blueberry-pie-baking contest was always great fun, although invariably there is an entrant or two who takes losing personally and becomes disgruntled, claiming that politics are behind some of the judges' decisions. One gentleman whose wife failed to win a ribbon went so far as to claim that someone must have "spiked" her pie to alter the flavor. It was a silly charge, of course, but made for an amusing piece in the *Cabot Cove Gazette*.

A call from my publisher, Vaughan Buckley, concerning a planned September promotional tour to coincide with my most recently published murder mystery made me forget about baking for the moment. I find that touring to promote my books is at once exhausting and exhilarating. I enjoy meeting my fans and signing books for them. Writing is a solitary endeavor, and I often wonder who is buying my books once they come to market. Touring and doing book signings is the best way to answer that question.

I was fingering through my recipe box and had just found a card with the ingredients for a pie made with "whortleberries," a close cousin to our bushes or perhaps just an old-fashioned name for blueberries, when Maureen Metzger called.

"I hear that you're going to enter one of the blueberry contests. Are you making a pie?"

The Cabot Cove grapevine in full flower.

"I haven't decided if it will be a pie or a tart," I said. "I assume you'll be entering."

"Sure. You know me, Jessica, I'm a real foodie, love contests. That's why I'm calling. Can we talk woman to woman and keep what I say a secret?"

"Oh my goodness. That sounds serious. I'll do my best," I said, tempted to add that if you want to keep a secret, don't tell anyone. *Anyone.*

"Great," she said. "I've been going crazy trying to come up with a blueberry pie that's really unusual, you know, something that will have everyone oohing and aahing."

"Have you? Come up with one?"

"I have. The problem is I need someone, a trusted friend like you, to give me an honest evaluation."

"Me?"

"Do you think it would be a conflict of interest?" she asked. "You know, with you and me entering the same division?"

I laughed. "Well, do you think you can trust me to be honest?"

"You're always honest," she said, making me regret

all the times I'd given faint praise to some of her more disastrous culinary efforts.

"I'm always willing to help out, Maureen, but—sure, go ahead," I said, wondering at the same time whether I had a good supply of Tums in the house.

"I've been experimenting using cream cheese and avocado in my pie."

"Oh. That's a—well, that's an unusual combination, Maureen." I didn't know what else to say.

"I saw some recipes online for blueberry and avocado smoothies, and I'm adapting them for the pie. I don't have the ratio of ingredients right yet, but I'm working on it. My third try is in the oven as we speak."

"Maureen, maybe Mort would be a better choice as your taster."

She laughed. "Oh, him. He wouldn't know a prize-winning pie from a hot dog. Besides, he's been on another diet lately, said he gains too much weight when I begin baking for the contest. I think he's just avoiding having to eat my mistakes."

I don't doubt it, I thought.

I finally agreed to taste her avocado–cream cheese–blueberry pie when she'd "perfected" the final version.

Having decided to reenter the world, at least the Cabot Cove world, I called Edwina and offered to return to volunteering one night a week at the shelter.

"How about tonight?" she said. "Barbara Hightower was scheduled but she's come down with a stomach virus."

"I'll be there," I said.

It felt good to be back in the swing of things. I'd missed my occasional evenings at the shelter and looked forward to becoming active again. During my hiatus, Edwina had told me that an increasing number of women had sought the shelter's services and that two had been relocated with their children to escape a volatile situation at home.

Edwina was already there when I arrived. As usual she'd brought cookies to serve anyone who might show up and had already made a pot of coffee and had a teakettle on the burner.

"It's good to be back," I said.

"And it's great to have you back, Jessica."

"Anything new on the Dick Mauser front?" I asked.

"Just what he wrote in the *Gazette*. I assume you read that."

"Yes, and your response."

"Why would a man as successful as Mauser make a cause célèbre out of this shelter?" she asked. "Doesn't he have better things to do with his time?"

I'd gotten up to pour myself another cup of tea when the doorbell sounded.

"Looks like we have a client," Edwina said as she went to unlock the door. She returned with a frail young blonde whose swollen lip said everything about why she was there. She'd given Edwina her name at the door, and Edwina introduced her as Carol Cogan.

"I'm just making tea for myself," I said. "Would you like some, or would you prefer coffee?"

"Just water," she replied. "Please."

I took her in as I drew a glass of water from the faucet. She reminded me of the time I'd rescued an abandoned puppy in a torrential rainstorm. Carol Cogan had the look of a lost dog. Her blond hair was stringy and needed a good shampooing. Her green eyes were vacant, the spark extinguished. She was thin; her gray sweatshirt and sweatpants hung loosely from her almost gaunt body. Despite the warm temperature outside, she had a wrinkled cotton scarf wound around her neck. And, of course, there was that swollen lip, which upon closer examination I saw was split in two places.

"We're glad you came," Edwina said. "You're safe here."

The young woman nodded and sipped her water.

"Would you like to talk about what happened tonight?" Edwina asked.

Carol started to answer but decided instead to sip again.

"You don't have to tell us why you're here," said Edwina. "That's completely up to you. We'll help you in whatever way we can."

The fingers that held her glass trembled, causing water to slosh over the side. Carol used two hands to place the glass on the table in front of her. After a false start in which she gulped in air, she cleared her throat and whispered, "I'm afraid."

"Of what?" I asked.

She shook her head. "Not of what," she said. "Of—of him."

"Who is it that you're afraid of?"

"My—my husband, Joe."

Edwina and I waited for her to continue. She coughed into her hand before saying, "He hit me something terrible tonight."

"Your lip," I said.

She ran her tongue over it. "He hit me so hard."

"May I take a look at it?" Edwina offered. She waited for Carol to agree before moving closer to her and examining her lip. "It's nasty. I think you might need a stitch. We can escort you to a doctor or the hospital if you like."

She shook her head vehemently; a lock of hair caught on the corner of her mouth and she brushed it away, wincing as she did.

I glanced at Edwina before asking, "Has your husband, Joe, hit you before?"

Carol swallowed hard and began coughing. "I'm sorry," she said.

"There's nothing to be sorry about," Edwina said. "When you're ready, try to tell us what happened tonight."

It took her a minute to pull herself together. We waited patiently until she whispered, "I wouldn't—I just wouldn't."

"Wouldn't what?"

"I refused to go to bed with him. He was drunk. I wanted him to sleep on the couch. He swore at me—he always swears at me—I hate that language—he swore at me and threw me on the floor. I yelled at him to leave me alone. He wouldn't. He kept pawing at me, so I took my pillow and went to sleep on the couch."

I winced at her description of the abuse she'd suffered.

"He wanted me to come back to bed with him, but I said no."

"Which you have a right to do," said Edwina. "You have the right to say 'no.' 'No' is a complete sentence."

Carol began coughing again and reached for her water glass. I picked it up and cradled her hands while she drew the glass to her lips. She nodded when she had taken a sip, and I returned the glass to the table. It was

then I noticed that her scarf had slipped a little, showing red and blue bruises on her neck.

"I haven't seen you around town," I said gently.
"Are you and your husband new to Cabot Cove?"

She nodded. "Eight months. We came from Chester.
That's near Bangor."

"A small town?" I asked.

"Very small, not even a thousand people, I think."

"Is it your hometown?" Edwina asked.

"Uh-huh."

"Did you and your husband work there?"

A nod. "I helped out in a fishing camp, waited tables. Joe worked at the paper mill, and he did some
guiding."

"Guiding?"

"Hunting and fishing. He guided sports in the summer."

"Sports?" Edwina asked.

"The rich ones," she explained. "Fishermen and
hunters. Joe called them 'sports.'"

She asked for a refill on her water and I got it for her.

"Children?" Edwina asked.

"No."

That's one good thing, I thought, but didn't say.

"Why did you move to Cabot Cove?" I asked.

"Joe got a job here. Said he'd make more money than
in Chester."

"Where does he work?" I asked.

"At the Mauser factory."

Edwina and I looked at each other but said nothing.

"And what does he do?" I asked.

"I'm not sure, probably moving heavy stuff. Joe was
a football player at school, always lifting weights,

showing off his muscles. He's not tall, but he's real strong."

The thought of this muscular young man beating up this fragile young woman was wrenching. My mind wandered back to the town council meeting, where a man whose appearance was similar to Carol's description of her husband stood up and defended Mauser's view of the shelter. He'd also been eyeing Harry McGraw's car that same night, the night that Harry's tires were slashed. We'd seen him again standing on the loading dock of Mauser's factory. I had a powerful hunch that he was Carol's husband.

"It must be difficult to leave your hometown to move somewhere unfamiliar," I said. "It must have been lonely for you at first."

Carol nodded sadly.

"Did your husband hit you before you moved to Cabot Cove, or is this new behavior?" Edwina asked.

"It's nothing new," she said.

"How long has he been hitting you?"

Carol sighed. "I didn't pay attention the first time. I thought it wouldn't happen again. He promised it wouldn't happen again."

"But it has. What happened tonight after you declined to return to bed with him?"

"Like I said, he was drunk."

"Alcohol is no excuse for hitting someone or pressuring them to do something they don't want to do," Edwina said.

"He followed me into the living room. I told him no. I don't feel good. I have a bug or something. That's when he grabbed my neck and hit me and threw me back on the couch. I told him I wasn't going to take it anymore, that I was leaving. He laughed and said I had nowhere to go. I told him I was going to the women's shelter. I'd read about you in the paper. I'm sorry. Maybe I shouldn't have come, but I didn't know where else to go. I don't know anybody here."

"You came to exactly the right place," Edwina said, putting her hand on Carol's.

"But," Carol said, her eyes even more woebegone than earlier, "but Joe said he'd—I can't use the words he used—I hate those words—he said he'd burn the shelter down and kill everybody in it, kill me, too."

Her comment was sobering. I had read of a women's shelter being firebombed somewhere out west by an angry husband who'd accused the shelter of having broken up his marriage.

"Do you believe he would do that?" Edwina asked.

"I don't know."

"Does Joe keep any weapons in the house?" Edwina asked.

"Just hunting rifles. That's all."

"Do you have someplace else to stay if you didn't want to go home tonight?" Edwina asked.

"I have to go home."

"Why?"

"If I don't go home, he'll be even madder at me."

"But he's threatened to kill you," I said. "He's threatened to burn the shelter office and anyone in it. He's a volatile man, Carol. You won't be safe. You'll be in danger of more beatings, or worse."

"What type of car does he drive?" Edwina asked.

Carol swallowed hard, setting off another coughing fit. I wondered whether there was an injury to her larynx. She leaned forward, her head in her hands, trying to get her breathing under control. "I don't know what to do," she said over and over.

"Please listen to me," Edwina said to Carol. "We're going to have to call the police. We take threats to the center and our clients very seriously," she said.

"You'll only make him more angry."

"I understand if I call the police, it will put you at greater risk at home, but I can't trust that he won't follow through on his threats. We can offer you shelter. We can relocate you to another town. We can make sure you're safe. Please, think about it."

Edwina had picked up the phone when the sound of breaking glass in the front of the building caused us to stiffen. She dialed 911 as I cracked open the door in the foyer that would afford me a view of the building's entrance. The man I thought could be Carol's husband stood on the sidewalk holding a tire iron in one hand, a plastic container in the other. I gasped as he tossed the liquid contents of the container through the broken front door and threw a lighted match after it. A sheet of flames flashed up from the floor. Edwina had come to my side and still had the 911 operator on the line. "That's right," she said into the phone, "he's smashed the window, and now he's setting fire to the building. Please hurry."

Cogan bellowed, "Carol," the way Stanley Kowalski yelled for Stella in *A Streetcar Named Desire*.

Edwina grabbed a fire extinguisher off the wall and I opened the door slightly. The fire was already abating. We couldn't see Cogan, and I fervently hoped he was gone. Edwina sprayed the lingering flames. Fortunately whatever accelerant Joe had used had burned up quickly, and while the floor and ceiling were charred, it didn't look as if the whole building would go up in blazes. We heard a siren and watched as a marked patrol car screeched to a halt in front of the building and two uniformed deputies piled out. They yelled through the broken glass. "Is there a rear door?"

"Yes," Edwina shouted back.

"Please leave by the rear exit," one deputy said. "And make sure everyone inside gets out."

As we backed away from the damage, a fire truck arrived, manned by four members of the Cabot Cove Fire Department.

Edwina and I walked through to the room where Carol Cogan sat cowering in a corner, her eyes wide with fright.

"It's okay," I said, kneeling in front of her.

"Was it Joe?" she asked in a feeble voice.

"I think so," I replied. "But it's okay now. The police and firemen are here."

Edwina and I escorted Carol outside, where an EMT offered to examine her. She sat on a bench behind the building, head bowed.

To my surprise, Mort Metzger, wearing civilian clothes, joined us. "What happened?" he asked. "I got the call at home and figured I'd better come myself, seeing as it's the women's shelter office."

"Carol, may I explain to the sheriff what happened?" I asked.

She nodded, and I gave Mort a rundown of the evening's events.

"It's her husband, huh?"

"She didn't see who was there."

"Know what kind of car he's driving?" he asked.

"No," I said, "but our client will know."

Mort squatted in front of Carol and used his softest voice to question her. She told him the make and year of the car. Pulling a two-way radio from his belt, he put out an APB. "You and Ms. Wilkerson will have to come down to headquarters and file a complaint," Mort said to me. "I hope you can get her to file one, too."

"We'll try."

"Okay," Mort said, "we'll roust a carpenter out of bed to put some plywood over that broken door. Looks like the fire's out, so no problem there. See you down at headquarters."

I joined Edwina, who sat with Carol Cogan. Edwina had explained Carol's right to make a statement, to file charges, and to ask for a protective order.

"I'm so ashamed," Carol said, "that he'd do something like this."

"You have nothing to feel ashamed about. It was his behavior, not yours."

"Has he ever been in trouble with the law before?" I asked.

She affirmed that he had. "He got into some fights back in Chester. I don't know what they were about. Someone dissed him and he knocked them out."

Edwina asked for and received permission from the firemen to reenter the rear of the building to collect some items. She brought out a bag containing donated clothing and toiletries for Carol, and the three of us climbed in her car for the drive to the shelter itself, making certain we weren't followed. Carol agreed to spend the night there until the situation could be sorted out. She thanked us profusely, and we left to go to the sheriff's office.

By the time we arrived, Joe Cogan was handcuffed and in custody.

"Wrapped his car around a tree," Mort said. "High as a kite, on alcohol and maybe something more."

Edwina and I gave our report, including that we'd both seen Cogan at the scene of the crime and that I'd witnessed him providing the flammable liquid and igniting it.

"Looks like Mr. Cogan has got himself a slew of charges to face," Mort said.

"You might ask him about slashing Harry McGraw's tires," I said.

"You know that he did it?" Mort asked.

"Just a guess," I said.

Edwina dropped me home and I locked the door, checking it at least twice. Later, in pajamas, robe, and slippers, I curled up in a comfortable chair downstairs, contemplating the events of the evening while sipping a glass of red wine. Not my usual routine, but it had been that sort of night and I was keyed up. Even with the wine, when I finally retired it took me until almost two in the morning to fall asleep. I was bombarded with weird dreams, one of which woke me with a start at six a.m.: I'd been sitting with Edwina at the women's shelter office, only I wasn't there as a volunteer. I was a battered wife, my yellow-and-purple face swollen, my lip split, and tears running down my cheeks. It was, I knew, just a nightmare. My late husband, Frank, was a loving, gentle man who captured insects in the house with a paper cup and delivered them safely outside.

I couldn't conceive of any husband striking a wife.

But some did. I'd seen it up close and personal, and my appreciation of the value of the Cabot Cove women's shelter was never higher.

Chapter Twenty-two

Edwina had left headquarters after we'd given the sheriff our statements about what had transpired that night, leaving Mort and me alone. As he reread my description of what occurred, Mort was receptive to my questions about the attack itself, and any wider meaning it may have had—namely, whether Richard Mauser was in any way involved.

"I'm just raising it," I said, "because it's a natural question to have. Cogan worked for Mauser. It's possible that Cogan slashed Harry McGraw's tires after Harry confronted Mauser at the council meeting. And if that's true—that Mauser at least knew about Cogan slashing the tires—it's also possible that he encouraged him, either overtly or through insinuation, to do damage to the shelter office."

"That doesn't hold water for me, Mrs. F. Cogan got himself a snoot full of booze and beat up on his wife. She came to the shelter and her husband came after her. How could Dick Mauser have arranged for *that* to happen?"

"I'm not saying that he did, Mort, at least not directly. But Mauser's ongoing animosity toward the shelter is very public. It could have inspired a similar hatred in Cogan. He knew his new boss wanted the shelter shut down, put out of business, and when Cogan's wife threatened to seek help at the shelter, his need for control and penchant for violence, fueled by alcohol, kicked in."

Mort sat back, raised his arms over his head, and yawned noisily. "Let's call it a night, Mrs. F.," he said. "Cogan'll sober up in his cell and have his day in court."

"And you'll question him to see if Mauser had anything to do with the tires, and with the incident tonight."

"First thing in the morning."

"Anything new with the Josh Wolcott murder?"

"Not on my end. The trial's coming up, but you know that. You're going to be called as a witness."

When I didn't say anything, he added, "And you're still convinced somebody else killed Wolcott, somebody he took for a financial ride."

"I'm not *convinced* of anything," I said, "but in my mind a reasonable doubt exists that Myriam Wolcott is guilty. I remember hearing that someone contacted her encouraging her to kill her husband, or even offering to do it himself—assuming it was a man."

"That's true. No secret."

I gave him my best tell-me-more look.

"Well," he said as we left his office and walked to his car, "I'll help put your mind at rest. The forensics folks finally managed to trace where those e-mails came from. Seems the sender logged in to be invisible online, sort of erased his identity. That might successfully hide him from most people surfing the Internet, but the forensic boys know how to get around it. They unerased the name, or at any rate the identification of the computer that the messages came from."

We climbed into his car and pulled away from the sheriff's office.

I thought about what Mort had said and began to laugh.

"What's so funny?"

"You've invented a new word, Mort."

"What word?"

"Unerased."

Mort grinned sheepishly. "Anyway, turns out those messages came from another house in the neighborhood."

"That's interesting," I said.

"The Wolcotts' neighborhood. A couple of blocks away. The Hanley family. We visited the house and talked to everybody there. They all swear they weren't the ones who sent those messages."

"Hanley? I know that name."

"The husband's a minister at a small church in that neighborhood, the wife's a nurse's aide, and the kid, Paul, he sounds like a straight shooter when he says he never wrote anything to Mrs. Wolcott."

"How old is the son?" I asked.

"Sixteen."

"Isn't he friends with Mark Wolcott?"

"Best friends, according to the father. They play video games together all the time."

"But if no one in the family sent those messages, Mort, then who did?"

"Beats me. The way I figure it, somebody hacked into their computer and sent 'em. Happens all the time, I hear, people hacking into other people's computers and causing mischief."

"Or," I offered, "the boys could be using the computer for something other than games."

"What are you getting at? You think the Wolcott boy wanted his mother to kill his father? I don't know, Mrs. F. It sounds pretty far-fetched to me."

"It does to me, too, when you put it that way, but it also seems far-fetched to think someone would hack into the Hanley computer to send messages to Myriam."

Mort pulled up in front of my house and left the engine idling.

"I appreciate your sharing that information with me, Mort. Thanks for the lift."

"No problem, Mrs. F. By the way, Maureen said you were entering a pie this year in the festival."

"If I ever get a chance to do some baking. How's Maureen's entry coming?"

Mort's sour expression said it all. "You ever taste a blueberry pie with avocado in it, Mrs. F.?"

"No, I can't say that I have, but Maureen has asked me to be a taster for her."

"Then I'll let you decide," was all he added about his wife's pie as he came around and opened the door for me. Among our sheriff's many attributes was loyalty to his wife.

Chapter Twenty-three

It came as no surprise that I found myself dwelling upon what Mort had told me about the messages urging Myriam Wolcott to kill her husband and how they'd been sent from a neighbor's computer—the same neighbor to whom Mark Wolcott often fled when things were difficult at home. Mort had ruled out members of the Hanley family as the source of those messages, including their sixteen-year-old son, Paul, who was Mark's friend. I was sure that Mort's reasons for his decision were valid. Someone might have hacked into the Hanleys' computer. But why would they have chosen that particular one? It was also possible that someone with access to the house could have used the computer to deliver those provocative threats. I didn't know the Hanley family, nor was I aware of others who may have spent time at their home. I could be sure of only one thing: Someone had sent Myriam those messages. The question was who.

But there wasn't much time to dwell on that or the

upcoming trial. The Blueberry Festival was suddenly upon us. The weather cooperated—the two-day event over a weekend was blessed with cooler temperatures, a cobalt blue sky, and a refreshing breeze off the water.

The festival drew more visitors than previous years. The town was chockablock with new faces, men, women, and children wandering from event to event, tasting the various blueberry concoctions, buying up arts and crafts offered by our more creative citizens, and bidding at the auction that was held in a large tent erected on the high school football field. Spirits were high. A thousand blue and white balloons lined the downtown streets, and store owners had followed through on the color scheme in their windows. Mara's restaurant on the dock had unfurled a huge sign proclaiming the best blueberry pancakes in the universe and offered mini–blueberry milk shakes for a dollar. The various musical groups alternated, providing toe-tapping tunes, and our local theater group put on a play set in the sixteen hundreds in which early settlers interacted with the local Indian tribes, the Abenaki, Penobscot, and Passamaquoddy. Members of the acting troupe had been working on their costumes for months, their efforts appreciated by the theatergoers.

The pie-baking contest was to take place on Saturday afternoon at four, with the pie-eating contest to follow. Maureen had sent me a sample of her entry, which Mort had dropped off. I'd told her as diplomatically as I could that I thought she needed to work a bit at the proportions, but she said that out of all her trials, this was the combination she liked the best. I wished her luck. My submission had come from an old recipe I'd unearthed. I made two, the first to be sure it came out well, and the second to enter in the contest. The pie had no exotic ingredients, just blueberries and a little lemon and vanilla. It tasted good to me—one of my better efforts, I told myself—but I didn't have any illusions about where I might place in the competition.

Due to the large crowds, Sheriff Metzger had canceled all days off and ordered his deputies to be on duty throughout the festival, augmented by a contingent of state police. He'd placed posters at strategic points throughout the town warning of the threat of pickpocketing and had told me on Friday that other festivals around the state had seen a sharp increase in the number of such incidents. Hopefully, it wouldn't happen to us. I heeded his warning and carried a small purse with a secure clasp and a long strap that I looped over one shoulder, allowing the bag to nestle on my opposite hip.

I ran into Mort as I exited the theater production.

"All going well?" I asked.

"So far. Everybody seems to be having fun and behaving themselves."

"Has Joe Cogan made his bail?" I asked. He'd been arraigned on a variety of charges, and Judge Mackin had set a high bail.

"Nope. That public defender assigned to him is screaming bloody murder over how high it is, but the judge is holding firm. I suppose you'd like to know that he was questioned about any connection to Dick Mauser, and he claims that Mauser had nothing to do with it. How's Cogan's wife?"

Edwina had told me that after a night in the shelter, and knowing that Joe was in jail, Carol Cogan had returned home and packed up her things. "She's been relocated out of town," I said. "She asked the shelter not to send her back to her hometown in Chester, for fear that's where Cogan will look for her first. I don't know where she is or what the future holds in store for her, but I think getting herself away from an abusive husband is a positive first step."

A local restaurant had set up a food stand and was selling a Maine staple, "lobstah rolls." Summer is when lobsters molt, shedding their shells. Cabot Covers know that "shedders," or soft-shell lobsters, are sweeter than hard-shelled ones and no nutcracker is needed, but the trade-off is there's less meat compared to the larger, hard-shelled lobsters. With my stomach rumbling in anticipation, I headed in the direction of the food stand and came upon Seth Hazlitt and Tim Purdy, who shared a bench, each enjoying a roll overflowing with lobster meat.

"Looks wonderful," I said.

"Ayuh, very tasty, Jessica," said Seth. "Everybody seems to make lobster rolls differently. This one is especially good, just the right amount of mayo."

"Mind if I join you?"

"Please do," Tim said, scooting over to make room.

Seth stood and handed me the paper plate on which his half-eaten roll rested. "Save our seats," he said. "I'll buy you one."

"No need to do that, Seth."

"Be my pleasure."

Seth joined a long line of others waiting to be served. It seemed that all of a sudden people had collectively suffered a yen for a lobster roll and had descended in droves on the stand. I felt guilty for making Seth wait so long to buy me lunch, but my attention was soon diverted to another line, where local Girl Scouts were selling their cookies, and where Cy O'Connor's right-hand lady, Sharon Bacon, stood in line.

I looked to see how Seth was progressing. He was now behind two other people waiting to place their orders, and a knot of people had formed behind him. I had to smile. Seth Hazlitt is one of the sweetest men I know. He can be crusty, even rude, at times, but he always means well. It would be a sad day in Cabot Cove when this self-proclaimed "chicken-soup doctor" decided to retire.

"Be back in a jiff," I told Tim as I set Seth's plate on the bench and fell in behind Sharon at the Girl Scout stand.

"Perfect day for the festival," I said.

"Sometimes you get lucky," she said.

"What's new in the office?" I asked.

Her raised eyebrows said much. She looked to her left and pointed to where O'Connor and Richard Mauser were having a conversation with a strikingly attractive young redheaded woman dressed in a skin-tight pants suit.

"Mr. O'Connor's latest hottie," she said.

I laughed. "Is she from here?" I asked.

"New York. He's been spending more time there than in Cabot Cove. She's a model, or so he says."

"She certainly is beautiful. Is he still representing Dick Mauser?"

"Sure. I never would have figured that they'd get along, but I suppose money talks, as they say."

"You and your new assistant must be busy getting ready for the trial."

It was her turn to laugh. "Judging from the time the

boss has spent in the office, you'd never know that a murder trial was about to take place. Oh, don't get me started, Jessica. Maybe I'm just old and out of touch with the way things are done these days."

"Age has nothing to do with it," I said. "Doing the right thing doesn't change no matter how old we get."

Our conversation ended as we reached the stand and bought our cookies.

"Enjoy the rest of your day," she said, "and, hey, good luck in the blueberry pie contest."

Sharon walked away and I felt a pang of sadness for her. She'd devoted herself to the O'Connor law firm and obviously knew that things were changing. I had thought she'd accommodated herself to the new circumstances, but apparently she felt she no longer fit in. Mauser had disappeared, but O'Connor and his model friend strolled by.

"Hello, Cy," I called out.

"Oh, Mrs. Fletcher." He introduced me to his date, Brigitte. "Taking in the fun?"

"Yes," I said. "I suppose you're up to your ears preparing for the trial."

"Actually," he said, "things are pretty much under control. I'm looking forward to it."

Brigitte looked bored. "C'mon, Cy. I want to see the rock band."

"Have to be going," he said. "See you in court."

A strange way to end the conversation, I thought.

By the time I got back to the bench, Tim was finished with his lobster roll and Seth had reached the young man at the stand and was placing his order. I was eager for him to return. I was famished.

As I chatted with Tim about how his revised history

of Cabot Cove was coming, a disruption suddenly ensued at the lobster-roll stand. I strained to see what had caused it and to see whether Seth was involved. He was.

I jumped up to see what had now become a full-fledged scuffle between a shabbily dressed middle-aged man and Seth.

"Give it to me," Seth yelled.

"What happened?" someone asked as Seth grabbed the man by the shirt.

"Let me go," the man said.

"You took my wallet," Seth bellowed.

The man swung at Seth but missed. Seth now had the man in the grip of both hands. He yanked him to the side and the man fell to his knees. Seth released his hold. The man scrambled away, got up, and pushed his way through the crowd in my direction.

"Stop him!" Seth yelled. "He's got my wallet."

The man came directly at me. He was wide-eyed, his face contorted as he tried to make his escape. I stepped back to avoid having him run into me. As I did, and as he passed, I stuck out my foot. He tripped over it and went sprawling to the ground, the wallet he clutched flying from his hand and skidding across the pavement. Two men in the crowd that had gathered pounced on him while I retrieved Seth's wallet.

I looked back to where the altercation had occurred. Seth was leaning back on a chair someone had thoughtfully provided, a group of people circling him. I ran there. His face was beet red and streaked with perspiration. I saw that he was breathing heavily, and I was afraid he was having a heart attack. I knelt at his side. "Seth," I said. "Are you all right?"

He tried to respond, but his breathing swallowed his words.

I touched his cheek, looked up, and said to those surrounding us, "Somebody, please call nine-one-one. Get an ambulance."

Seth managed to collect himself. He waved an arm in the air. "No, no ambulances," he said. "I'll be fine, just shaken up, that's all."

"No," I said, "I think that you should . . ."

Now he was pushing on the seat with both hands. "Help me up," he said.

Seth Hazlitt is no lightweight, and it took another person in the crowd and great effort on both our parts to help get my friend to his feet. The tan slacks that he wore were a bit grubby now, and his flowered Hawaiian shirt was dark with sweat.

"He got my money, the filthy bugger," he said.

"No, he didn't," I said, producing his wallet and handing it to him.

"How'd you get it?" he asked.

"I tripped him."

I looked back to where I'd upended the pickpocket. A uniformed deputy from Mort's office had handcuffed the man and propped him against a tree, and the sheriff, who'd been enjoying a sausage sandwich at a nearby kiosk, walked over to join us.

"That hooligan gaffled my wallet," Seth told Mort, his breathing now back to near normal.

"He did *what*?" Mort asked.

"Gaffled my wallet," Seth said, not trying to disguise his annoyance. "You never will learn to speak like the rest of us do, will you, Sheriff? Gaffled. Stole my wallet. Ripped me off. Picked my pocket."

"Sorry about that, Doc, but cool your jets. We've got the perp in custody, and you've got your cash and cards back. But you'll have to come down to headquarters to file a complaint against him."

"Which I will happily do. But first I'm going to buy this lady a lobster roll and get another one for myself. I deserve an extra treat after this kerfuffle. Then once I've gone home, showered, and changed out of my untidy outfit, I'll present myself at your office."

"Fair enough," Mort said. "No rush."

I watched them escort the pickpocket away, and while I was happy that he'd been caught and that Seth's wallet had been returned, I felt a twinge of pity for the thief. He looked like a man who'd fallen on hard times, his eyes vacant, his posture one of abject defeat. That didn't excuse his behavior, of course, and he'd undoubtedly broken the law many times before. Hopefully being apprehended and facing jail time would change his perspective and prompt him to go on to live an honest, productive life.

Seth returned from home wearing fresh clothing and rejoined a group of us at the pie-baking contest, which had attracted a standing-room crowd. The four judges included the owners of Peppino's, a cookbook writer who'd been imported from a nearby town, and Charlene Sassi of Sassi's Bakery. The pies were lined up on a long table with only numbers in front of them; the bakers would remain anonymous until the winners were announced. I frankly never have understood how judges in a pie-tasting contest could manage to consume so much, but they all dug in with enthusiasm. Meanwhile, those of us in the crowd who had an entry in the contest tried to ascertain the judges' reactions based upon facial expression.

"I'm so excited I can hardly stand it," Maureen Metzger said.

"Easy does it, hon," Mort, who'd joined us, said.

"Easy for you to say," Maureen said. "You haven't spent half your life getting ready for the bake-off."

Mort glanced at me but said nothing. I knew what he was thinking: that he'd be glad when it was over.

After the judges had tasted all the pies, they conferred for fifteen minutes before handing the results to Mayor Shevlin to read off the winners.

"We'll start with our third-place winner. No need to prolong the *mystery*," said the mayor, grinning. "Third place goes to Aunt Edna's Whortleberry Pie, baked by our own mystery lady herself, Jessica Fletcher."

"I don't believe it," I said, genuinely shocked. I looked at Maureen, who forced a wide smile and hugged me, then pushed me forward to accept my yellow ribbon. I thanked the mayor and judges before taking my place again standing next to my friends. "What a nice surprise," I said.

"Who's Aunt Edna?" Maureen asked.

"I have no idea," I replied. "I found the recipe in my old card file. Someone must have given it to me years ago."

The mayor rapped his gavel on the table. "Second place goes to Best Blueberry Pie Ever," Mayor Shevlin drew out his announcement.

"Oh, that's me," I heard behind me.

"Nate Swisher. Where is Mr. Swisher?"

"Right here."

The audience clapped politely. I was glad Mr. Swisher had won a ribbon. He was a retired senior citizen whose wife had died the previous year. As he accepted his second-place red ribbon, he told the crowd that his wife had taught him everything he knew about baking.

"Isn't that sweet," Maureen said.

"And now for our first-place finisher," our mayor said. "Drumroll, please."

Someone pounded on the table, imitating a drum. Next to me, Maureen bounced up and down in excitement.

"For baking Hurtleberry Magic, the blue ribbon goes to Barbara Franklin."

Cheers went up as the first-prize winner, wiping away tears, stepped out of the crowd to collect her prize, a silver cup to go along with her blue ribbon.

"She's a good baker," Maureen said gamely, as Mort gave his wife's shoulders a squeeze.

"You'll be the big winner next year," I told her.

"I must not have had the correct amount of avocado," Maureen said. "Don't you think? You liked it. Right?"

"Perfection takes a while to achieve," I said, hugging her. "You'll figure it out next time. Let's watch the pie-eating contest."

With the remains of the pies from the contest in front of them, the three contestants ate furiously during the allotted time. When the mayor hit the fire bell with his gavel, signaling the contestants to stop eating, last year's winner, a chubby teenager with blueberries all over his round face, had prevailed again.

We gathered at Seth's house that evening. Maureen

had gotten over her lack of acknowledgment and spoke earnestly about how she'd do better next year. Everyone was in a good mood. Seth's experience with a pickpocket was the only one that had been reported, and spirits were high as he recounted his battle royal with the thief, who had mysteriously grown in size and muscle in the ensuing hours. Aside from a few folks who had had too much to drink and made fools of themselves, the festival had been a rousing success.

By the time I got home that night, I was still buoyant from having been with my friends and actually had a ribbon to hang on my office wall. Things were good, very good.

Except that Cabot Cove, and yours truly, would no longer have a blueberry festival to occupy our collective thoughts.

Myriam Wolcott's trial was about to begin.

Chapter Twenty-four

Most trials in Cabot Cove are fairly mundane; there's not a lot of drama in run-of-the-mill DUI and DWI cases, petty theft, traffic violations, or the occasional assault case. It had been years since a murder trial had taken place, and the notoriety of the Wolcott murder had ensured that the courtroom would be packed to capacity. *The Hour*'s broadcast had obviously helped pique interest, as did a series of articles in the *Gazette* leading up to the day of the trial.

The district attorney had filed a pretrial motion to bar all witnesses from attending the trial until after they'd testified. But Judge Mackin ruled against her, allowing Edwina and me to join Tim Purdy and Richard Koser in seats in the middle of the courtroom. Edwina and I wore small purple ribbons to indicate solidarity in supporting the women's shelter, and I was pleased to see many other women in the room wearing them, too.

Richard Mauser was also there. He sat at the other

end of the row from us, his full, ruddy face set in a menacing scowl.

Judge Ralph Mackin, who'd been on the bench for many years, was an interesting study in contrasts. In person he was easygoing and extremely amiable, laughing easily and fond of puns and limericks. But once he donned his black robe and came to the bench, he was all business, and heaven help the attorney who crossed him. Still, despite ruling the courtroom with an iron fist, he was unfailingly fair, the picture of what a good judge should be.

Mackin and I had become good friends over the years. His wife, Lorraine, and I were involved together in a number of civic endeavors, and I belonged to a book group she'd started many years earlier and that flourished to this day. I often turned to the judge when researching courtroom procedure for my crime novels, and he'd become a valuable resource for me. Once, a few years ago, I'd come across information that shed a new and different light on an arson case he was hearing, my additional insight causing him to declare a mistrial. He often joked with me that if Mort Metzger were ever to resign as sheriff, he would put my name up for consideration.

We all stood as the judge entered the courtroom and took his seat behind the bench. After some preliminary legal matters were dispensed with, he instructed the bailiff to bring in the jury. I recognized a few of the twelve men and women, although the majority were unfamiliar to me. In order to expand the potential jury pool, the call had gone out to registered voters in the county in which Cabot Cove is located. The panel was equally divided, six men and six women.

Judge Mackin directed that the defendant be brought in. Two female officers escorted Myriam Wolcott to the room and led her to the defense table, where Cy O'Connor sat with Sharon Bacon. Seated in the first row directly behind them were Myriam's brother, Robert, Myriam's two children, Mark and Ruth, and her mother, Mrs. Caldwell. There had been a debate about whether attending their mother's trial would be too traumatic an experience for the children, but Cy O'Connor had insisted that they be present, undoubtedly to garner sympathy from the jurors. I'd heard that Myriam had pleaded that they be spared the experience, but her mother overruled her, which came as no surprise.

If the months of house arrest had taken a toll on Myriam, it didn't show in her physical appearance or how she carried herself. She was dressed fashionably in a simple pale blue dress; around her neck she'd tied a thin purple scarf. Whether she chose the color to show solidarity with those wearing purple ribbons was conjecture, but I liked to think that she had.

Judge Mackin asked whether Diane Cirilli was prepared to begin the prosecution's case. She said that she was and addressed her opening remarks to the jury.

I was impressed with Ms. Cirilli's demeanor and oratorical skills as she summed up the case she intended to present against Myriam. She cited the evidence that she would offer and told the jurors that she trusted their fairness and impartiality. "The defense will have you believe that the defendant, Myriam Wolcott, shot her husband because she feared for her life and for the lives of her children. She will portray her husband as a monster who routinely abused her and their children to the point that she had to kill him to protect herself. You will hear from expert witnesses for the defense who will claim that battered women become shell-shocked—the so-called Stockholm syndrome—and are unable to do what any rational person would do under the circumstances, call the police or file for divorce. The truth is that of nearly four million women abused each year, only five or six hundred of them resort to murdering their abusers."

"*Only* five or six hundred?" Edwina whispered to me.

Ms. Cirilli continued. "Under our laws, a self-defense plea is only valid when the defendant is in danger of suffering *imminent* bodily harm and must use deadly force to protect herself. You will see through the testimony of law enforcement officials who responded to the scene that this was not the situation on the night Josh Wolcott was brutally gunned down. The state will also introduce evidence, including photographic evidence, that the relationship between Mr. and Mrs. Wolcott was not as grim as she would like you to believe, photos of them as a very happy couple over the course of their marriage. You will also learn that the victim in this case, Joshua Wolcott, died leaving a life insurance policy with his wife as the beneficiary. While the sum left to her isn't large, it further provides a motive for her to have killed him.

"Your job is to weigh the facts and the evidence and come to a just and unanimous decision. I know that you will live up to this awesome responsibility. Thank you."

It was time for Cy O'Connor to make his opening remarks. He made a splendid appearance as he positioned himself in front of the jury box; he looked like a model for a high-end clothing store in his custom-tailored striped gray suit, white shirt, and maroon tie. He smiled, welcomed them, and echoed what the DA had said about trusting them to do the right thing. "And the right thing," he said slowly, "is to find Myriam Wolcott not guilty because she acted in self-defense. As the trial progresses you'll undoubtedly hear a great deal of debate about what constitutes an 'imminent threat.' The prosecution would have you believe that it demands that a weapon of some sort be held to the defendant's head at the moment that she defended herself. But that flies in the face of reason. The defendant, Myriam Wolcott, was the victim of constant, unrelenting physical and psychological abuse by her husband, Josh Wolcott. You'll hear testimony from leading citizens of Cabot Cove who will corroborate this. The defendant's husband possessed a collection of firearms, and in days before the event had made a point of leaving them around the house as an implicit threat to his wife—and by extension her two children, Mark, who is sixteen, and Ruth, age twelve. The situation in the Wolcott household had deteriorated to the point that . . ."

O'Connor spoke for another fifteen minutes, addressing various points made by the prosecutor before thanking the jurors for their service and rejoining Myriam at the defense table.

Ms. Cirilli slowly and methodically began presenting her case, starting with the introduction of various reports from the police and forensics experts. Her first witness was one of the deputies who'd first responded to Myriam's 911 call. His written report was entered into the record, and she questioned him at length about every detail he'd seen and heard the night of the shooting. "Please tell the jury the position of the body when you responded that night."

"He was lying by the side of a car in the driveway."

She asked him to describe the car, which he did. She then introduced photographs taken of the scene, using an overhead projector. I looked to where the Wolcott children sat and saw that they'd lowered their heads to avoid having to witness the grim scene.

"What was the position of the car?" the DA asked.

"It was—what do you mean 'the position'?"

"What direction was it facing?"

"Out. I mean it was backed into the driveway.

"What about the doors? Were they open or closed?"

"Closed. I mean except for the driver's door. That one was open."

"And you've testified that the body of the victim was right beside that open door."

"Yes, ma'am."

"Did you surmise that he was about to get in the car when he was shot?"

"Objection!" O'Connor called out. "That calls for speculation on the witness's part."

"Sustained." Judge Mackin said to the deputy on the stand, "Only testify to what you know, Officer, not what you think might have happened."

"Yes, sir."

Cirilli had called three other witnesses to the stand by the time the judge granted a lunch recess, admonishing the jury not to discuss the case with anyone, or among themselves, or to read anything or watch coverage on TV. Court was adjourned until one thirty.

I was back inside the courtroom on time for the afternoon session. As it turned out, the judge declared a recess after less than an hour's worth of testimony, something having to do with motions that had been filed by the attorneys during the lunch break.

"We'll convene tomorrow morning at nine thirty sharp," Mackin said, again instructing the jurors on what they were prohibited from doing.

I called Seth when court let out. He had just finished seeing his last patient for the day.

"I've been sitting so long, I can use a good walk," I told him.

"Capital idea. Mind if I join you?"

"It would be my pleasure. I'm going to stroll over to browse the window at Charles Department Store. Why don't you meet me there?"

"Sounds like Mrs. Wolcott's self-defense plea might not work," Seth said after I filled him in on the proceedings while we'd made our way down to the docks after getting together on Main Street. "If her husband was about to get in his car and drive away, that sure doesn't constitute an imminent threat to her."

"My reaction, too," I said.

"How did Mrs. Wolcott look?" he asked.

"Very calm and composed. She took notes and whispered something into her attorney's ear now and then."

"And what about the children?"

"They sat and listened calmly, too, except when pictures of their father in a pool of blood were shown. They avoided looking at them."

"Glad that they did. Sitting through their mother's trial is bad enough. You and Ms. Wilkerson are testifying tomorrow?"

"It depends on when the district attorney finishes

presenting her case. We're witnesses for the defense. We come second."

"Nervous?"

"No. Cy O'Connor will ask me questions about the night Myriam visited the shelter office, and I'll answer them truthfully. By the way, Ms. Cirilli petitioned the judge not to allow Edwina and me to be in the courtroom while the other is testifying. He agreed. I think Cy will call her first since she's the shelter's director."

"Well," said Seth through a yawn, "from what I've heard and know, the outcome is pretty much preordained. I don't see much chance of Mrs. Wolcott getting off."

"I hope you're wrong," I said. "I still don't believe she killed him."

Later that night, after Seth had driven me home, I kept seeing Myriam and her children in the courtroom, her fate—and certainly theirs—on the line. On reflection, I was sure that Seth was right, that the outcome would not be favorable. Getting over the legal definition of "imminent threat" was too high a hurdle.

The start of the trial had inspired much discussion in Cabot Cove in the usual places around town and online. When I opened my computer to check e-mail, there were a bunch of messages about the first day in court. There was also a message from Harry McGraw. I opened it first.

"Business is slow," his e-mail said. "Thought I might take a ride up to Cabot Cove and see what's happening in our favorite murder case. See you tomorrow."

Chapter Twenty-five

Edwina picked me up the next morning, and we arrived at the courthouse at nine. We hoped that the district attorney would conclude her case before the day was out and that we would be called to testify. But it wasn't to be. Ms. Cirilli had received permission the previous day from Judge Mackin to bring in two expert witnesses on domestic abuse and spent considerable time that morning establishing the credentials of one of them for the court and the jury. The first testified at length, basically debunking the theory that an abused spouse should be excused for killing the abuser, days, even hours after an incident in which abuse took place, in effect supporting the "imminent danger" theory of the prosecution. His testimony upset Edwina, but she had the good sense not to violate courtroom decorum by verbalizing her objection. Cy O'Connor did object a few times when he thought the witness had exceeded his area of expertise, and Judge Mackin upheld his objections. O'Connor also asked during his cross-examination whether the witness was being paid by the prosecution, and how much. He acknowledged that he was a paid expert witness and also confirmed that he made a substantial proportion of his income testifying around the country, in almost all cases paid by the prosecution. Whether that resonated with the jury in Myriam's favor was pure conjecture.

The lunch break was from noon until one thirty. The second expert witness would testify when court reconvened.

As Edwina and I left the courtroom to head for a local deli, the two Wolcott children appeared in the hallway. I was surprised to see them without an adult at their side and debated greeting them. I decided to.

"Hi," I said." I'm Jessica Fletcher. I'm a friend of your mother."

Ruth, the twelve-year-old, cast her eyes to the marble floor, but her teenage brother, Mark, said, "Hello. I kind of remember your name."

"Is your friend Paul Hanley here with you?" I asked, looking around as though I might recognize him.

My question seemed to startle him.

"Your mom mentioned how close you two are and that you spend so much time together. It must be tough when you both want to use the computer to do homework. Who gets to go first?"

"Computer?" he mumbled. "Why are you asking that?"

"I know that your mom received some messages on her computer that had been written on your friend's computer. I thought maybe . . ."

He looked up at his grandmother, who'd suddenly appeared behind me.

"What are you doing?" she asked sternly.

"Having a conversation with your grandson," I said.

"How dare you," she said to me. She then said to the children, "Come with me. You are never to speak with anyone without my being present. Do you understand?"

"I didn't think there was anything wrong in simply saying hello to them," I said.

"Well, you are wrong, Mrs. Fletcher, *very* wrong!"

Edwina started to say something, but we were joined by Cy O'Connor. "Problem?" he asked.

"Please instruct Mrs. Fletcher and her friend that the children are off-limits. They are not to be approached by them and—"

"I'm sure Mrs. Fletcher meant no harm," said O'Connor.

"I will be the judge of that," Mrs. Caldwell said. With that she grabbed both kids by their arms and whisked them away.

"She's uptight," O'Connor said. "I'm sure you can understand that."

"She's certainly protective," I said, "but she is also is a remarkably rude woman."

As Edwina and I headed out for lunch, she asked me what my questioning of the young Wolcott boy was all about. I deflected her query by changing the subject, to which she didn't object.

The second expert witness testified until almost four o'clock, taking up the rest of that's day's court time and pushing off our testimony until the following day—hopefully. Edwina and I left the courtroom with friends who'd attended the trial. We'd reached the sidewalk when I saw Harry McGraw climb out of his car and head in our direction.

"Harry," I said. "You *did* come."

"Yeah, sure. Nothing jumping in Beantown. Besides, my bookie is getting antsy with me. I made a couple of bad bets lately. Just need a little time to recoup."

Among Harry McGraw's myriad human weaknesses is a fondness for betting on horses—or anything else, for that matter.

As we chatted, Myriam Wolcott emerged from the courthouse accompanied by her mother, brother, and two children.

"There's the old battle-ax, huh?" McGraw said.

Mrs. Caldwell aimed furious eyes in my direction, causing my blood pressure to rise.

A contingent of press had set up just outside the courthouse, including Evelyn Phillips and her new hire, James Teller, as well as reporters from neighboring towns. A TV remote unit from Bangor had arrived in Cabot Cove the night before and had parked its mobile van, with its satellite antenna jutting from the roof, next to the print media's camp. They tried to corral Myriam and her family for a comment but were rebuffed. Myriam's brother, Robert, rushed them into a waiting car. But a moment later Richard Mauser exited the building and walked directly to the press. I sidled closer to hear what he had to say.

"Mr. Mauser," a reporter called out, "as a member of the town council you've blamed the Cabot Cove women's shelter for Josh Wolcott's murder. Do you still stand by that?"

"You bet I do," the councilman replied. "That shelter and its people fed ideas that were poison to the defendant, Mrs. Wolcott—filled her with the justification for killing her husband. You heard what the expert witnesses said inside. She could have just walked away from him if she was so unhappy, gotten a divorce. The poor guy was getting into his car when she gunned him down. You call that 'imminent danger'?" He guffawed. "If you do, I've got a bridge to sell you."

With that he went to his Cadillac, which was parked in a spot reserved for town council members, and drove away.

Evelyn spotted me and ran to where we stood. "What's your reaction to what transpired in the courtroom today, Jessica?"

"I don't have any comment," I said.

"I do," said Edwina. "Richard Mauser is trying the defendant before the trial is even over. He puts himself forward as judge and jury all by himself. Grrrrr."

Evelyn made notes in the pad she carried and turned to me once more.

"I trust in the judicial system," I said. "Let the jury decide."

"The word around town, Jessica, is that you don't think Mrs. Wolcott shot her husband. What do you base that on?"

"I prefer not to respond to rumors, Evelyn." I cocked my head at McGraw. "Come on, Harry. Time to go."

"Wait a minute, Jessica," Cy O'Connor called to me as he hurried down the courthouse steps. He was breathing hard. "Sorry you and Edwina have had to hang around so long."

"That's all right," I said. I didn't add that I was content merely to attend the trial. I felt a kinship with Myriam Wolcott and wanted to be there to support her, as unstated as that support might have been.

"I'm afraid you'll have to wait even longer to testify," Cy said. "Judge Mackin has canceled tomorrow's proceedings."

"Why?" I asked.

"Something to do with new evidence being introduced by the prosecution." He glanced at his watch. "Ms. Cirilli and I are due back inside in a half hour to meet with him in chambers."

"What is the new evidence?" I asked.

"I don't know yet, but I thought you'd want to know about the change in plans. Enjoy your day off."

Evelyn Phillips tried to corner O'Connor as he returned to the courthouse, but he walked briskly past her and disappeared inside.

"What could this new evidence be?" Edwina asked.

I shrugged. "I suppose we'll find out soon enough," I said.

"I'll be grateful for the extra time," Edwina said. "Sitting on those benches all day is hard on my back. Would you like a lift home?"

"Thanks, Edwina, but I need to spend a little time with Harry. I'll give you a call tomorrow."

"Where to?" Harry asked as we walked to his car. "Wherever it is, I hope it won't take long. My stomach is rumbling."

"There's something I'd like to do."

"Tell me."

"Cy says there's new evidence. If so, Sheriff Metzger will be aware of it. I'd love to know what it is."

"And you want me to find out."

"If you wouldn't mind."

"Nah, I wouldn't mind, but I think you should be with me if I drop in to see him."

Police headquarters was only a few blocks away, and we walked there.

"Is the sheriff in?" I asked the deputy on desk duty.

"Yes, he is, Mrs. Fletcher, but I don't think—"

"Would you be good enough tell him that I'm here and that Harry McGraw is with me?"

"Okay, but he's up to his neck today."

The deputy disappeared through a door leading back to Mort's office. To my surprise, he returned with the sheriff.

"Hello, Mrs. F.," he said. "McGraw. To what do I owe this honor?"

McGraw looked at me. When I didn't say anything, he jumped in. "Mrs. Fletcher was told this afternoon that court is canceled tomorrow because of new evidence."

"Who told you that?"

"The lawyer, O'Connor," Harry said.

"Figures. Let me guess. You want to know what the new evidence is."

"Just curious," I said.

"You're the most curious person I've ever known, Mrs. F. But you know what? I'm going to tell you because you'll end up reading about it in the paper tomorrow morning anyway."

My expression mirrored my surprise.

"Yeah," he said. "Somebody in the state police blabbed about it to some media type, and Mrs. Phillips at the *Gazette* was told about it. I just got off the phone with her."

McGraw and I waited for him to continue.

Mort shook his head and smiled. "Can't believe it myself, but we think we've found the murder weapon in the Wolcott case."

"You *think*?"

"Good chance that it is."

"Well, that *is* big news," I said. "Where was it?"

"Might as well tell you that, too," he said. "Some fisherman fifty or so miles west of here caught the weapon on his hook instead of a bass and turned it over to the state boys."

"What kind of weapon was it?" McGraw asked.

"Oh, you're curious, too," Mort said. "Must be catching from hanging around with Mrs. F. It'll be in the paper, too. Deer rifle. Satisfied? I have to get home. Maureen's having guests for dinner."

"I wouldn't want to keep you," I said. "Oh, one more thing, Mort. You said this fisherman was fishing fifty miles west of here. Any chance it was near Gorbyville?"

"Good guess, Mrs. F. It was right outside it. Good fishing there, I'm told. Well, nice seeing you again, McGraw. Have a good night, Mrs. F."

Harry and I didn't have anything to say to each other during the walk back to his car. Once we were on our way to my house, he said, "Goryville, Maine. That's where the defendant's brother lives."

"It's Gorbyville, Harry, and yes, it's where we visited Myriam Wolcott's brother, Robert, and his wife, Stephanie."

"I figure I'm thinking the same thing you are," McGraw said.

"I'd be shocked if you weren't, Harry," I said. "Let's take care of those hunger pangs. I'll make you a home-cooked dinner—food for thought."

Chapter Twenty-six

When we arrived at my house, there was a message on my answering machine from a court clerk advising me that although court proceedings had been canceled for the following day, I was to be reachable at all times in the event the judge decided to reconvene. I was glad that I'd given my cell phone number. It meant I could leave the house and still be available to take a call.

McGraw and I debated what to do with our suspicion that the weapon used to kill Josh Wolcott might have been removed from the murder scene by Myriam's brother, Robert. We had no proof of that, of course, but it made sense. The question was how to bring our theory to the court's attention. And would it contribute to or refute my thesis that Myriam hadn't been the one to pull the trigger? I didn't see any direct connection, but it was an avenue to be explored.

We decided that we would get together in the morning and make a visit to Cy O'Connor's office, who was the obvious person to hear our conclusion.

Sharon Bacon was at her desk when we arrived.

She tilted her head in the direction of his office. "Mrs. Caldwell is with him."

"Do you think he'd find time for us after she's gone?" I asked.

Sharon's shrug was her response. "You've heard, I assume?"

"Oh, dear. What now?"

"They've found the murder weapon. It was in the paper this morning."

"Yes, I'd heard that, but my paper hadn't been delivered before I left."

She handed me that morning's *Gazette*, the front page of which heralded the discovery.

"I understand that no one is certain if it *is* the murder weapon," I said. "Has Forensics made that determination?"

She glanced at O'Connor's closed office door before saying, "It was unregistered, or so I'm told. But that's not unusual with hunting rifles."

"I'd been led to understand that Josh Wolcott registered most of his weapons, including rifles."

"Maine laws don't require it," Sharon said. "He elected to do it."

"But he didn't elect to do it for *all* his weapons?"

Sharon shrugged.

"Fingerprints?" McGraw asked.

"I don't know," she replied. "Cy told me that Forensics worked all night examining the weapon. They faxed him their preliminary report first thing this morning. He grabbed the pages from the machine before I had a chance to read them."

"Did he say anything about where the weapon was found?" I asked.

She looked at me quizzically.

"I just thought that Cy might find it interesting, that's all. Sheriff Metzger said it was found by a fisherman near Gorbyville."

"That's what it says in the paper," Sharon said. "They quoted the fisherman."

"Myriam Wolcott's brother lives in Gorbyville," I said, "and he was at her house the night of the shooting. She called him before she dialed nine-one-one."

"I know," Sharon said, sighing. "The prosecution is making a big deal out of that."

The door to O'Connor's office opened, and he emerged with Mrs. Caldwell. Their expressions mirrored their surprise at seeing us.

"I was hoping to steal a few minutes of your time," I said to O'Connor.

Mrs. Caldwell shot a stern look at O'Connor, clearly questioning why he would even consider the request. She walked brusquely past us, leaving O'Connor with a sheepish grin.

"Just a few minutes," I said.

Reluctantly, he ushered us in. "I don't have time to waste," he said. "What do you want?"

"The weapon that was found," I said.

"What about it?"

"We understand it was found up near some hick town called Gorbyville," McGraw said.

He'd gotten it right this time.

O'Connor's face was a blank.

"Where Myriam Wolcott's brother lives," I said.

"I know that," O'Connor said.

"Doesn't that strike you as a strange coincidence?" I asked.

"Not at all," he said. "I've already talked to Robert Caldwell. He knows nothing about it."

"According to him," McGraw said.

"Yes, McGraw, according to him. Besides, it's irrelevant. Nobody even knows yet whether it *is* the weapon used to kill Josh Wolcott. Some fisherman drags it up and everybody jumps to conclusions, starting with the media."

"Was it the same caliber weapon that was used to shoot Josh?" I asked.

"Yes, which means nothing. There are plenty of those deer rifles, hundreds, maybe thousands in Maine. We're having a hearing this morning with Judge Mackin concerning the weapon." O'Connor's temper had surfaced. "Case closed," he said. "Is there anything else I can do for you? If not, please excuse me. I've got a busy day ahead."

We accepted our dismissal and retreated to the waiting room.

"That was quick," Sharon said.

"Too quick," I murmured as Harry and I said goodbye and headed for his car.

"This doesn't make sense," he said. "They find this rifle in some body of water and right away claim it's the murder weapon. But the gun wasn't registered to anybody, so why jump to that conclusion? There's gotta be something else."

"Sharon didn't know whether they found fingerprints on the weapon. Maybe they *did*."

"That'd be my bet," said Harry.

Based upon his history as a betting man, I didn't take his faith as encouraging, but I withheld my editorial comment. Of far greater concern was whose fingerprint might have been found on the rifle, if any. If Myriam's print was there, it didn't bode well for her. But maybe the print, if there was one, belonged to someone else who could be identified.

Like someone who'd been fleeced by Josh Wolcott.

Harry dropped me home and said he was going to drive back to Gorbyville to ask around about Robert Caldwell, see whether he fished in the same waters where the weapon had been found, maybe even find a local citizen who possibly heard Caldwell make some revelatory comments about his brother-in-law's murder. It was a long shot, of course, and I declined the invitation to accompany him. But I was pleased that McGraw, as cynical and nonconforming as he is, wanted to forge ahead on my behalf to discover the truth, no pay involved. I was glad to have him on my side.

I tried to use what was left of the day editing chapters from my latest book, but waiting for my cell phone to ring distracted me. It was like having set an alarm for early in the morning and staying awake all night waiting for it to go off. The call from the clerk at the court came at four that afternoon. The trial would resume the following morning at nine, and all witnesses were expected to be there—and on time.

McGraw called me at eight that evening to report that he'd found someone in Gorbyville, a fisherman, who said that Robert Caldwell often fished in the same water in which the weapon had been found. "The guy told me he wished he'd found the rifle because he would have demanded a reward," Harry told me, laughing. "Nice old guy. He says Caldwell is a lousy fisherman, stands where the fish are." Another laugh. "He talked funny like all you people do up here in Maine."

The next morning, word had gotten around that a rifle had been found that might be the murder weapon. Evelyn's front-page story the previous day, and a follow-up story in that morning's edition, ensured that the courtroom would be packed. A line had formed outside by the time Edwina and I arrived.

We avoided the press and were escorted into the courtroom by a sheriff's deputy, who directed us to seats reserved for witnesses and others with an official reason for being there. I took note that Myriam's brother, Robert, was not with the family that morning. Mrs. Caldwell sat staunchly between Mark and Ruth Wolcott behind the defense table, where Cy and Sharon Bacon waited for the trial to resume. Richard Mauser was ushered in just before the bailiff called, "All rise!" Judge Mackin entered the room, took his chair behind the bench, and invited us to take our seats. As I waited for Myriam to be brought in, I wondered what had transpired between the attorneys and the judge yesterday. So much of what happens at a trial takes place backstage; decisions made in the judge's chambers can, and often do, have a dramatic impact on the outcome.

Myriam made her appearance at a few minutes past nine. She looked less composed and put together than when I'd last seen her in court. She glanced around nervously, smiled at her children and mother, caught my eye, and held the gaze until returning her attention to O'Connor and Sharon.

The judge apologized for abruptly canceling yesterday's session, saying that an urgent matter had been brought before him that had to be resolved. He asked Ms. Cirilli whether she was ready to proceed.

"Yes, Your Honor."

"Fine. Call your first witness."

"The People call Dr. Melvin Weeks of the Maine Central Forensics Laboratory."

O'Connor got to his feet. "Your Honor," he said, "I renew my objection of yesterday, and I've prepared a written objection for the record."

"Objection noted," Mackin said. "Call your witness, Ms. Cirilli."

Dr. Weeks was a kindly, soft-spoken older man who detailed his background, his experience, his professional affiliations, and the peer-reviewed articles that he'd written. When he and the prosecutor had gone through that pro forma exercise, the DA asked whether Dr. Weeks had examined the weapon found near Gorbyville, Maine.

"Yes, ma'am. I was called in to the lab at night for that purpose."

Ms. Cirilli asked a court officer to hand the weapon to the witness.

"Is this the weapon you examined?" she asked.

"Yes, it is."

"What tests did you perform?"

"Ballistics, as well as tests looking for trace evidence that might indicate who had handled it."

"You mean fingerprints?"

"Yes, ma'am."

"The weapon you examined had been submerged in water for a period of time," Ms. Cirilli pointed out. "Does this affect whether prints can be found on a weapon?"

"To some extent," he replied. "It depends upon the material being tested. A wood stock, for example, might retain a fingerprint even after being submerged. The same holds true of metal surfaces that had been oiled."

"And during your examination did you detect any fingerprints?"

"Yes, I did. There were fragments of various prints on the weapon, but only one that was readable."

The tension in the room was palpable, and people leaned forward in their chairs.

"Would you please tell the ladies and gentlemen of the jury about that fingerprint?"

"Of course. It was unusual because of its size."

"Size?"

"Yes. It was relatively small. It's my professional opinion that it was left by someone of less than average size."

"A child?"

"Not necessarily a child, Ms. Cirilli. But as I said, someone with a small hand."

"And did the print match one of the defendant's fingerprints?"

"It did not."

All eyes focused on the defendant's table as O'Connor asked permission to approach the bench. Judge Mackin approved, and O'Connor and Cirilli walked up, along with the court stenographer, who would record what was discussed.

Edwina whispered to me, "I don't understand. Why would the DA introduce evidence that might get Myriam off the hook?"

"From what I know about Ms. Cirilli, she's a dedicated officer of the court, more interested in getting to the truth than adding another conviction to her belt the way too many prosecutors do," I said. "What I *don't* understand is why Cy objected to having the weapon introduced. If Myriam's prints aren't on the gun, it could help exonerate her."

"Do you think it could be a child's fingerprint?" Edwina mused in a hushed tone.

The bench conference ended and Ms. Cirilli asked a few more questions of Dr. Weeks before ending her direct examination.

To everyone's surprise, O'Connor said that he didn't have any questions for the witness, and Dr. Weeks was excused.

Ms. Cirilli also called to the stand someone from the forensics unit who'd examined Myriam Wolcott's computer files. He confirmed that she had written in one of her postings that she'd wanted to kill her husband. O'Connor was effective in his cross-examination, pointing out that the particular computer posting had not been read in its entirety: "My client added after saying that she *sometimes* wanted to kill him, 'No, don't mean that,' and further said that it's not right to hate anyone." The expression on the faces of some of the jurors said that he'd scored a point with them, especially after he'd gotten the witness to admit that people often say that they want to kill but don't mean it.

It was one thirty when, after presenting a few more witnesses for the prosecution, Ms. Cirilli announced, "The People rest, Your Honor."

"All right," said the judge. "I suggest that we all do the same. Have some lunch and we'll resume at two thirty."

After the lunch break, Cy O'Connor began his case by calling Edwina to the stand. I'd noticed sitting next to her how nervous she was, and I'd gripped her hand as her name was called.

"Your Honor," the prosecutor said, "I remind the court that the second witness to be called, Jessica Fletcher, is not to be present during Ms. Wilkerson's testimony."

I immediately got up and followed a court officer to the hallway, where I sat on a bench just outside the double doors and awaited my turn. I'd brought a book with me and started reading it. I wasn't ten minutes into it when what sounded like a chorus of anguished voices erupted from behind the doors. Within seconds the doors flew open and two officers raced past me, numerous exclamations of "What's happened?" trailing behind them. I got up and looked into the courtroom. People now stood. A cluster of them surrounded an area of the courtroom on the opposite side from where Edwina and I had sat. She stood in the witness box, and the judge stood, too. "Please, everyone stand back," he said over the din of other voices, pounding his gavel to gain attention. I turned at the sound of footsteps on the marble floor. Two white-coated EMTs carrying a small gurney ran by me and into the courtroom.

I slipped through the doors to see what had occurred. Edwina had stepped down from the witness stand. She was crying. I asked her what had happened.

"Look," she said, pointing to where the EMTs were attending to someone on the floor. They shifted position, allowing me to see their patient. It was Richard Mauser.

"I was testifying, answering a question, and he let out a moan, then a louder one, stood up, and then came crashing down over the people sitting in front of him. He must have had a heart attack."

Everyone moved back to allow the EMTs to wheel Mauser from the courtroom to a waiting ambulance.

Judge Mackin pounded his gavel to quiet the crowd. "In light of this unfortunate incident, I suggest we take a short recess to allow everyone time to calm down and refocus on the proceedings at hand," he said. "Court will resume in sixty minutes. Bailiff, please remove the defendant from the court. I'll be in my chambers."

When the trial resumed an hour later, those in attendance were still shaken by what had occurred, but the commotion in the courtroom had shifted from a loud roar to a conversational buzz, and, following the strike of the judge's gavel, to a mere rustle of movement.

I waited outside again until Edwina completed her testimony, and then took the stand.

After establishing that I'd been at the women's shelter's office the night Myriam Wolcott arrived, O'Connor led me through a series of questions regarding her demeanor and physical condition that night.

"She'd obviously been struck by someone," I said, "and she told Ms. Wilkerson and me that her husband had hit her."

"Did she indicate whether her husband had hit her on other occasions?"

"Yes."

"The prosecution has made a point that the defendant was free to leave the house, seek shelter, get a divorce. Had you and Ms. Wilkerson offered such advice to Mrs. Wolcott?"

I paused as I tried to recollect what we'd said to Myriam that night. "No," I answered, "I don't recall saying that to her. Ms. Wilkerson did suggest that she stay the night at the shelter, but . . ."

"Objection," Ms. Cirilli said. "It's hearsay. Please direct the witness to testify only to what *she* said."

"Objection sustained," Mackin said.

I had wanted to explain that Edwina had encouraged Myriam not to return home that night and that Edwina had later informed me that it was typical of battered women to minimize their abuser's behavior. But O'Connor moved on to other questions, which I answered to the best of my ability.

After I was excused, I left the courtroom and went into the hallway, where Edwina sat on a bench. She looked terribly distraught, and I joined her, putting my arm around her. "Are you all right?" I asked.

"I feel terrible," she said, shaking her head.

"Testifying can be very stressful," I said, "but it's over now."

"No. That went fine. I mean I feel terrible about the horrible thoughts I've had about Dick Mauser. I hated him—I wanted him to suffer, to hurt bad, to . . ."

"Your thoughts had nothing to do what what's happened to him," I said. "You and he had a conflict of opinion, and it's only natural to think bad things about someone who's been such a foe, and a nasty one at that."

"Yes, but I wanted to kill him. And now I hope he doesn't die."

Chapter Twenty-seven

Edwina had already left for home when Harry Mc-Graw bustled down the hall in my direction.

"Hi," I said. "I was wondering whether you'd show up."

"Wasn't sure I'd get here myself, Jessica. I just came from Gorbyville. I stayed overnight. Creepy little motel with a lumpy bed. I kept thinking of *Psycho*."

"You stayed there? Why?"

"Well, I got friendly with a local gal who works at a local bar and grill, a grungy place with a sticky bar top and dusty animal heads on the wall. Anyway, I stopped in for something to eat after I found the fisherman who knew Caldwell, and this lady and I hit it off."

Spare me the details, I thought.

"So I'm eating my hamburger—can you believe they had moose burger on the menu?—and getting philosophical with my new friend when guess who walks in."

"I can't imagine."

"The young Mrs. Caldwell. Stephanie Caldwell."

"Did she recognize you?" I asked.

"She looked at me strange-like, as though she recognized my face but couldn't place it. So I go over to her at the bar where she's sipping some drink mixed with Coke and remind her."

"I don't imagine that she was pleased to see you again," I said.

"She was actually pretty friendly. Catch this, Jessica. She ends up telling me that she and her loser hubby are calling it quits."

"I can't say that I'm surprised," I said. "What else did she tell you?"

"I'm glad you're sitting down," he said. "Mrs. Stephanie Caldwell has herself another drink, which results in a loose tongue. Never seen it to fail. Forget truth serum like they use in espionage movies. Rum and Coke'll do it every time. Anyway, she starts talking about the night her brother-in-law was killed and how they raced to the Wolcott house. I didn't press because I sensed that she wanted to get something off her chest, so I said the right things, like it must've been real upsetting to see Wolcott lying in a pool of blood, things like that. So what does she say then?"

"Tell me, Harry."

"She says that she pleaded with her husband not to do it."

"Do *what*?"

"Take the rifle and put it in his car."

"Whoa," I said, looking around to make sure we were alone. "She actually said that?"

"Uh-huh."

"Did she say what he did with the rifle after they left?"

"No. I suggested that maybe he tossed it in some pond or river, but she clammed up, ordered another drink. She wanted to dance."

"Did you dance with her?"

"Me? Are you kidding? My dancing days are behind me. Besides, the only music the jukebox played was old country-and-western songs about dogs dying and husbands leaving home. My new friend, the waitress, was getting jealous, so . . ."

"I get the point," I said.

"Yeah, well, now you know what happened to the weapon. What do you want to do about it?"

"We have to make it known to the court and to the attorneys."

"O'Connor?"

"For starters."

McGraw grunted.

"What?" I asked.

"I'd say that this takes everybody else off the hook. I mean, the people who Wolcott scammed. Looks like you guessed wrong, Jessica. Looks to me like the rifle was used by Mrs. Wolcott."

"Or maybe her brother," I said. "Certainly someone in that family. But I still stand by my conviction that Myriam didn't shoot her husband."

Harry looked at the closed double doors. "Trial's still going on?"

"Yes. They'll probably conclude in a few minutes. The judge seems to prefer ending the day at four. By the way, you missed the latest incident. Richard Mauser had a heart attack."

"He's dead?"

"He's at the hospital. Hopefully he'll pull through."

Ten minutes later the doors opened and people filed out. I looked inside to where Myriam was speaking with her mother and children, and where Cy O'Connor and Sharon Bacon were returning papers to his briefcase.

"Let's talk to him," Harry said.

"I have a better idea," I said.

We entered the courtroom and approached Judge Mackin's law clerk, Gary Lauder, whom I'd known for years. "Got a minute?" I asked.

"Sure, Jessica."

Gary and I went back a long way. When he wasn't functioning as Ralph Mackin's law clerk, he wrote poetry, which had developed a certain kinship between us. I'd edited a book of his poems that he'd self-published, and he and his wife were devoted fans of my books. "Gary," I said, "this is Harry McGraw. He's a private investigator who worked for Mr. O'Connor but who is now helping me."

"Helping you? With what?"

"Helping me get to the bottom of the Wolcott murder."

"I didn't realize that you were involved," he said, "aside from testifying."

"I'm not involved—officially. Do you think Judge Mackin would grant us some time in chambers? Mr. McGraw has come up with new evidence that has a direct bearing on the case."

Lauder looked quizzically at Harry, who shrugged and grinned.

"New evidence?" Lauder said. "You should take it to the DA or the sheriff's office."

"I know that would be the usual route, Gary, but I really would prefer that the judge be made aware of it. While this is an unusual imposition, I really think the judge will want to hear it. I assume that both attorneys will be present. Would you ask the judge if he'd grant my request?"

Gary grimaced before saying, "Sure, Jessica. Wait here."

O'Connor and the prosecutor, Ms. Cirilli, were still in the courtroom, and O'Connor eyed me with suspicion, although he didn't approach us. The law clerk reappeared. "Judge Mackin says he'll see you in chambers provided the attorneys agree."

"I'd appreciate it if you'd see if they will agree," I said.

He conferred with O'Connor and Cirilli, both of whom asked him questions. Finally, he returned and said, "I'll take you to the judge's chambers. The attorneys will be in shortly."

Judge Mackin was in a good mood. He greeted us warmly and pointed to red leather armchairs across the desk from him. "I just finished your latest novel, Jessica," he said. "A hell of a good story. I never saw the ending coming."

Moments later, O'Connor and Cirilli arrived.

"What's this all about?" the prosecutor asked.

"Mrs. Fletcher has asked for this meeting," said the judge. "This gentleman is . . ."

"I know who he is," O'Connor said sharply.

Harry stood and extended his hand to the prosecutor. "Harry McGraw, PI."

She took his hand briefly and eyed me curiously.

"Okay," the judge said. "Go ahead, Mr. McGraw. Tell

the attorneys about this new evidence you say you've discovered."

Being in the judge's presence seemed to unnerve Harry. He cleared his throat a few times before saying, "I know this is unusual, Your Honor, but . . ."

"Get to the point," Mackin said.

"Well, it's like this, Your Honor. I was up in Gorbyville snooping around and I met this waitress in a bar where I stopped to . . ."

"Harry!" I said.

"Yeah, okay. Sorry. You see, there's this Caldwell dame. She's married to the brother and she lets it be known that her hubby took the murder weapon and put it in his car so the cops won't find it. She says she begged him not to do it, but they're pretty much on the outs, so he ignores her."

Judge Mackin listened carefully to what McGraw said. When the private detective was finished, the judge said to Ms. Cirilli, "I'd say this is a valuable piece of evidence, wouldn't you?"

"Yes, it is," she replied. "If what this gentleman says is true, the defendant's brother is guilty of impeding a homicide investigation and lying to authorities."

"Yeah, but what bearing does it have on the case we're trying?" O'Connor said.

I turned to Ms. Cirilli and said, "Your witness, Dr. Weeks, testified that the only fingerprint he found on the weapon came from someone with a small hand. While Mrs. Wolcott is slender, she's hardly what you would call 'small.' Wouldn't that in itself cast doubt on her guilt?"

"Oh, come on, Jessica," whined O'Connor, "the witness said he found fragments of other prints. One of them could be my client's."

"I hope you're going somewhere productive, Mrs. Fletcher," Judge Mackin said.

O'Connor addressed the judge: "Your Honor, the basic truth is that my client, Myriam Wolcott, has admitted that she shot her husband. The trial isn't to refute that. We acknowledge that she pulled the trigger. The question is whether she had a right to defend herself against her abusive husband."

"I'm sorry to disagree with you, Cy. I don't believe and never have believed that Myriam Wolcott shot her husband. I think that she has pleaded guilty to protect someone else."

All eyes focused on me.

"Are you suggesting this brother of hers?" the judge asked.

"No, Your Honor, I'm not, although it's a possibility. What I *am* suggesting is that to go forward with the trial without exploring new possibilities would be—well, I don't think justice is being served."

"And do you have information about these 'new possibilities' you think the court should consider?" Mackin asked.

"I object to this, Your Honor," O'Connor said. "Mrs. Fletcher is simply speculating without anything to back her up. I'm in the middle of my defense, and to interrupt proceedings at this juncture would be not only inappropriate; it could be the basis for a mistrial."

Mackin sighed, sat back in his leather chair, laced his fingers on his chest, and said, "I don't think it would be untoward to declare a one-day recess to give me time to sift through this new evidence, and to hear more of Mrs. Fletcher's concerns—with you and Ms. Cirilli present, of course. I know, I know, it's an unusual situation, but nobody ever said that the law is perfect. If it was, you wouldn't need me." He looked hard at Cy and added, "Do you want to declare a mistrial now, Counselor?" The way he said it left little doubt that he would not be pleased if O'Connor raised another objection. When he didn't, Mackin summoned his clerk, Gary Lauder, and informed him that court would be dark the following day. "Please inform the principals of this change," he directed Lauder. "But I'd like the defendant and other significant parties at the court at nine in the event I wish to speak with them."

"Who does that include, Your Honor?" Lauder asked.

"The family."

"The children, too?"

"Yes."

To us he said, "I'll see you here at nine sharp." With that he rose and disappeared into another room.

O'Connor's red face and tight lips testified to his anger. He glared at me, started to say something, got up, and stormed from chambers. The prosecutor was less dramatic with her exit. She smiled at me and said, "I'm looking forward to hearing what you have to say, Mrs. Fletcher."

"I appreciate that," I said, "and I promise not to take too much of anyone's time."

I left the courthouse with McGraw feeling pretty good about myself. I'd never expected that the judge would go to the extent of canceling a day in court in order to hear me out and to ponder his next move.

But after Harry dropped me home and I had a chance to do some pondering myself over a cup of steaming green tea, I realized that I'd put myself in an extremely awkward position. All I had to present to the judge the following day was a series of suppositions with little to back them up. In effect I was now expected to present a case of my own, and I knew I'd better put my thoughts together overnight.

I'd started doing just that when the doorbell rang.

Chapter Twenty-eight

A black Lexus sedan sat in the driveway. I opened my front door.

"Good evening, Mrs. Caldwell."

"Good evening, Mrs. Fletcher. May I come in?"

"By all means."

If she was at all concerned about having stopped by unannounced, she didn't express it. She walked past me, stood in the middle of my living room, and said, "Charming little house. Have you been here long?"

"Yes, I have. Won't you sit down?"

She hesitated as though debating whether to choose a chair or the couch. She opted for a chair, in which she sat ramrod straight, her knees pressed together, the same pose she'd adopted when Edwina and I had visited Myriam right after the murder.

"Would you like tea?" I asked.

"Thank you, no. This isn't a social call."

"Well, then," I said, taking another chair, "the obvious question is *why* are you here?"

"I should think it would be obvious," she said.

"Perhaps to you, Mrs. Caldwell. Please educate me."

My air-conditioning was on, but I didn't need it. She'd brought with her sufficient BTUs to cool an armory.

"I'll get right to the point," she said. "I've been informed that you have convinced the judge to delay my daughter's trial."

"I don't think that I've convinced him of anything. He made a decision based upon his own judgment. By the way, you're free to call me Jessica."

If I expected her to suggest using her first name, I was mistaken. It would be Mrs. Caldwell.

"I also understand," she said, "that this private investigator of yours has implicated my son in some minor aspect of the trial."

I couldn't help the laugh that came from me. "'Minor aspect'?" I said. "I hardly think that removing a murder weapon from the scene of the crime is a 'minor aspect.'"

"That information came from Robert's wife, Stephanie," she said with distaste, as though having sucked on a lemon wedge. "My soon to be former daughter-in-law is a common woman, Mrs. Fletcher. Nothing she says is to be believed."

"I'm sure that the judge will come to his own conclusions."

She relaxed slightly, leaned back, and exhaled an exaggerated sigh. "You don't understand," she said.

"Understand what?"

"Understand the need for a family to stand shoulder to shoulder in times of great need."

"Please continue," I said.

"You seem like an intelligent woman," she said in a tone reserved for expressing exasperation at a slow child.

"Thank you," I said.

She came forward. "It is imperative that Myriam take responsibility for Josh's murder."

"Why?"

"Oh, for God's sake," she said, "for the good of the family. I can't believe that you are blind to this."

"Mrs. Caldwell," I said, "I'm not blind to the need for justice to be done, fair justice, legal justice. Our judicial system isn't something to be manipulated for an individual's sake, or any family's sake. No one is above the law."

Her first smile of the evening was a dismissive smirk. "How lofty that sounds," she said into the room. "How lofty—and naïve."

I'm by nature a patient person, but my patience was running thin. "Mrs. Caldwell," I said, "just what is the purpose of your visit?"

"I want you to stop your infernal snooping and intrusion into what is none of your business. I and my family have gone through a terrible ordeal. We don't need you, or anyone like you, making it worse. I'll be candid, Mrs. Fletcher."

As though she hadn't been.

"I'm sure that you have faced financial difficulties, as all writers do. I will pay you to stay away from my family. How much will it take?"

I managed to keep my anger in check as I stood and said, "I think our conversation is at an end, Mrs. Caldwell. Good evening."

She, too, got up, straightened her skirt, and said,

"You are a foolish woman, Mrs. Fletcher. A *very* foolish woman."

She left, got in her car, and backed out of the driveway. I realized that I was trembling and urged myself to calm down. If she'd thought that her visit and insults would cause me to think twice about backing off, she was wrong.

I was certain that she had coerced Myriam to plead guilty in order to protect someone else, and I had a good idea who it was. Now I needed to gather my thoughts and make notes of them before meeting with Judge Mackin in the morning.

The two attorneys were in Judge Mackin's chambers when I arrived after a fitful night. McGraw had wanted to be there but was tied up with business obligations he needed to attend to. However, he'd already informed the judge of what he'd discovered in Gorbyville, and while I would have greatly appreciated his moral support, his presence wasn't strictly necessary.

"I want you to understand, Mrs. Fletcher," Mackin said, "that this turn of events is somewhat unusual in a murder case. Then again, it's been an unusual case from the beginning, so I'm willing to hear what you have to say. It's evident to me that you've devoted considerable time and effort attempting to get at the truth. That's what this courtroom is all about—getting at the truth. I'm also aware after having lived in Cabot Cove for many years that your reputation as not only a best-selling author, but as an investigator without credentials, precedes you. The floor is yours."

"Your Honor, before Mrs. Fletcher starts," O'Connor said, "I'd like to make it clear that the Wolcott children are not to be included in any of these proceedings. They were questioned at length immediately following the murder and had nothing to offer in the way of evidence. Ms. Cirilli and I agreed not to call them as witnesses, and that is still the case."

"I'm aware of that agreement between you and Ms. Cirilli," Judge Mackin said, "but considering these new circumstances, I might want to negate it. Is the defendant's brother present outside?"

"No, sir," O'Connor said.

"Issue a bench warrant for his arrest," Mackin ordered his clerk. He then asked O'Connor whether the Wolcott children were on hand.

"Yes, sir," O'Connor answered. "They're with their grandmother. The defendant is present also. She's with my associate, Ms. Bacon."

"Fair enough," Mackin said. "Go ahead, Mrs. Fletcher."

"Thank you, Your Honor." I pulled notes from my purse. "I first became involved when Mrs. Wolcott visited the women's shelter office seeking refuge from her abusive husband. I was there as an unpaid volunteer. A few days later, Mrs. Wolcott's husband was shot dead in front of his house, and the focus of suspicion naturally fell on his wife. She proclaimed her innocence for days following Mr. Wolcott's murder until, for no apparent and logical reason, she changed her story and declared that she had, indeed, killed her husband.

"Of course, it was possible that she had pulled the trigger. But somehow I couldn't square that with my instincts. I set off on the theory that someone who'd suffered financial loss at the hands of Mr. Wolcott was the real killer, and I worked with the private investigator who was here yesterday to prove that thesis. I was wrong. Once Mr. McGraw learned that the defendant's brother had taken the murder weapon from the scene and discarded it in a body of water near where he and his wife live, it became obvious to me that the weapon had indeed been fired by someone in the Wolcott household."

"There you have it, Your Honor," O'Connor said. "She's admitting that my client killed Josh Wolcott."

"I'm admitting nothing of the kind," I said.

"I'm going to object again at allowing Mrs. Fletcher to, in effect, testify here in chambers without the benefit of a formal legal setting," O'Connor said sternly.

"Would it be more amenable to you, Mr. O'Connor, if I swear her in?"

"You can do that?" I asked.

Mackin smiled. "I can do anything I wish," he said. "This is, after all, my chambers and my courtroom." He reached into a desk drawer, brought out a Bible, and extended it to me. "Place your right hand on it," he said, which I did, and he administered the standard oath all witnesses in a courtroom are obligated to take.

"Done," the judge said. "You're sworn in, Mrs. Fletcher. Proceed with your statement."

Did I detect the hint of a smile on his craggy face?

I continued. "Mrs. Wolcott's sudden and unexplainable switch from pleading innocent to pleading guilty to the shooting raised a red flag with me. That was reinforced as a result of confrontations I had with the defendant's mother, Mrs. Warren Caldwell, who I believe had choreographed this change in plea in order to protect someone else in the family.

"Who could that be? I wondered. Was Myriam protecting her brother, or perhaps her sister-in-law? They

were there the night of the murder, although they supposedly responded to her call *after* Mr. Wolcott was
shot. Was that true, or had they arrived earlier?"

O'Connor loudly guffawed. "This sounds as though
Mrs. Fletcher is writing one of her murder mystery
novels," he said scornfully.

Judge Mackin gave O'Connor a withering look.

I pressed on. "The defendant's brother certainly had
a motive to kill Josh Wolcott," I said. "He had been the
victim of his brother-in-law's financial shenanigans,
along with others. But it didn't make sense to me that
Myriam would plead guilty to a crime she hadn't committed to save *him*."

I paused. No one said anything, so I added, "Much
as I regret to say this, that left two other possibilities—
the Wolcott children."

"I've had enough of this nonsense," O'Connor said.

"Calm down, Mr. O'Connor," Mackin said. "You
know, I knew your father. He was a fine lawyer and a
true gentleman, and I never had to admonish him in
court. I suggest that you keep his demeanor in mind."

"My father was . . ."

Mackin directed his next words to me. "So you suspect that Mrs. Wolcott might be trying to protect her
children."

I thought before making a definitive statement. "Yes,
Your Honor, I do."

"That's a serious accusation," Mackin said.

"I'm well aware of that," I said. "But let me explain
further. Myriam Wolcott participated in an online forum for abused women. The police discovered that a
message from another participant on that forum had
come from a neighbor's house. I believe if you press

him that Mrs. Wolcott's sixteen-year-old son, Mark, will tell you that he was the source of the angry messages to his mother in which he suggested that she kill her abusive husband."

Mackin looked to Ms. Cirilli for a response.

"The sheriff made me aware of that possibility, Your Honor," she said, "but it was never substantiated."

"And it still is unsubstantiated," I said quickly, "but maybe it can be substantiated by speaking with Mark Wolcott."

Judge Mackin pondered my request. Finally he said, "Of course, the young man has no legal obligation to discuss this with me, but there's nothing to lose by trying."

"Your Honor!" O'Connor said.

Mackin ignored him and asked Gary Lauder to bring Mark Wolcott to chambers.

O'Connor stood and followed the clerk out of the judge's chambers and into the courtroom. It was only a minute or two later that he returned with Mark, his sister, Ruth, and Mrs. Caldwell.

"I didn't expect a crowd," Mackin said.

"I am the children's grandmother," Mrs. Caldwell said, "and I strenuously object. You have no right to subject a young boy to this charade created by this—this—this woman." She pointed a long, red-tipped finger at me, like a talon about to spear a rodent.

"I simply wish to have a private chat with this young man," Mackin said. "As his grandmother, you're certainly invited to stay—I have grandchildren of my own—but you and everyone else will have to be quiet. Understood?"

Mackin indicated a chair in which he wanted Mark

to sit. The young man, whose small stature made him seem even younger, tentatively sat, his hands clenched into a fist on his lap. The chair seemed to swallow him. I looked at twelve-year-old Ruth Wolcott, who was perched on the edge of a chair, her doting grandmother's arm around her.

"I know that you and your family have been through a great deal," Judge Mackin said in a friendly tone, "and I certainly don't want to make you feel even worse than I'm sure you already do. Have you ever been in a judge's chambers before?"

"No—no, sir."

"It's a little different in here from the courtroom, less formal, fewer rules. You can just consider this a friendly chat, nothing more."

"Yes—yes, sir."

"All right, then. There's some confusion about what happened the night your father died. You were there?"

Mark looked to his grandmother, who shook her head. Mackin noticed it and said, "Although we're less formal in here, young man, the rules regarding telling the truth prevail. It's my job, along with the attorneys, to get at the truth. Now, your mom has said that she was the one who killed your father. Is *that* the truth?"

Mark's eyes filled with tears.

"Telling the truth is always the best thing," Mackin said. "We always feel better after we have."

"That's enough!" Mrs. Caldwell said, standing.

Mark, whose head had been lowered, looked up at her. "I don't want to lie anymore," he said. "I don't want to."

"I'll have you disbarred," his grandmother told the judge. "You have no right to put him through this."

Mark's pained scream filled the room. "She didn't do it! She didn't. Don't send her to jail. He was so bad. He was a monster. He hit her all the time. I hated him! I hated him and I'm glad he's dead."

For the first time since we'd met, Mrs. Caldwell lost her regal bearing. She slumped back into her chair and pressed her hands to her face.

I looked to Judge Mackin to say something. When he didn't, I felt I needed to fill the gap. My stomach was churning. It was distressing to have suspected that a child could pick up a gun and kill his father. But I knew his mother was *not* the murderer, and the truth needed to come out. I moved to where Mark sat sobbing, placed my hand on his shoulder, and said, "It must have been terrible for you to shoot your father, but you did it because of what he'd done to your mother. The court will understand."

Suddenly Ruth, who'd also begun to cry, jumped up from where she was sitting and ran to her brother, flung herself across his lap, and said, "It's okay, Mark. He won't hurt anybody anymore." She disengaged from him, stood, looked at Judge Mackin, swiped the tears from her cheeks, and declared, "I shot my father. I'm the one who did it."

To say that I was shocked was a classic understatement. I looked at Mark, then at Ruth, and felt tears welling up. Could it be that I was so wrong in believing that Mark had shot his father? I'd been right about their mother—that she was lying when she claimed to have pulled the trigger and that she'd done it in order to spare her children.

But which child?

I had been certain it was Mark. I had been wrong.

Mrs. Caldwell answered that question. Dry-eyed and having again maintained her composure, she came to me. Her face, set in stony anger, was only inches from mine. "Are you satisfied, Mrs. Fletcher?" she said. "Are you satisfied that through your meddling, a twelve-year-old girl might be sent to prison?" She turned from me and addressed the judge. "We had it all worked out," she said. "I convinced my daughter and Mr. O'Connor that if Myriam claimed that she'd killed Josh, it would protect this precious child and that she would never be found guilty by a jury because she'd acted to protect herself and her family from further abuse. Doesn't that make sense? What was the harm in it? He was dead and deserved to die. The child would be spared, my daughter would be free, and that's the way it would have ended were it not for Mrs. Fletcher's intrusion." She again looked at me. "May you rot in hell," she said as she grabbed Mark and Ruth and herded them through the door to the courtroom where Myriam and Sharon Bacon waited.

Cy O'Connor, who'd said nothing during the wrenching events of the past few minutes, also headed for the door.

"Just a second, Mr. O'Connor," Judge Mackin said. "As an officer of the court, you are entrusted to seek the truth. It sounds to me as though you've been involved in a scheme to thwart justice, which will have consequences. I dread to think what your father would have said."

O'Connor started to respond, but no words came. He slunk from Mackin's chambers and quietly closed the door.

Chapter Twenty-nine

What occurred in Judge Mackin's chambers that day had a profound impact on me. I'm very much a glass-half-full person who seldom gives in to depression. Yet I spent the days immediately following the confrontation—and the sad truth that emerged—in a funk, questioning myself and what my efforts had resulted in.

Mrs. Warren Caldwell's words—"May you rot in hell"—stayed with me like a sore that wouldn't heal. Intellectually I knew that she was wrong to assign blame to me for uncovering the true circumstances of the case, that her twelve-year-old granddaughter had wielded the weapon that killed her father. Ruth's grandmother had tried to circumvent the law in her misguided belief that she was above it and that she was entitled to choreograph everything having to do with her son-in-law's murder. She was wrong in that assumption, of course, but I understood what drove her. I might have been tempted to do the same thing were a grandchild of mine in a similar circumstance. But being tempted is different from taking action. She was wrong, and I hung on to that truth.

Harry McGraw visited me before heading back to Boston. Seeing him boosted my spirits; he has that effect on many people. We joked before he left: "That offer to hook up with me in my agency still stands, Jessica—McGraw and Fletcher, private investigators."

"I still prefer Fletcher and McGraw," I countered, and we both laughed.

Naturally, what came out of that day in Judge Mackin's chambers was the talk of Cabot Cove. Evelyn Phillips and her young reporter, James Teller, badgered me for comments, which I declined to give. The articles they would write were compelling enough without any editorial input from me.

Myriam Wolcott recanted her story that she'd killed her husband and issued a statement in which she said she'd assumed blame in order to shield her young daughter. She pleaded for the child not to be judged harshly and pointed out that Ruth had become sick at seeing her mother physically and verbally abused over the years by her father. Myriam acknowledged that the night of the shooting, Josh had been especially brutal in his attacks on her, threatening to kill her in cruel ways, and describing how he would dispose of her dead body. Both Ruth and her brother, Mark, had pleaded with him to stop. When he persisted in his threats, Mark had run upstairs and grabbed his own deer rifle, an unregistered gun that his father had given him. Mark had pointed it at his father and demanded that he stop the abuse. But Josh laughed at him, and Mark couldn't go through with it. Ruth, in hysterics, wrestled the weapon from her brother's hands, followed her father out to the driveway, and pulled the trigger. She hadn't aimed; she was incapable of that. But the single shot that was discharged remarkably found its mark. Josh Wolcott fell to the ground mortally wounded.

Seth Hazlitt instinctively knew the conflicting feelings I was suffering and made it a point to stop by.

"Stop beating yourself up, Jessica," he told me after arriving with a box of pastries from Sassi's Bakery. "You did the right thing."

"But I can't help feeling that because of me this lovely little girl now has to live for the rest of her life not just with the horrible memory of having killed her own father, but the certainty that everyone around her knows what she did. The impact on Mark Wolcott is equally profound. I questioned myself long and hard before going into the judge's chambers and pointing an accusatory finger at Mark Wolcott. I kept asking myself was I doing the right thing. I knew I had to do it, but . . ."

"The children will receive the best psychiatric and psychological care," he said. "You know that. What happened inside the Wolcott house that led to this tragedy was beyond anyone's ability to intervene."

"But we should have done more," I said. "Myriam came to the women's shelter office looking for help, and we didn't provide it."

"From what you and Edwina have said, you suggested that she leave the house, told her it was a dangerous situation. She didn't listen. Damn shame what happened, but you didn't cause it. Get over it, Jessica. You knew what was goin' on in court was wrong and you made it right. Sometimes innocent people get hurt when someone else does the right thing, but that doesn't mean you don't do it. Heah?"

"Yes, Seth, I h-e-a-h." His words, plus the bear hug

he gave me, did wonders for my psyche and snapped me back into a semblance of the person I usually am.

Later that day, I received a call from Edwina Wilkerson.

"Richard Mauser died," she said.

I'd known that he'd remained in critical condition since suffering his coronary and that Edwina had kept track of how he was doing through frequent calls to the hospital.

"I'm sorry to hear it," I said.

"I don't think I'll ever get over the hatred I felt for the man."

I remembered Seth's advice to me. "Knock it off, Edwina," I said in my best impression of Seth Hazlitt, and proceeded to give her the sort of pep talk I'd received from my physician friend. It seemed to help, and we promised to get together in the coming days.

Two other visits bolstered my spirits.

The first was from Sharon Bacon, Cy O'Connor's right-hand woman, who had come by to help put my mind at ease.

"The attorney assigned to defend Ruth Wolcott has worked out a plea with the district attorney," she told me, "and Judge Mackin has approved it. Ruth will be treated as a child and placed on probation while receiving counseling. When she reaches twenty-one—and providing she does everything expected of her by the court—her record will be expunged. The court recognizes that she acted impulsively and reacted to her father's abuse of the mother. It's not an excuse, of course, but there are plenty of extenuating circumstances that weigh in her favor."

"I'm pleased to hear that," I said. "And I hope Mark receives similar help, as well. What about the others, the grandmother, who pressured her daughter to file a false plea, Myriam's brother, who removed the weapon from the scene, Myriam herself, and Cy O'Connor? They were all involved in a scheme of sorts."

"The grandmother's off the hook," Sharon said. "She never lied to authorities or in court under oath. The brother faces charges of obstructing justice. The DA is charging Myriam with conspiracy and lying under oath, but considering the circumstances, a plea deal is likely to be worked out. As for Cy, there's a real possibility that disbarment proceedings will be discussed by the Maine Bar Association. He told me the other day that he's closing up his practice here in Cabot Cove and moving to New York City."

"Where does that leave you, Sharon?" I asked.

Sharon laughed. "His leaving has forced me to make up my mind about what to do with my life. I'm looking forward to a pleasant retirement."

"Well deserved," I said. "It was really good of you to stop by. I feel better knowing that Ruth Wolcott won't be treated too harshly."

"Sometimes our legal system does the right thing," Sharon said.

The second visitor was a complete surprise to me. When I opened the door I was faced with a friendly-faced middle-aged woman wearing a gray-and-black dress. I didn't know her. A car with a driver was parked at the curb, its engine running.

"Yes?" I asked.

"Mrs. Fletcher? My name is Laura Mauser. My husband was Richard Mauser."

"Oh, dear," I said. "I was so sorry to hear about your husband's passing. I intended to go to the wake, but . . ."

"Please," she said, "there's no need to explain."

"Won't you come in?"

"I'd rather not," she said. "I know I'm intruding and don't want to take up your time. I just came by to give you this."

She extended an envelope to me.

"I considered giving it to Ms. Wilkerson, but in light of the problems between her and my husband, I thought better of it."

I hesitated to open the envelope, but when it was clear that she was waiting for me to do just that, I slid my finger under the flap. Inside was a check made out to the Cabot Cove women's shelter in the amount of one hundred thousand dollars.

"I don't understand," I said.

"It's in Richard's memory," she said. She managed a small smile. "He could be difficult, but he wasn't as bad as some made him out to be. Use it well, Mrs. Fletcher. The shelter is much needed here in Cabot Cove."

It took me a while to get over the shock of the check and what the sentiment behind it meant. When I had, I picked up the phone and called Edwina Wilkerson.

"Thanks for the pep talk the other day," she said. "I needed it."

"Edwina," I said, "I'd like to start volunteering at the shelter again one night a week."

"Wonderful. How about tonight?"

"Tonight sounds fine. I'll be there along with something I think you'll be both surprised at and delighted with."

"What is it?"

"Just a reminder that life can be good. See you at seven."

AUTHORS' NOTE

Authorities tell us that most cases of domestic violence are never reported to the police. Yet one in four women will experience domestic abuse in her lifetime. For children, being a witness to domestic abuse is the strongest risk factor for the perpetuation of violence from one generation to the next. If you know someone who is being abused, help is available twenty-four hours a day. Please reach out to the National Domestic Violence Hotline at 1-800-799-SAFE.

Read on for a peek at the next original
Murder, She Wrote Mystery,

CLOSE-UP ON MURDER

Available in hardcover in October 2013
from Obsidian

Hollywood, California

"You should be flattered that she chose to play the character from your book," the executive producer, Terrence Chattergee, told me. "Vera Stockdale has been offered many plum parts over the years." His eyes roamed the room even as he addressed his comments to me. "But none of them were up to her standards." Chattergee was a handsome man with a dusky complexion and thick black hair going gray at the temples. He had made a name for himself as a producer in what was then Bombay, and had brought his Bollywood sensibility to California with great success.

"For some reason she took a liking to your story," Chattergee continued, sending a smile and raised eyebrows to the director, who'd just entered the room. "Vera is very particular."

I was in Hollywood to attend a read-through of a screenplay Chattergee was producing. It was based upon one of my mystery novels, *A Deadly Decision*. I had developed the story using a real-life incident that had taken place in Cabot Cove about half a dozen years ago. A local judge, Ruth Harris, had ruled against a husband in a custody case. The husband, a man with a hair-trigger temper, had denounced Judge Harris in the courtroom and warned of retribution. A week later, while the judge was out walking her dog, she was shot in the back by an assailant. There were no apparent witnesses other than the dog, but the spotlight of investigation shone brightly on the angry husband and his threats against the judge's life. When it was determined that the man had a solid alibi, focus shifted to the judge's husband, Neil Corday, a shady attorney with a string of lawsuits against him. He had been playing footsie with a waitress at a local café, among other women. Although I'd been skeptical, evidence piled up against the waitress, Jenny Kipp, who'd reacted with fury when the marriage proposal she'd expected from the judge's husband never materialized. She confronted Corday—and his new lover, Tiffany Parker—with a gun, the very weapon, it turned out, that had been used to shoot his wife, the judge. Jenny Kipp was convicted and sent away for life.

Vera Stockdale, who was playing the judge, had been a big star decades earlier and had come out of retirement to take this role.

"She wouldn't accept just any part," Chattergee said. "She wanted one with gravitas and a chance to show her dramatic range."

The lady under discussion sat halfway down a long rectangular table. Her platinum mane was styled in a smooth pageboy, not a hair out of place, and she wore a pink cashmere sweater set and rhinestone-adorned black-framed eyeglasses attached to a gold chain, which rattled against the table as she leaned over to peer at her lines in the open script in front of her. In one arm she held her Chihuahua; the other rested on a book, *Famous Actors' Famous Monologues*, that she'd been hugging to her chest when she arrived. It should have warned me of what was to come.

"So, here we are, Jessica Fletcher," Chattergee said, "about to make a movie of your book."

"I'm delighted to be here," I said. "Thank you for inviting me. I look forward to seeing Ms. Stockdale in the role."

Without bothering to respond to me beyond a grunt, he turned abruptly, walked along the table, and placed himself in a chair opposite the star and next to the director.

Frankly, I didn't see how the role of the judge served as an especially good opportunity for the actress's triumphant return to the silver screen—after all, she gets murdered in the first half of the story—but I knew enough from past experience with movie productions not to question the opinion of the executive producer, at least not to his face.

The case had been prosecuted in Cabot Cove, and the state of Maine offered production companies financial incentives to film there, so the Hollywood types were going to shoot "on location" and make our town a giant set. But before the production moved to the East Coast, the cast and principal production executives had gathered in Hollywood for a preliminary review of the script, and I was among them.

"Not exactly the hail-fellow-well-met type, is he?" said Hamilton Twomby, the screenwriter, who had introduced me to Chattergee. "But as an executive producer, he's done okay. We should be in good hands."

Twomby and I had worked on the script long-distance, mostly by e-mail, occasionally by phone. More precisely, he'd written the script based upon my book, and I, as "script consultant," was permitted to review it and to make suggestions. Not that many of my suggestions had found their way onto the page. It would be easy to chalk it up to difficult communications. "Ham," as Twomby was called, didn't have a landline telephone, so our conversations often began with "Can you hear me now?"

Twomby smoothed a hand over his mouth and left it there. "Vera, on the other hand, is a diva," he said in a low voice. "At least she was before she retired. Should be interesting to see if the leopardess has changed her spots. If she's really itching to get back in the game, maybe she'll be more accommodating than she was when she had top billing." He waved at a tall woman with a mass of curly hair. "I have to say hello to someone," he said. "I'll be right back."

Vera hadn't spoken to me herself—she'd merely nodded when we were introduced—but her personal astrologer was eager to assure me that the movie was the "perfect property" to relaunch the career of the former star. "I have studied her chart," Estelle Fancy confided as the rest of the cast and production company officials filed into the room and took seats at the table. "She has a close alignment of intellect and self-expression. Her high ability to transmute ideas, inspiration, and artistic potentials into actualities will carry her through."

"That sounds impressive," I said. "Have you told Ms. Stockdale?"

"Oh, yes. She knows I endorse this venture. Venus is approaching retrograde and is slowing down. It's an auspicious time for her to advance her goals, also an incredible chance for major healing and forgiveness. I advised her to go forward, and I'm to accompany her on location. I doubt she would have done it without my approval or, for that matter, at another time in the universe." Before I could come up with an appropriate response, she drifted away like some ghostly apparition and took one of the chairs lined up along the wall for those not invited to sit at the table.

"Don't you just love that baloney?" a deep voice murmured in my ear.

I turned sharply to face the smile of actor Walter Benson, the male lead in the film, who was playing the judge's husband.

"Vera's astrologer has been trying to get her a part for years," he said, winking at me. "No one was interested."

"I wasn't aware that finding roles for clients was the responsibility of an astrologer," I said.

"It is if you want to get paid. Ms. Fancy, Vera's resident stargazer, finally hit the jackpot with Chattergee. Rumor has it that our esteemed producer owes Vera a fortune in back child support, and paid Ms. Fancy a handsome sum to persuade our star to accept the role and drop her claim against him as a deadbeat dad. Not that he doesn't have the money. But he knew Vera would be willing to let him off easy for a starring role."

"They've been divorced for years, if I remember correctly," I said. "Aren't their children adults?"

"Child. Yes, she must be by now. Awkward little thing—at least she was before they shipped her off to boarding school. But while the battle is over, the war rages on."

"And how do you know this?"

"Oh, my darling girl," he said, holding out a chair and bowing toward me, "inside knowledge is the coin of the realm in Hollywood."

"I'll keep that in mind in case I'm ever in the market for some ready cash," I said, acknowledging his gesture by sitting down.

Benson took a seat next to Vera, picked up her book on monologues, and began leafing through it. I mulled over what I knew about him. He was a virile leading man who'd spent most of his time on-screen with his shirt off. At least that was my impression from having seen a few of his early films. The screenwriter had made a snide comment about Benson's being typecast as the philandering husband of the judge—"His most bankable asset is a strong jaw and a sculptured set of pectoral muscles, although he's getting rather long in the tooth for bare-chested roles," Twomby had said. The Hollywood business magazine *Variety* had reported that it had taken numerous auditions and screen tests for Benson before he'd won the role. I'd shown the article to Twomby when I arrived.

The screenwriter squeezed himself into the chair next to mine. He was a hefty man with a thin mustache and a narrow beard that ran along his jawline, leaving his cheeks clean-shaven. "Benson should be grateful he's here," Twomby said, continuing his catty comments about the actor. "His acting abilities were never in question, but his penchant for pursuing every would-be starlet here in La-La-Land almost scuttled his chances for the role."

"I wouldn't think that was so unusual in Hollywood," I said.

"Oh, it isn't at all, if you're subtle about it, or even if you're not. However, on Benson's last film, several production assistants charged him with sexual harassment."

"Oh, dear, that's certainly not good."

"There's nothing quite like a lawsuit to cast an actor in a poor light with producers who want to keep a tight fist on the budget—and that's all of them."

"How did Benson get into their better graces?"

"That's the good part," Twomby said, lowering his voice again, although it was doubtful anyone could overhear us above the buzz of conversation filling the room. "His agent maneuvered two glitzy magazines into putting him on their covers. Even bad publicity has a positive effect on an actor, especially when his prowess in private matters translates to profits at the box office."

Chattergee tapped his coffee mug to attract the group's attention and to start the meeting. I decided on the spot that the gossip shared by Benson and Twomby, while grist for the tabloids, was not an area in which I was especially interested or even comfortable, and I resolved to do everything in my power not to contribute to the movie business rumor mill.

Not an easy resolution to stick to when "surrounded" by Hollywood.

"I have a complaint," Vera said, once the room had quieted.

"Yes, Ms. Stockdale," the producer said, addressing his ex-wife.

"I don't like this scene on page fifteen."

There was a rustle of papers as everyone turned to that page.

"What's wrong with the scene?" The question came from Mitchell Elovitz, the director.

Vera shifted her dog from her right hand to her left so she could point at the page. "Frankly, this dialogue feels insipid and unfinished. You're talking about a sitting judge. Wouldn't someone in her position have more to say when the district attorney is making his case?"

"Want to give us an example of what you mean, Vera?" Elovitz said.

"I know this is only your second—is it?—film, Mr. Elovitz," she replied, "but even you should be able to see that the judge should be expressing her dismay at the husband's behavior, lecturing him on what it means to be a good father and how he should conduct himself." The actress pulled her glasses down her nose and sent a withering glance in Chattergee's direction. "In addition, we need an internal monologue here to fill out her character," she said, her right hand now resting on her book. "Something meaty and with meaning. I will not portray someone who is wishy-washy, and that's what I see on the page."

"I think the scene is fine as it is," Chattergee said. He looked around the room for confirmation, but avoided Vera's gaze.

"Let's let the screenwriter comment," Elovitz said. "Ham? What do you have to say?"

Twomby shifted in his seat. "I . . . I don't know," he

replied. "That's not what the scene calls for." He frowned as he ran his index finger down the page, scanning the lines. "Ah," I heard him say and his face brightened. "Actually this dialogue came straight from the book. I didn't change a word here." He sat back with a smile.

All eyes in the room focused on me. *Oh, boy!* I thought, mentally calculating how the scene had played out in real life and whether I had missed something in my dramatization of it.

"Mrs. Fletcher, would you like to add anything?" Elovitz asked.

"I would," I said. "Some of the dialogue in my novel, as in this case, was lifted from the actual trial transcript. But in general, a judge doesn't make a lot of comments while a trial is ongoing. She rules on objections and may clarify a point of law, but she is supposed to be *listening* to both parties so she can make a fair judgment at the appropriate time."

"I have to do more than just *listen*," Vera said. "I'm not coming out of retirement just to listen." A low growl came from her dog, as if echoing her annoyance.

"I understand," I said, "but the judge usually reserves her comments until she delivers her decision. I think you'll find she shares her opinions quite eloquently later on in the script."

"I don't care what she *usually* does. I want her to be eloquent right from the beginning," Vera said, glaring at me. "I don't see her personality coming through here." She closed the script. "If I'm to play this role, I need to have more background on this woman, her likes, dislikes, the way she thinks about her position and its importance in the courtroom. I expect that to be added here." She thumped her palm on the script, and switched her gaze to Chattergee. "It's ridiculous to expect me to play this part as it's written. Brannigan has more lines in this movie than I do, for crying out loud. And she's just the tart who's cheating with the judge's husband."

"I don't have more lines than you," said Lois Brannigan, who was playing the mistress, and who sat three seats down from Vera. "But I'd be delighted to switch roles if you're not happy."

"Don't think I wasn't informed that you coveted my part, dearie," Vera said acidly. "But you don't have the box office value I do. And you never will. The role of the judge was written for me, and I'm keeping it. But I want Twomby and Fletcher to bulk it up."

"We'll work on strengthening the part, Ms. Stockdale," Twomby said, frantically scribbling notes to himself in the margin of the script.

"See that you do. I'll expect a better version by the end of the day." She rose, taking her dog and her book with her, and left the script on the table.